BATS
IN THE
BELFRY

BATS
IN THE
BELFRY

A London Mystery

E.C.R. Lorac

With an Introduction by
MARTIN EDWARDS

This edition published 2018 by
The British Library
96 Euston Road
London NW1 2DB

Originally published in 1937 by Collins

Cataloguing in Publication Data
A catalogue record for this publication is
available from the British Library

ISBN 978 0 7123 5255 0

Typeset by Tetragon, London
Printed and bound by CPI Group (UK) Ltd, Croydon CR0 4YY

BATS
IN THE
BELFRY

INTRODUCTION

This reissue of *Bats in the Belfry* ushers back into print a hidden gem from "the Golden Age of Murder" between the two world wars. The pseudonymous author, E.C.R. Lorac, enjoyed a successful if low-key career spanning more than a quarter of a century. Yet this particular novel seems to have aroused little attention, either on first publication or subsequently, despite its quality.

Two aspects of the book lift it well above the ordinary. The first is the plot. By the time this novel appeared in 1937, Lorac was an experienced, highly professional writer of whodunits, and had developed the crucial skill of being able to shift suspicion from one character to another without allowing interest to flag. The opening scene, set on an evening in March, introduces us to most of the people who will play a central part in the story, including Bruce Attleton and his glamorous wife Sybilla, their friends Thomas Burroughs, Neil Rockingham, and Robert Grenville, and Bruce's ward Elizabeth. They have gathered following the funeral of Anthony Fell, a young architect from Australia, and "a cousin of sorts" of Bruce's, who has been killed in a car crash. Before long, the conversation turns to the subject of how to dispose of a body. This proves to be significant...

We learn that Bruce is being plagued by a mysterious stranger called Debrette, but the nature of the connection between them is unclear. When both Bruce and Debrette go missing, Robert Grenville tries to find out what is going on. Before long, a corpse ("fashionably headless and handless" as Milward Kennedy put in when reviewing the novel for the *Sunday Times*) is found in the spooky, derelict Belfry. The plot thickens nicely from there; this is a good example of "fair play" detection, and Lorac's generosity with clues gives the alert reader every chance of working out the solution to a well-constructed mystery.

The second key ingredient of the story is its atmosphere. During this phase of her career, Lorac set many of her novels in central London; *Murder in St John's Wood* and *Murder in Chelsea* both appeared in 1934, and they were followed by *The Organ Speaks*, in which a corpse is found in a music pavilion in Regent's Park. She knew the city well, but perhaps never captured its dark side better than in this novel. The sinister Belfry Studio, also known as "the Morgue", is nicely evoked: "A gaunt tower showed up against the lowering sky, which was lit by the reflection of Neon lights in the West End. At the corner of the tower gargoyles stood out against the crazily luminous rain, and the long roof of the main body of the building showed black against the sky."

Lorac wrote the book in August 1936, while staying with her mother, Beatrice Rivett, at Westward Ho! In a copy she inscribed to her mother, she recalled their "lovely holiday", and memories of the sun on the Burrows, and the sands of Bideford Bay. She was fond of the north-west coast of Devon, and in 1931 had used it as a setting for the opening scene of her very first novel, *The Murder on the Burrows*. *Bats in the Belfry*, with its very different locale, was published rapidly, in January 1937, by Collins Crime Club, the prestigious imprint under which many of her books appeared.

The Lorac name concealed the identity of Edith Caroline Rivett (1894–1958), who was born in Hendon and educated at South Hampstead High School and the Central School of Arts and Crafts. She was generally known as Carol Rivett, and when she published her first novel, she reversed that name to disguise her identity (when inscribing another Lorac book, she described her authorial persona as "Carol in the Looking Glass"). Probably she, like other women writers of the day—Lucy Malleson, who wrote as J. Kilmeny Keith prior to adopting the pen-name Anthony Gilbert, was a prominent example—thought it preferable to imply to readers that she was a male author. Most of the reviews assumed that Lorac was a man. Indeed, the critic and author H.R.F. Keating wrote in his enjoyable monograph *Murder Must Appetize* (1975) of "my slight sense of shock on discovering that this trenchantly logical, pipe smoke-wreathed hero of my boyhood was Miss Edith Caroline Rivett, elegant practitioner of the arts of embroidery and calligraphy with a stitched tunicle and an illuminated book of benefactors to be seen in Westminster Abbey".

The young Keating associated Lorac with Freeman Wills Crofts, master of the methodical, well-constructed police story, and creator of Inspector Joseph French, a Scotland Yard man whose amiable manner and quiet persistence were shared by Lorac's Inspector Macdonald. Macdonald, like French, is a character far removed from omniscient superstars of detection such as Sherlock Holmes, Hercule Poirot and Lord Peter Wimsey, and his cases benefit from at least a surface element of realism. Conversely, he was much less memorable than his most illustrious fictional predecessors. Even Lorac seems to have forgotten his first name—in his debut appearance, his first name is James, but mysteriously, it soon became Robert.

As Keating implies, Lorac was a member of that generation of crime writers who eschewed personal publicity, and little has

been written about her life. Lorac was elected to membership of
the prestigious Detection Club in the year that *Bats in the Belfry*
appeared, and later served as the Club's Secretary. She never
married, and she bequeathed her literary estate to her sister.

Lorac was a prolific novelist, and perhaps to avoid flooding
the market with books under the same name, in 1936 she began to
publish under the name Carol Carnac. Most of the Carnac novels
feature Chief Inspector Julian Rivers, a policeman in the same
mould as Macdonald. By the time of Lorac's death in 1958, she
had produced more than seventy books, but in the last sixty years,
her reputation has—inevitably—faded. Nevertheless, her books
have long commanded interest from collectors, and early first
editions in dust jackets command high prices. Since 2013 there
has even been an E.C.R. Lorac discussion forum on Facebook. I
hope its members, as well as many readers unfamiliar with this
accomplished author, enjoy the long-awaited reappearance of
Bats in the Belfry.

MARTIN EDWARDS
www.martinedwardsbooks.com

I

"As funerals go, it was quite a snappy effort. No dawdling, well up to time and all that, but, my godfathers! what a farce to have to go to it at all. Didn't make a ha'porth of difference to the party concerned."

Bruce Attleton mixed himself a whisky and soda calculated to reduce funereal impressions to a minimum, and swallowed it rather more quickly than was customary in such a gathering. Neil Rockingham holding in his own hand a glass containing a milder version of the same drink, raised an angular eyebrow as he replied:

"Well, funerals never worry me. One good point about them—and weddings too, for that matter—is that they do get on with the doings—preamble, main theme, and blessing for curtain, and there you are. Snappy, as you say. Not like some of these infernal parties where you stand on one leg and wonder when you can decently depart. I do like a focus-point to an entertainment."

Bruce grinned, and his dark, sardonic face lighted up as he threw himself into a comfortable chair by the log fire. It was March, and the evenings were cold, so that the warm, slightly scented air of Sybilla Attleton's drawing-room struck a man as cosy after the raw air outside. A nice room, this of Sybilla's, meditated Rockingham. Peaceful, well-designed, chairs large enough to sit in, and plenty of them, not too many fallals for a man to trip over, and yet definitely a woman's room, with its colour scheme of faint grey and silver, lilac and deep blue. A sociable room, but not the right spot to swill down whisky like that nervy blighter, Bruce, was doing.

Sybilla, an exquisite figure in silver lamé with a short ermine cloak round her shoulders, lighted a Balkan Sobranje, and made a little face at her husband.

"I gather the funeral did make you shed a tear after all, Bruce—not for sorrow about our dear departed brother, but a tear of self-indulgent sympathy, that you should have been called upon to make the frightful effort of standing by a grave-side."

"Caustic, what?" Robert Grenville, a little embarrassed by the tone of Sybilla's voice, decided that jocularity was the vein to follow. "If it's not being unreasonably inquisitive, who was the party concerned, so to speak? The bury-ee, or interee, or what you call him."

"The 'dear departed' or the 'late lamented' is the accepted term," replied Bruce amiably enough. "On this occasion, it was a young chap named Anthony Fell—a cousin of sorts, though I can't tell you the exact degree. Family ramifications always beat me. However, this one turned up from Australia a few months ago—architect, hearty sort of chap. Doing quite nicely in the interim, building large-scale blocks on the modern housing principle, complete with the best in plumbing. Unfortunately he didn't manage the plumbing of his own car as well as he did that of his working-class flats. Came blinding down Porlock Hill in a fog, in a last year's racing model—a yellow sports car that made me sick to look at it. His brakes failed just when he needed 'em at a pinch and he somersaulted—what ho, she bumps!" He picked his glass up again and looked towards the tantalus. "So that was that, and we buried what was left of him to-day. Old

Neil here, came in as best man—very sporting of him. Not my idea of a good day, though."

"Miserable business," said Rockingham soberly enough. "Fell only showed me the car a few days ago, gassing about how he always vetted it himself. Whale of a chap with engines according to his own estimate."

"Poor young man—and you grudged him a few hours at his one and only funeral," put in Elizabeth Leigh. She was sitting on the lilac tuffet, warming her beautiful slim legs at the good heat of the cedarwood fire. Red-headed, white-skinned, with the round face of very young girlhood, Elizabeth appeared fit for a Da Forti halo and lute when she looked pensive, as now. "Dead in a strange land, and no one to shed a tear. If you'd told me about it, I'd have come myself, and cast rose leaves on the coffin." *not in March*

"And what good would that have done, Eliza?" inquired Bruce. "Nix, and you know it. Our family doesn't seem to have any staying power. They all pop off early, except the Old Soldier. He's about a hundred, and still going strong. Some one told me he bought an annuity when he was fifty-five, and got it cheap because he'd a dicky heart. The company he bought it from have written him off as a bad debt. They've given up hoping he'll die, and call him the Old Soldier. They don't, you know."

"Oh, but he must, sometime," put in Sybilla. "Some one said to me the other day that when you're born there's only one thing which can be said about you with any certainty, and that is that you'll die—sometime. Nothing else is certain, but that is."

"Cheery thought." Thomas Burroughs had been sitting silent, just behind Sybilla, until that moment, and the sound of his voice made Bruce Attleton scowl. It was a deep voice, and resonant, but Bruce said it sounded fat, "reeked of money"—and the rather stout, heavy-jowled Burroughs certainly was not hard-up.

"Nice way of greeting the son and heir," went on the latter. "Here you are, little 'un, and you're for it one of these fine days. Just a matter of time, what?"

"And the beautiful part is that no one knows when their time will be up," said Elizabeth, in her sweetest voice. She disliked Burroughs—one of the few things she had in common with her guardian, Bruce Attleton. "A slip, a skid, a fit, an aneurism, a syncope, and the lustiest becomes a mere bury-ee. I like that word," she added, her ingenuous blue eyes gazing hard at the wealthy stockbroker.

"Food for worms," put in Robert Grenville blithely. "I say, jolly topics we seem to be on. All flesh is grass, I know; still, it doesn't do to ponder over it."

"By way of cheering you all up a bit, I'll tell you of a competition that's been set for the monthly evening at my club," went on Elizabeth, averting her eyes from Burroughs' heavy face with a nicely calculated little moue of distaste. "We always have an intellectual exercise of sorts, and notice is given of it beforehand. The problem this month is as follows: If you were landed with a corpse on your hands, by what method could you dispose of it so as to avoid any future liabilities? Highest marks will be given for a method which is not only ingenious, but possesses the elements of practical common sense."

There was an outbreak of exclamations. Robert Grenville chuckled, and said, "By Gad, that's a corker!"

Attleton laughed and refilled his glass, saying, "Give us a moment to think it out, Liza."

Burroughs expostulated. "Rotten morbid ideas you modern girls go in for. Club, indeed! You want spanking and sending to bed."

Sybilla said languidly, "Don't be Victorian, Tommy. Everyone plays these murder games. Just use your wits as though there were money in it."

Rockingham, standing by the fire, smiled down at Elizabeth. He was a tall fellow, very fair, looking older than his forty-two years by reason of premature baldness. He had a very fine head, and the smooth lofty brow sloped back slightly to meet the magnificent domed skull. His hair, fair and smooth, was thick enough at the back, but his baldness gave him a professorial look, at odds with his fresh-skinned face. Rockingham took Elizabeth's problem quite seriously in the manner of one who loves a problem for its own sake.

"We need some more data," he said to her. "Are we to assume that we've corpsed the subject ourselves, or are we just obliging a friend?"

"I asked that too," said Elizabeth, replying to his friendly twinkle with a smile of angelic virtue. "It is assumed that one has created the corpse oneself, either by accident or malice aforethought, as may be most convenient."

"It's a nice point," said Bruce. "Imagine that I'd done some one in, here on this hearth-rug, and I wanted to get 'em clear out of the way, so as not to leave a trace—not too easy."

"I think you're being too casual." This time it was Grenville who spoke. It was Elizabeth's problem, and he particularly wanted to stand well with Elizabeth. "Never go and murder any one in a hurry—that's the first axiom. Think it all out carefully."

"Go on," said Elizabeth. "Elaborate. I want ideas."

"Assume that I'm going to murder a chap named Tom Brown. I've got to work it so that no one will know I was the last person whom he was seen with. I can't make an appointment with him in case any one else hears about it." Grenville was leaning forward now, his chin on his fists, his brow corrugated in thought. "I'd go to one of those dud car-marts—one of the places where you can get something that'll go for a couple of hundred miles for about ten pounds. I'd pay a deposit and drive out with some old car one wet evening, and I'd meet old Tom Brown on his way home from the station or something and say, 'Rotten evening, old boy. What about a lift?' Once he'd got in. I'd bat him one on the boko, and drive on to a little place I'd have taken on the edge of the outer suburbs—simple life and all that, every tenant builds his own house. I'd have got the garage up, and a nice hole ready in the floor, and I'd bring old Tom in and shift a bit of concrete on top of him, and then return the car to the mart and pick up my deposit. No connection between me and Tom, and the car."

"Not too good," said Elizabeth; "and rotten as a story. It might work, but I couldn't hope to win a prize with a garage floor as depository."

"That's perfectly true," said Rockingham; "though the touch about giving Tom a lift unexpectedly on a wet evening appeals to me as simple and effective. Pass that, cut out the garage floor, and drive Tom out to one of those dene holes some where and just tip him in. They're said to be almost bottomless."

"You tire me." It was Sybilla's languid voice which uttered this deflating phrase. "If there are such things as dene holes, they must be about chock-full with fictitious corpses. I'm tired of them."

"Well, what's yours?" asked Elizabeth eagerly.

Sybilla drew in a long breath of cigarette smoke.

"I'm not up to batting people over the head," she said dreamily. "I have a fancy for electricity. I'd connect up the power to the water in the wash-hand basin and say, 'Darling, do have a wash,' and when all that was over..." She tilted her head up meditatively. "A sunk bath, in the floor, you know. Tilt him in, and then concrete, plenty of it, and the bath mat on top. All quite simple."

"Good God! Sybilla, I wouldn't have believed you'd have thought about anything so—so—" gasped Burroughs, and Attleton laughed.

"Gives you a turn, old boy? Quite in the Borgia and Lady Macbeth tradition, when you thought Sybilla only played drawing-room comedy?"

"Never mind that," put in Elizabeth. "I think Sybilla's got more originality than you others."

"Quite a nice touch, that, about setting old Tom into the permanent fabric of the establishment," murmured Attleton, and Rockingham, seeing Burroughs' bulging eyes, put in:

"It's only a matter of exercising the imagination, Burroughs. Don't you read thrillers?"

"But I say, Elizabeth, you haven't told us your brain-wave yet," said Grenville. "Out with it! I bet it's pretty grim."

"It is," said Elizabeth complacently. "Much grimmer than Sybilla's, then. You know there are a lot of those big Georgian churches in London with lovely crypts—where they put people in family vaults? I know one in Bloomsbury. The furnace for heating is in the vaults, and it's quite easy to find the way down and slip in without being noticed. In my story, you get old Tom to come exploring with you, and bat him over the head at the further end of the vault, where it's *very* dark, and you come back next day and hide till night, and then you get busy unscrewing one of the old coffins—they're on ledges, you know, and just pop Tom in and do it up again."

"Good lord! The kid's got ideas, Neil. What about that for a Grand Guignol sketch? You're a dramatist. Can't you see the possibilities?"

"I certainly can," said Rockingham slowly, "but the theme's almost too macabre for production. It has the makings of a good short story, Elizabeth. Why not try it?"

"It wouldn't work—not in practice," said Burroughs, helping himself to another drink. "You'd have the deuce of a time getting the screws out of the coffin, and there'd be a lead lining inside."

"I'd thought of all that," said Elizabeth calmly. "A drop of oil in the screws, and garden secateurs for the lead lining. Would you like to come there with me just to get the atmosphere?" She smiled impudently at the heavily-built, well-tailored stockbroker, and Bruce put in with a laugh:

"Don't you risk it, Burroughs. She might feel disposed to put her theory into practice. Thanks for the tip, Liza. I'll bear it in mind in case of need."

"If you want to visit the scene of the projected crime, why not invite me?" Grenville pleaded to Elizabeth. "I'd make the perfect collaborator—and if the actual murder wasn't necessary, we might screw a column out of the idea and share the boodle."

"If ever you take to crime, Elizabeth, take my tip and play a lone hand," said Sybilla severely. "All this accomplice business is childish. Meantime, if you can bear it, my child, come and read over that new script of Vine's. I'm not sure if I like my part. The men can have a rubber of bridge to amuse themselves."

She got up with the deliberate grace characteristic of her, and with the calm determination which Rockingham had long noted as being an essential of her apparently lazy make-up, said good-night to her guests.

"Good-night, Tom. I shall be out of town till the end of the month, remember. Half-past one at the Berkeley Grill on the 1st—All Fool's Day. Good-night, Mr. Rockingham. Thank you for holding Bruce's hand at the funeral. Good-night, Mr. Grenville. Leave Elizabeth to her own murders. Come along, angel face."

She drew Elizabeth's arm through her own and they went out of the room, leaving the four men standing by the fire. Burroughs made no bones about taking his departure once Sybilla had gone.

"I've got to go down to my club to see a fellow—" he began, and Bruce Attleton cut in:

"... about a dog. That's all right, Thomas. Good-night."

Burroughs pursed up his mouth in a manner that deepened the heavy lines running from nose to lip and replied, "That's about the size of it. Good-night, Attleton. You don't look too fit. Cut up about that young cousin of yours. Shocking thing. Too much wild driving about. Safety first's my motto. 'Night, Rockingham. 'Night."

He nodded to Grenville and Bruce strolled to the door with him and chatted casually while the stockbroker got into his coat. Returning to the drawing-room, he said:

"Come along into the library, Neil, and you, Grenville. It's more comfortable in there."

Rockingham shook his head.

"No. We'll bung off. You don't want us here, I know that. I'm sorry you were cut up about that accident to young Fell. I feel a bit unhappy about it. He *did* show me his damned car, and

I know a sight more about them than he did. I ought to have looked at his brakes."

"Oh, rot! That's hair-splitting in an attempt to blame yourself, old man. Besides, I don't believe in theories of accident. I'm a fatalist. Young Anthony had got his ticket, his time was up, and if it hadn't been faulty brakes on Porlock Hill, it'd have been a train smash or a pneumonia bug. It's quite true, I *was* cut up. I liked the beggar, what I saw of him, and considering how our whole family's been at loggerheads for generations, it was rather refreshing to find a cousin I liked. They all quarrelled like Kilkenny cats. Old Uncle Adam began it—the Old Soldier. He quarrelled with the whole clan and later generations kept it up. We're a nice crowd!"

He turned away from the fire, adding, "I was damn grateful to you for coming. I loathe funerals. I'll go and wash it off, soak in a Turkish bath for an hour or two. Good-night, old boy. See you in Paris next week." He turned to Grenville, adding, "And look here, young fella me lad, I'm always glad to see you here, but don't go imagining I've changed my mind. I haven't. Cheer ho! Weller'll let you out."

Weller was the butler, who presided over his duties in the Attletons' picturesque little house in Park Village South with the air of a pontiff, and a skill which was half the secret of the perfectly run house. Every one liked Weller, and particularly the servants who worked under him, consequently Sybilla Attleton was able to keep a contented domestic staff in a house which had basement kitchens and awkward stairs and cellars.

Just as Bruce Attleton opened the drawing-room the butler appeared and glanced at his master, who said, "Well, what is it now?" in his quick irritable way.

"I didn't get the opportunity of telling you earlier, sir. A gentleman named Debrette phoned while you were out."

"Oh, he did, did he?" snapped Attleton. "If he rings up again, tell him I'll bash his bloody head in. Got that? No other answer."

Rockingham took Grenville's arm and urged him towards the hall, and the butler followed them and busied himself with their coats, apparently quite unconcerned at his master's outburst of ill-temper. Grenville, who had caught sight of Attleton's face when he spoke, had been considerably taken aback. Bruce was frequently nervy and jumpy, but to answer a servant in such a manner, and in the presence of guests, betokened something more than ordinary ill-temper.

Rockingham, however, seemed quite unperturbed, and chatted cheerfully to Weller as he put on his coat and muffler.

"It's turned into a real nasty evening, sir," the butler was saying. "The fog's thickened a lot. Always bad in the park, and now it's just pouring in from over there. Chilly as Christmas."

"It is that, and it was damn' chilly in that graveyard this morning, Weller," replied Rockingham. "Hope Mr. Attleton hasn't caught a chill. Miserable business."

"It was indeed, sir. I felt badly over it. A nice cheery young gentleman he was, too. No relatives to speak of, I understand, barring Mr. Attleton. At least that saved breaking the news."

"You're right. Rotten job sending condoling cables. Good-night, Weller."

"Good-night, sir. No taxi?"

"Not for me. In a fog like this I'd rather walk. What about you, Grenville?"

"I'll come along with you, if I may. Ugh! What a climate!"

The two men stepped out into a cold, white mist, in which all sound seemed to be muffled, as is the curious paradox of fogs. In actual fact the silence was due to the slowing down of the traffic.

"Nervy beggar, Bruce. That business of Anthony Fell's death shook him up rather."

Rockingham spoke absent-mindedly, but Robert Grenville replied with some heat:

"Nervy he is, I grant you, but I'm more than a bit mad with him. I don't see why I should suffer permanently from his caprices. He's Elizabeth's guardian, and he's right to take his duties seriously, but confound it, if she's willing to marry me, and lord knows, I'm crazy to marry her, why should he exert his powers to prevent us marrying? It's not as though she's a big heiress. I'm not fortune-hunting. I've got enough income to ensure that she'll be comfortable, over and above her own little fortune. What's he got against me, Rockingham?"

"I don't suppose he's anything against you, my dear chap. In fact, I know he hasn't. He likes you, but Elizabeth's a very young thing. Probably Bruce thinks it'd be a mistake for her to get tied up before she's seen enough of the world for her to know her own mind."

The two men had at first followed the curve of the Outer Circle as they made their way from Park Village South towards Mayfair, where Rockingham had his abode, but when they reached Park Square they turned towards the Marylebone Road and crossed over to Park Crescent, thereafter walking diagonally across the network of streets between Portland Place and Baker Street. Crossing the Marylebone Road, Grenville burst out:

"Well, I call it damnable! Elizabeth *does* know her own mind now, and he's just giving her the chance to get unsettled. I hate all this feminist club business, and Sybilla may be a corking fine actress in modern comedy and satire, but she's no sort of example to an unsophisticated girl like Liza. Take the way she runs merchants like that fat blighter, Tom Burroughs—spoiling the Egyptians! I like Bruce all right, or I would if he'd only be reasonable, but Sybilla and her push make me sick. Wouldn't it be better for Liza to be married and have a home of her own, than to go trailing round with all these over-sophisticated, man-hunting, pseudo-intellectual females who see life all awry?"

Rockingham chuckled a little. "I can see your point, of course, though it's not up to me to criticise Sybilla. She's Bruce's wife, on the one hand, and as an actress she knows her stuff. Let's leave her out of it. You say you like Bruce. The fact of the matter is, I'm worried over him. I think he's got something on his mind, and it's probably that that's making him awkward over you and Elizabeth. His mind refuses to cope with more than one problem at a time."

"What is it? Money?—or the Debrette gentleman to whom he referred so genially just now?"

"What do you know about Debrette?"

"Nothing—except that Sybilla mentioned his name one day, and Bruce went off into the devil's own fury over it."

"H'm. Look here, what about coming into my place for a drink, if you've nothing else to do? We might talk things over a bit. I'm in a bit of a quandary, and you're no fool, Grenville. Besides, you might get a line on the fellow, with your journalistic experience. I don't like talking in this fog. Gives me the feeling that Mr. Debrette may be prowling around like the hosts of Midian. Come in and talk for a bit."

"Thanks. I'd be glad to. I've often thought of writing your house up as a unique example of history crystallised in the West End. It's an amazing spot."

"Good spot, but it'll be too damned expensive for me if I don't strike it lucky with a new play soon. Hell! I swear there *is* some one following us, Grenville. Listen!"

Rockingham stopped dead, holding his companion's arm, and Grenville said:

"Yes. I heard footsteps. They've stopped now. Wait a jiffy."

He plunged suddenly into the fog, leaving Rockingham standing under the blurred light of a street lamp, looking warily round him. There was something absurd about the feeling of tension that possessed him, here in the heart of the West End, with the smug-looking door-plates of fashionable specialists all around him. He lighted a cigarette and shrugged his shoulders, but breathed a sigh of relief all the same when Grenville appeared again beside him, saying:

"I lost the bloke in the fog. Funny do, what? Let's make for your quarters. I agree with you, a fog's no place to discuss odd doings."

Rockingham's little house lay in the angle between Park Lane, Culross Street and Shepherd's Market. To reach the entrance it was necessary to walk through a narrow archway at the end of a mews; this opened on to a surprising little square of greenery where stood a tiny square house of two stories, built as a country cottage, perhaps, or an annexe to some manor house in the latter days of Queen Anne's reign. How the comely little building had survived, built around on all sides, was one of the puzzles which delight the heart of the London antiquarian, but there it was, of pleasant rose-red brick, with a tiny forecourt of crazy paving, and a great plane tree towering behind it in the garden of some lordly house which still survived the devastating hand of the modern flat builders.

In the fog, as Rockingham and Grenville passed under the archway, it looked more fantastic than usual, with its square lantern shining above the bleached oak front door, and a gleam of orange light above the fanlight.

Letting himself in with a latchkey, Rockingham led the way up the little straight staircase to his panelled sitting-room on the first floor, and invited Grenville to sit down while he poured out drinks at a side table.

"It's this business about Debrette I want to talk about," he began abruptly. "I shouldn't have mentioned it if you hadn't, but I'm glad to have the chance of discussing it with some one. You know Attleton well, and you've a vested interest in his welfare, so to speak, because of Elizabeth. Can you find out who this Debrette is? Have you ever heard the name in connection with any Art Exhibition, or anything of that kind?"

Grenville shook his head. "No. Never. Have you ever seen the chap?"

"Once only. I answered the telephone once while Attleton was out—Weller told me there was some chap who seemed anxious for an answer, and this man Debrette was cursing at the other end of the line, saying he'd got to speak to Attleton, or the heavens would fall. That gave me a chance to hear Debrette's voice—he's a foreigner, undoubtedly. Then a few days later I was just turning into Park Village with Attleton when I heard the same voice over my shoulder saying, 'Just a moment, Mr. Attleton. It's for your own sake, you know.' I saw him that time, a queer-looking dago with a pointed beard and huge convex lenses set in the widest rimmed specs I've ever seen. He's a noticeable chap because he's got a streak of white in his beard. You may wonder why I'm telling you all this. Quite frankly, I want to find out who this Debrette johnny is. Attleton won't tell me. He shuts up like a clam when I mention the subject. I've known you long enough to trust you, Grenville. You know how to hold your tongue."

"Lord, yes. I know that. If I split on some of the funny yarns I've hit while searching for copy I might have made a spot of trouble—for myself as well as other people." He lit another cigarette and studied Rockingham's frowning face. "Having trusted me so far, you'd better trust me a bit further. I'm game to look into the Debrette gentleman's antecedents provided you give me adequate data—and reason."

"Right. You can use your own imagination as easily as I can use mine. If Attleton's in a frenzy of nerves over this chap, and yet won't tell his own friends anything about it, the answer's easy. Attleton's being blackmailed, or threatened in some way. Now if that's so, the cure's easy too—police. Any sane man ought to know that it's safer to turn a blackmailer over to the police than to bargain with him. My position's this. I can't get anything out of Attleton, so I want to run this bird to earth so that I can get him dealt with if need arises. The story's too nebulous at present. It sounds like a penny dreadful—a dago with a beard uttering crazy warnings. I'm a plain man—don't hold with this stuff off-stage. Besides, it's second rate."

The disgust on Rockingham's severe face made Grenville laugh.

"Yes—but you didn't feel so complacent in the fog just now. Funny things *do* happen in London—don't I know it?—and the police don't always get there in time. Now, I'll accept your reasoning. You want your bird run to earth so that you can lay a hand on him in case of need. Now for your data. You've got something more to go on than the chap's name, and a beard with a white streak in it, I take it?"

"Yes, I have." Rockingham hesitated a little and then said, "I don't know if I shall wake up in the morning and curse for having spread myself like this. However, no use shilly-shallying. I've a notion the chap hangs out in a studio somewhere in Notting Hill. I was out to dinner there last week—a damned rotten dinner, too—and I turned into a quiet pub on my way to the station to have the whisky I'd longed for all the evening and hadn't got. The pub was called The Knight Templar—somewhere off the Alton Road. I saw Debrette go out as I went in." Rockingham got up and stood by the fire.

"You may well ask why don't I run him to earth myself. It'd be easy enough, assuming that he lives somewhere in the Alton Road district. The point is this. Debrette knows me by sight. He saw me with Attleton and he's talked to me over the phone. If he sees me on his trail in his own neighbourhood, he may do a bunk, so that I shall lose sight of him. He's never seen you, presumably, so if you come into contact with him he'll have no grounds for smelling a rat."

"That's quite sound," agreed Grenville. "Well, I'm game. As you say, it oughtn't to be difficult to run him to earth. Now say if I spot him—what d'you want me to do? Scrape an acquaintance?"

"Lord, no! I only want to know where he hangs out. I may be being a damned fool to interfere at all. It's probably more sensible to mind one's own business, but I'm fond of Bruce. He's got no more sense than a child, in spite of all his wit and learning. If

ever a man wanted a nursemaid, he does. But look here. Don't
for God's sake go butting in and getting yourself mixed up with
that Debrette merchant by going to see him, or anything of that
kind. I tell you frankly I don't like the look of him. I'm not of
a nervous disposition, but if I needed to have any dealings with
Mr. Debrette, I'd see to it that I left my note-case behind and
took a stick with me to help reason in case of need. I don't want
to have *you* on my conscience."

"And another funeral, with Elizabeth strewing rose-leaves
and never a spray of yew," laughed Grenville. "Don't you worry.
I'm quite capable of looking after myself. However, I gather that
the commission on this occasion is merely to find the blighter's
address?"

"That's it, Grenville. It's in your own interests, in one respect.
If we can get this tom-fool business of Debrette out of the way,
perhaps Bruce will see reason over your marrying Elizabeth.
Anyway, trust me to do my best for you—but it's no use talking
to him when he's as nervy as St. Vitus."

"Thanks. Jolly decent of you. By the way, when shall I report
progress—if there's any to report? Didn't you say you were going
over to Paris in a few days?"

"Yes—on Wednesday, the 18th, to see the premiere of that
new Maudet farce. I shall be away about a week or ten days. I'll
let you know for certain later. A letter here will be safe enough.
As a matter of fact, there's no hurry. Bruce is going to run over
to Paris while I'm there. Perhaps it'd be better to put off this
little sleuthing do of yours until we came back."

The irresolution in Neil Rockingham's voice made Grenville
laugh. "'Letting I dare not wait upon I will.' It's not like you to
temporise."

"No. The fact is I've let the whole silly business get on my nerves a bit. Don't know now whether I wasn't a fool to set you on to it. Anyway, for God's sake don't go asking for trouble!"

"I won't. Any old how, it won't do any harm to collect the bird's address. You've trusted me to do a job for you. I won't make a mess of it."

"Stout fellow! What about another night-cap?"

"Make it a short one. I've got to get home to Chancery Lane on shanks' mare. There won't be a thing moving in this fog. Come and see my quarters some time. They're not in the stud-book neighbourhood like yours, but they're not un-amusing. A cottage off Fleet Street, complete with grass plot in front."

"Good lord! Funny city, this is. Never know what you'll find in it. I'll come and look you up when I'm home again."

"Good. Good-night—and thanks for letting me in on the story. I rather like my part of the job."

"I'm glad—only no funny stuff, remember!"

"Right you are. I'm the world's most discreet. Cripes! What a night!" and he plunged off into the blanket of fog.

30 years before the Clean Air Act, making smokeless fuel compulsory in London

II

IT WAS TWO NIGHTS LATER, ON THE EVENING OF THE DAY
when Neil Rockingham had gone to Paris, that Grenville
began his researches into the matter of Debrette's abode.

Walking home in the fog, after his talk with Rockingham,
Grenville had done some hard thinking. The story he had heard
struck him as peculiar, but he had sensed something odd about
Attleton's behaviour of late. When Grenville had first met him,
three years ago, Bruce Attleton had been a cheery soul, a bit
caustic in wit, perhaps, a little on the precious side, but good
company, and full of mirth. Recently his good humour had
deserted him and he had become increasingly irritable and
nervy, so that his friends found him a trial and his wife grew
tired of his captiousness. Grenville, observant and keen-witted,
guessed that the charming house in Park Village South was
kept up mainly on Sybilla's money, for Bruce Attleton had not
sustained his early success as a writer. Two bestsellers and then
flop, meditated Grenville. Didn't do to succeed too early. Better
build up a reputation slowly.

Nevertheless, he thought to himself, there was no reason why
Attleton should be so intransigent over the matter of Elizabeth's
marriage. She was nineteen, by no means too young, to know
what she wanted, especially in these days when the young
arrived at early conclusions as to the problems of life, and as
for Grenville, he was as much in love as a healthy young man
of thirty could be. Wait for two years, till Elizabeth attained
her majority and was free of her guardian? Two years? Hell!

Grenville guessed that his chance of marrying her would grow steadily less good with every day of those two years.

As he walked eastwards through the fog it was not unnatural that something inside his head asked, "Anything for me in all this?" If all was fair in love and war, what was against him, Robert Grenville, discovering some lever to move the obstinacy of a guardian over that hedged-in privilege of powers concerning his ward? Grenville was fair-minded and honest enough, but he was very much in love, and his blood was hot within. Small wonder that he scorned the cautiousness of that careful old stick, Neil Rockingham, and let his mind wander afield over the possibilities latent in that queer conversation. Blackmail? suggested a voice inside him, realising that what he contemplated was not far removed from that unsavoury practice. Well, damn it, this ward and guardian business was a species of slavery, anyway, and a man had no business to be a guardian at all if he were susceptible to the activities of blackmailers.

"No harm in looking into it, anyway," Grenville had said to himself. "It's probably all a mare's nest, anyway. Someone dunning Attleton for a gambling debt, and trying to frighten him into paying up. Rockingham's got rattled over young Fell pipping off like that, and he's just looking for trouble."

Nevertheless, when Grenville had got into bed that night he admitted to himself that it wasn't like Rockingham to get rattled. He was generally the most level-headed of men.

It was on a Friday evening that Grenville paid his first visit to The Knight Templar, which he found by asking a newspaper vendor at Notting Hill Gate Station. Even with the very precise directions given by the knowledgeable paper-man (and Grenville was quick to recognise an authority on pubs when he met one) it took him a long while to find Mulberry Hill where this particular pub was situated. It was a horrible evening, raining miserably with an admixture of sleet, and Grenville cursed the quiet little roads of Notting Hill as he trudged along, raincoat buttoned up to his chin, pipe turned downwards in his mouth.

Mulberry Hill, when he reached it, seemed the most improbable road on earth to boast a public house. It was a wide, quiet street—what the house agents would call "a good residential quarter," with pleasant little stucco-covered houses, well set back in gardens, and shady with trees. Grenville knew enough about the neighbourhood to know that there were plenty of studios hereabouts. Gittings, the portrait painter, had a big place nearby in Burdon Hill; old Sir George Crampton had lived in the same road, and Delaney, the black-and-white man, had his place in Burdon Place—though why the deuce Rockingham supposed his dago was connected with the arts, Grenville couldn't see.

Just when he was feeling most depressed, and apparently miles away from any pub of any kind, Grenville saw the lights and the signboard of the very discreet-looking tavern which called itself The Knight Templar. It appeared to have got there by mistake, and looked more like an ordinary residence than a public house, standing back in its little garden, with a few modest signboards to betoken the beers it proffered.

Once in the bar, Grenville was quick to decide that as pubs went, this was a good pub, and with a double whisky inside him felt more amiably disposed to this quarter of London. They were a mixed lot in the saloon bar—a couple of men in dinner jackets arguing earnestly together, one or two prosperous-looking tradesmen, discussing greyhound racing with a fellow whom

Grenville took to be a bookie, and a tall man in rather shabby clothes who looked a somebody in spite of an ancient coat worn over an old pullover. It was to the latter that Grenville addressed himself, getting on to the topic of renting a studio. He knew enough artist's jargon to keep his end up, and was soon able to bring in the name of Debrette, who he believed "hung out somewhere in the neighbourhood." The painter to whom he was talking cocked up an eyebrow.

"Debrette? Sculptor, isn't he? Friend of yours?"

"Umps... so so. Friend of a friend," replied Grenville.

"Quaint bird—and he's got a damn' quaint corner to roost in. Shouldn't care for it myself. I should drink myself blind if I lived in that place."

"Where does he live exactly? I want to look him up."

"Lord, you'll have a fit when you see it. Some wag called it the Morgue. It's the devil of a fine studio, but enough to give you the blue jimmies. I forget who built the place, some rum sect with a religion of their own, and a private Messiah. Must have had pots of money. Anyway, it was a place of worship way back in the nineties, then the sect died out, or the money died out, and it was derelict for years. Eventually some chap bought it and turned it into a studio, but it's too big and too expensive, and it's just been mouldering with occasional tenants in it for years. I believe it's sold now, and they're going to pull it down in a few months' time and put flats up. I say, Melisande" (this to the barmaid), "who was the last chap who had the Morgue before old beaver took it on? That sculptor chap?"

"Mr. Lestways," replied the lady in question. "He was a one, he was. I was told not to serve him at last. Half seas over all the time, he was."

"Lestways, that was the chap. Hung himself to a beam in the jolly old place. Don't wonder. There's a tower at one end where owls nest, and bats. Great snakes! It's a looney sort of hole."

"Sounds jolly," replied Grenville. "What about old Debrette? He dotty too?"

"Well, if he's not a particular pal of yours I'll admit I think he's borrowed a bat or two from the belfry. Comes chasing in here and gets outside a couple in double quick time and goes chasing off again. Rum bird. Doing some big stuff, I believe, and wanted an adequate sized place. Well, he's got it! I reckon you could seat five hundred in that barn, and it leaks like a colander in rainy weather. He says he's fixed up a tarpaulin to keep his clay dry while he's working."

"He must be a bit dippy," said Grenville, and the other replied:

"That's about the size of it to my mind. You go and see him. It's worth a visit. First on your right when you leave here, you can't miss it."

"Thanks. I'll go and have a look-see," replied Grenville. "I reckon it's worth the walk."

He paid for the drinks and buttoned up his coat again, feeling distinctly more cheerful than when he had come in, and walked out again into the chill, wet darkness. His mind was busy trying to sort things out and make sense of them. What could be the connection between a sculptor "with bats in the belfry" and Bruce Attleton, that distinguished ornament of the Authors' Club, husband of the beautiful Sybilla? A doubt flashed through Grenville's mind. Could this sculptor chap be another Debrette, a connection perhaps, of Rockingham's "dago"?

"'Run and find out'—like the mongoose," said Grenville to himself, and took the first on the right as indicated.

The road he found himself in was wider than Mulberry Hill and planted with plane trees, and he soon caught sight of the building described by the painter in The Knight Templar. A gaunt tower showed up against the lowering sky, which was lit by the reflection of Neon lights in the West End. At the corner of the tower gargoyles stood out against the crazily luminous rain, and the long roof of the main body of the building showed black against the sky.

It was a queer-looking building to find among the prosperous houses of that pleasant-looking road, and Grenville was aware of a feeling of apprehension, quite unreasonable, at the sight of the dark massive structure. "The Morgue"—and a sculptor who hanged himself from a beam. "Jolly!" he said to himself, but having got so far he wasn't going to funk that dark-looking pile. He went up to the iron gate which stood between the two imposing stone pillars and shook it, and found that it swung to his hand. Pushing it open, he went in, up a stone-flagged path, and found himself faced by an arched doorway, so overgrown with ivy that it was obvious it could not have been opened for years. He turned down the path which led by the side of the long hall and saw a light in a window at the end. Rehearsing to himself the story he had fabricated of a friend who wanted a portrait bust, he walked on until he found a doorway close below the lighted window. Here were deposited empty milk bottles and a tin dustbin—sure signs of occupation. In some way their appearance gave him confidence. Milk bottles. Nice and homely and commonplace. Perhaps the chap wasn't batty after all. He glanced back at the lamp-lit street and heard the steady tramp of a constable on his beat, the hoot of a passing taxicab, and laughed at his own premonitions of a moment ago.

Still—"odd things do happen in London," he heard his own voice saying, and was glad that he had brought a good heavy stick. With that thought he raised his hand and gave a tug to the bell chain beside the door.

Hearing the clang of the bell inside, Grenville also heard his own heart beating. It was absurd, but the place was uncanny, something out of the normal. He heard footsteps on a stone floor within, and then a small panel was opened in the upper part of the door and light fell on Grenville's face. He could see a dark shape against the light—a man's head, but it was in silhouette, and he could not make out any detail.

"Yes, who is it?"

The voice from the open panel had an unmistakable accent— the "who" had no aspirate in it, and Grenville felt encouraged.

"Is that Mr. Debrette? I've been asked to look you up. A man I know wants a portrait bust done."

"And who is your friend?"

"Chap named Martin. Never mind if you're busy. It's damned wet out here, and I'm not a philanthropist, nor yet a performing seal."

The aggressiveness in Grenville's voice seemed to please the other. He laughed and replied in a more friendly way:

"Milles pardons! This place is the 'ome of tramps. Wait. I will open the door. I am alone. I 'ave to be careful."

There was a rattle of bolts, and then the door opened and a blaze of light from an unshaded bulb shone in Grenville's face. He saw a man's figure against the light, and was able to perceive that the man's face was bearded and that he wore very large spectacles. Then the unexpected happened. A hand was raised, and the contents of a tumbler were shot in Grenville's face. The tumbler contained whisky and soda, and the journalist staggered back, momentarily blinded and bewildered by the unexpected attack.

"Go back to your friend Attleton and tell 'im to go to the devil," shrilled the bearded man at the door. "As for you, go! Allez vous en! Diable! Pah!"

With a final sound like a spitting cat, the man slammed the door, leaving Grenville out in the rain with whisky running down inside his collar, his eyes streaming with the smart of the spirit, and his temper very much in evidence. He heard a cackle of laughter before the sliding panel was closed, and in a fit of unreasoning rage he began to kick the solid door, mainly with the desire to vent his temper on something.

This unprofitable occupation was interrupted by a deep voice from the gate by the road.

"Now then, what's all this about? Steady on there!"

Grenville found his handkerchief and wiped his eyes as a police constable appeared on the path.

"The damned blackguard chucked a glass of whisky at me."

"Now you'd better get this straight," said the constable firmly. "Any charge to make?"

Grenville collected his wits, which had been bemused by the unprovoked attack. He didn't want complications with the police as the sum total of his evening's activities.

"No. Sorry, constable. I expect I asked for it. He emptied his glass over me, dirty dog. Made me mad for a minute. I like whisky all right in the proper place. Smell my coat if you don't believe me—and then the blighter laughed. Wouldn't you have been mad yourself if any one played you a dirty trick like that?"

"Well, I'm not saying I wouldn't," replied the other gravely. "You artist gentlemen, you're all the same. Better go home and sleep it off, sir."

Grenville laughed. He couldn't help it.

"I'm a damned great fool! Right-o, constable, only these little things get one's goat."

The large policeman led him down the path and finally shut the gate firmly behind him when they stood on the pavement outside.

"Now then, sir, you go straight home," he admonished, and watched Grenville as he set off at a good round pace from the scene of his ignominious encounter.

III

NEIL ROCKINGHAM DID NOT STAY LONG IN PARIS. A WEEK after he had left London he was back again in his little Mayfair house, and the first thing he did on his return was to ring up Robert Grenville. The latter hailed the call with satisfaction.

"I say, I'm jolly glad you're back. I've got some news for you, of a sort. Can I roll round now? I want to talk things over."

"Good. Come straight here. I can give you a scratch meal of sorts. Don't bother to dress. In about half an hour? Excellent!"

When Grenville was ensconced in Rockingham's room—it was then about seven o'clock, the latter having reached Charing Cross Station at six—the dramatist said abruptly:

"Any luck in the matter of our friend Debrette?"

"Well, so-so. I ran him to earth. Before I spill my yarn, I wish you'd tell me this. Did you see Attleton in Paris?"

"No, I didn't. I'm worried to death about him, Grenville. He booked a room at the Bristol, but he didn't turn up. I rang up Sybilla to find if he'd changed his plans, and she said no. He was in Paris, or if he weren't, she didn't know where he was."

"I see. Well, wherever else he went, I'm prepared to wager he didn't go to Paris."

"What the deuce do you mean?" Rockingham held a lighted match in his fingers, preparatory to lighting his pipe, but Grenville's sentence made him forget all about the pipe, and the match burnt down to his finger so that he dropped it with an oath as the flame touched him.

"It's a longish story. I'd better begin at the beginning."

With a neat turn for narrative, Grenville described his visit to The Knight Templar, and his subsequent exploration and discomfiture. He laughed aloud as he told of the whisky which so unexpectedly greeted him at the strange doorway of The Morgue, but Rockingham's fair face did not lose its frown of troubled expectancy, and Grenville hurried on with his story.

"When I woke up next day, I can tell you I felt pretty mad. No one likes to be made to feel such a sanguinary ass as I felt when I heard that blighter cackling behind his sported oak. I thought I'd like to get even with him."

"If you'd only not butted in," began Rockingham in a school-masterly voice, and Grenville sat up and fairly let fly.

"Look here. You can sit there like an animated bust and lecture the book shelves if you like, and I'll buzz off home and leave you to it, but don't expect too much of human nature. You ask me to do the donkey work, and then expect me to switch off like an automatic gramophone and forget the last record. It won't do, old boy! You gave me a hand to play, and I played it in my own way. If you don't like it, say so. I'll keep my scoop to myself and be damned to you."

Rockingham hastened to apologise. "Sorry, Grenville. The fact is I'm worried, and consequently unreasonable. Go on, for God's sake, and get to the doings, whatever they are."

"Right oh!—and not so much about butting in," said Grenville, his square chin tilted up aggressively, but a grin on his wide, good-humoured mouth. "Thinking it over I decided I'd go and call on Mr. Bloody Debrette next day—with a pepper-pot. I woke up full of beans, pocketed the pepper-pot, and round I mooched to The Morgue. When I got there I met a young fella in a billycock hat coming out of the door. 'And what might you require?' sez he, for all the world like a draper. I said I wanted my friend Debrette, and he says, 'Oh, he's gone. Lease up yesterday. He's left no address.' 'Sorry about that,' sez I, and made for the gate, not wanting this young house-agent's errand boy on my heels. After a diplomatic circuit of the neighbourhood I came back to The Morgue. Place fascinated me—I wanted to get inside. On further inspection I found a sort of trap-door effect that led to a coal cellar—quite unfastened, and in I popped. I won't bore you with descriptions of the place—you can wait till you see it—but I'll just tell you this. The place I got in was a coal cellar, pretty foul and all that, but there was a smart leather suitcase lying in one corner. I opened it—a liberty, perhaps, and all that—but it intrigued me. You see, it was Bruce Attleton's suitcase."

"Hell!" Rockingham fairly jumped in his seat. "Good God, man! Don't you see this may mean something ghastly! It's no joke, Grenville. Heavens above!"

"Keep your wool on, old man," replied Grenville. "This is where you need a cool head—and remember the bit about fools butting in." He grinned, not without malice. "I don't know what Bruce is up to, but maybe it's some little game of his own that he won't thank you to publish. I've often wondered whether Bruce hadn't some little affair of his own on when Sybilla was so snorty to him."

He looked Rockingham straight in the face and saw him flush. "Thought as much. We're not all of your equable temperament. However, that's as may be. I tell you I opened the suitcase. All neatly packed, pyjamas, sponge-bag and what nots, a copy of the *London Mercury*—*and* his passport, in the pocket inside the lid. Wherefore I say—he's not gone to Paris. Perfectly sound, what?"

Rockingham bent and knocked out his pipe on the bars of the grate with a deliberation which was almost exaggerated. His lofty brow was creased in thought, and his eyes, when they met Grenville's again, were very troubled. He spoke quietly this time.

"Perfectly sound." His voice was dry. "This has got to be looked into, Grenville. I'm not misjudging you, I know your flippancy's just skin deep—like my censoriousness. This may mean the deuce of a lot of trouble, putting it at the lightest count. It may mean something much more grim—in which case, God help us! Now you say that you broke into this damned place—last Saturday, wasn't it? Presumably what you did once, we can do again."

"Undoubtedly," replied Grenville, "but I think we'd better have all the cards on the table this time. First—are you going to make a police matter of it right away?"

"No." Rockingham's deep voice was very decided. "Not until—or unless—we make some further discovery which will take the matter out of our hands. Don't misunderstand me. I'm a law-abiding man, not one of those half-baked fools who think criminal investigation is the province of the amateur. But first, I'd like to decide that there *is* a case for the police. If Bruce is just up to some of his wild-cat games, the less muck-raking the better."

"Ker-wite. Meaning I heartily agree. Next. A straight question. How much do you know about this Debrette?"

Rockingham met Grenville's inquiring eyes squarely.

"Nothing at all, barring what I told you, absolutely nothing. I saw the chap on the occasion I mentioned, and I heard his voice on the phone. I couldn't get a word out of Bruce about him."

"Right. Now for the house-breaking." Grenville produced a key from his pocket, a remarkably large, clumsy affair. "That, oh reverend senior, is the key of Ye Morgue. Having done a spot of investigation it occurred to me that it might be as well to legalise the position. I'm like you—all for law and order—on occasions. I climbed out of the cellar and then went and called on the leading house-agents nearby in that very desirable neighbourhood. As I told you, the place is at the fag end of a ground lease. In a few months it goes to the housebreakers—quite time, too, and the chap who's got the end of the lease on his hands would let it to the devil himself for tuppence. The agents are bored stiff with it, but quite willing to rake in an extra commission. They made no bones about letting it to me for three months at a pound a week, tenant responsible for his own interior decorations. My aunt! I laughed till I rocked over that! I paid twelve quid down as rent in advance, thinking it might be bread cast upon the waters, and I've been camping out there at night, if you'll believe me, waiting for Debrette—or Bruce Attleton—to come and retrieve the suitcase. Thoughtful, what?"

"Very thoughtful." Rockingham's quiet voice was grateful this time. "I apologise again for what I said about butting in, Grenville. You've been extraordinarily decent and sensible over the whole show, though I can't help regretting that you didn't take that bobby at his word, and make a charge against Debrette for unprovoked assault. Then we might have got him where we could find him."

"D'you know, I've thought that once or twice myself, in the interim," admitted Grenville. "But it was infernally difficult, you know. You'd warned me not to make too much palaver, and I didn't want you to come home cursing me to hell for getting the whole show into the limelight. After all, I didn't know—I don't know now—what Bruce has been up to. If Debrette's got hold of any murky secrets about Bruce's affairs, the latter wouldn't have thanked me for running the blighter in. Besides, I had myself to think about. When it comes to brass tacks I hadn't a leg to stand on. I *was* trying to interview the chap under false pretences, when all's said and done. Still, it's a nice point as to whether I should have done better to try to get him run in."

Rockingham got to his feet. "No use going over 'ifs'," he said. "You've done uncommonly well, and it was a damned good idea to get possession of that blasted place. By the way, what've you done about that coal hole?"

Grenville grimaced. "When I come away I fasten it up," he said. "When I'm in residence I leave it open—with a booby trap of pails and what nots to give the alarm if anybody gets in. Still, I admit it's a nervy business sleeping there."

"Good God! I should say it is," exclaimed Rockingham. "Well, there'll be two of us to see to it in future. Now what about a meal? It'll be out of tins, I warn you. I don't keep any domestics on the premises—can't be bothered with 'em. I have a saturnine dame who comes in and does the place in the mornings. She hardly ever speaks to me, thank God, and we suit one another admirably."

He led the way downstairs to a tiny dining-room—there were only two rooms on each floor of the little house—and soon the two men sat down to the scrap meal. Since this was produced out of Fortnum and Mason's dishes, Grenville had no fault to find with it, and the bottle of Liebfraumilch which accompanied it was of a quality no man could cavil at.

Grenville started talking about what he chose to call "l'affaire Debrette," but Rockingham shook his head.

"Do for God's sake leave the whole show alone for a bit. Honestly, I'm as puzzled as you are, but it's no use hazarding suggestions. There are a dozen explanations which might fit, all equally far-fetched. Let's give the subject a miss until we get to the blasted place."

"Blasted just about suits it, with no exaggeration at all," chuckled Grenville. "It's got a blight on it. The roof leaks in so many places that the walls have grown a species of green mould. It's clammy and mouldering and mildewed, and yet it has an awful air of fallen grandeur, of sanctity debased."

"Chuck it," groaned Rockingham. "Don't try your journalistic gifts on me. They're wasted. If you want to show your intelligence, tell me what you think of dramatising the Brontë works."

Grenville found himself being hurried through one of the best arrangements of quails in aspic he had ever tasted. There was Stilton cheese, too, and a prime one at that, but no time to do it justice. Rockingham produced some old brandy, however, that Grenville sniffed lovingly at as he tilted it in its Venetian goblet. He guessed that his host was glad of that fine drink to enable him to keep up his pose of studied detachment. For all his superior air, Neil Rockingham was worried and he was less able to conceal his perturbation than Grenville.

Swallowing down his drink in a manner that did it much less than justice, Rockingham said:

"We'll take a taxi to Notting Hill Gate and then walk. Better not take the car. Might be noticed if we left it nearby."

"If we left your Lagonda standing outside The Morgue I think it's likely it might attract a little attention," drawled Grenville. "Contrast a bit too striking, what?"

It was fine when they reached Notting Hill and they strode through the quiet streets at a great pace. When they reached the corner of Mulberry Hill and Rockingham saw the gargoyles at the angles of the tower he said:

"Good Lord! There's no end to the fantastic things you come upon in London. If this were set in a woodland clearing you'd swear it was ages old."

"Whereas it's set in Notting Hill, and in daylight you can see it's the most lunatic jumble of Victorian Gothic mixed with Oriental detail and debased Byzantine embellishments," said Grenville airily. "This way, old man, and watch your step! The paving's none too even."

Opening the door at which he had suffered his repulse five nights ago, Grenville fumbled for a switch, and Rockingham found himself in a porch with a vaulted roof, the walls of which had once been stencilled with Oriental patterns, but which were now discoloured and mouldy. Having shot the bolts on the heavy door, Grenville opened another door in the farther wall of the porch, pressed down a switch inside and flung the door wide, saying:

"Well, here we are! I never thought to possess a studio of my own, let alone one so spacious."

Rockingham stood by the door post like a man petrified.

"Good God!" he exclaimed. "Good God!"

It was a weird sight. Two immensely powerful electric bulbs hung from the lofty roof and shed their naked rays over the vast hall. The floor was littered with the remains of a sculptor's craft, chips of marble, lumps of clay, unfinished models, filthy wrappings. One or two ancient modelling stands and a drunken-looking easel were there, together with a crazy-looking camp bed, half concealed by torn curtains hanging from rods, and a dirty sink was set against one wall. On a low platform at the farther end stood an old concert grand, very long and gaunt, and above the centre of the floor a tarpaulin had been rigged up, fastened by cords reaching out to the side walls. Beyond the platform the groining of a shadowy apse was visible, and when Grenville switched on the lights there was a flutter of wings in the darkness of the beamed roof overhead, and the call of a startled bird.

"Well, I'm absolutely and completely damned!" said Rockingham. "I've never seen anything so demented looking in this world. My dear chap, you don't mean to say you've been *sleeping* here?"

"Well, more or less," replied Grenville. "I've spent the night here, anyway. I thought if Debrette *did* come back, he'd be more likely to come by night than by day. I'm not troubled with nerves, and this crazy place has actually fascinated me a bit. There's a gas-ring, you see, and water laid on, and a stove if you care to light it—all modern conveniences, in short. Then there are mice, nice appealing little beggars, not too shy, and cats who get in God knows how, and birds who roost in the beams up there, to say nothing of the owls in the tower—quite a nice rural touch about that. I brought my own blankets, but the camp bed seemed quite clean. It's in a good strategic position. The roof doesn't leak over that bit."

Rockingham walked slowly down the littered floor, looking almost fearfully to left and right.

"That any one should *live* in such a place is simply inconceivable to me," he said, but Grenville replied:

"Oh, you're an epicure, spoiled with the flesh-pots of Mayfair. I've seen many a studio in Paris which was a long chalk worse

than this one. I wish I'd got a pile of money, I'd buy the place
and do it up properly. Gorgeous place to live! I tell you I got
a fright one night. That jolly piano up there is rusted all to
glory, most of the strings bust, but one of the remaining bass
strings took it into its head to snap just after I'd turned the
lights off. It was uncanny. First a report which sounded as
loud as a pistol shot, then the quiver and hum of the string
springing back, and that woke the echo of every remaining
string—the dampers have all rotted to glory—and the whole
thing seemed to sing. Then a cat began to howl in accompaniment and the owls woke up and hooted. Very pretty! A sort of
diabolic concert."

Rockingham shook his head. "Well, I've never thought I was
a coward. I went through the war like other folk, but I'd rather
put up with a night's bombardment than spend one here. It's
beastly—uncanny."

"Oh, rot! A whole succession of chaps have lived and worked
here. If Mr. Dago-Face wasn't afraid of the creeps, why should
I be? As a matter of fact, the bed was in the vestry, or robing
room, or high priest's chamber—a cubby hole over there, but I
somehow preferred to be in the open if you see what I mean."

He led the way across the hall and pushed open a door
leading to a small room less than half the height of the main
building. "This is what the agents describe as bedroom, bathroom and kitchenette. Fact! There's a bath in the cupboard
effect beyond, and a range of sorts. The cellar stairs are through
here."

He stopped and glanced back over his shoulder.

"Shall I turn out those lights in there? We're advertising our
occupation to folks outside."

"No matter," said Rockingham. "In any case, I want to have a good look over the place, and we can't do it in the dark. Be damned to whoever is outside."

"Now if you were Bruce Attleton, I should expect you to behave just as you're behaving now," said Grenville. "You've made up your mind that something ghastly's happened."

"I can't help it, my dear chap. There can't be any normal explanation of Bruce's suitcase, unlocked, in a cellar in a place like this. The fact that Debrette has bolted makes it all the more sinister."

"Rotten word that. Anyway, how d'you know that Bruce isn't tailing the other bird? The steps are down here. I've left the suitcase where I found it. Take my flash lamp. There's no light down there." Rockingham went forward to the door which the other indicated, and turned his light on to the stone steps which led downwards, and began to descend. Grenville added:

"Be careful of the steps, they're slippery. Hell! What's that?"

A sound of something falling came from the hall behind them, and the younger man turned back, saying, "Confound it! I know I bolted the damned door. There's no other way in." He sprang across the little room and lunged out into the hall—and then the lights went out.

Rockingham, at the bottom of the shallow flight of stairs, let out a yell.

"Here, stay where you are until I come, you fool!" His words were drowned by a crash up above, and then equally incomprehensibly the lights flashed out again.

His heart pounding, Rockingham dashed up the mildewed stairs, slipped, came down on one knee, swore, recovered himself, and gained the body of the hall to see Grenville sitting on the floor, his hands touching a red weal on his forehead.

"The bastard!" he said thickly. "Caught me one on the head in the dark. Bat me one over the boko, as I said to Elizabeth."

"Look here, I've had about enough of this," said Rockingham disgustedly. Having bent over Grenville to ascertain the extent of his injuries, he stood up again and glared round the dishevelled-looking studio. It was empty save for their two selves, and the door by which they had entered remained shut. "I don't believe in spooks and what nots," he said. "There's somebody in the damned place, and I'm going to find them."

"It wasn't a spook that biffed me," complained Grenville, struggling up on to his knees. "Got a flask on you, old chap? I can see myriads of stars and all that."

"Brandy's no good to you then," replied Rockingham severely, speaking in that schoolmasterly tone of his which always made Grenville feel obstreperous. "Stay where you are till the dizziness goes off. I'll get a cold compress on that thick head of yours. Is the water in that tap drinkable?"

Grenville grinned feebly. "Water!" he protested disgustedly. "Good to wash in, you blighter."

"It's all you'll get from me. Never give a head injury spirits. I studied medicine for a bit once, if it interests you."

He went to the sink and drenched his large silk handkerchief under the tap, as cool now as he had been rattled when he first came in. Grenville, still feeling sick and shaky, grinned feebly and demanded, "What do you do if the lights go out again?"

"They can't—not while I've got my eye on those switches," retorted Rockingham. "I told you—I've no use for spooky theories. The lights went out because someone turned 'em out. Hold on to that flash-lamp and keep your own wool on!"

He returned with the wet handkerchief and a cup full of water, and tied up Grenville's head with skilful fingers.

"Now you stay where you are, young fellow, while I mooch round. I'm going to consider the door fastenings first."

"He's not such a frightened auntie as I thought him," meditated Grenville, swallowing the cold water quite gratefully. "Funny—show him a spot of something that looks like danger, and he's as cool as a cucumber. Blast my head! It's just spinning."

Rockingham was thorough in his survey. He found that there were three doors in all—one to the porch, one to the bedroom-kitchenette, and one to the tower. Of these, the porch and tower entrances had their bolts shot on the inside. The great west door, which Grenville had seen from the outside, overgrown with ivy, was boarded up on the inside. The only possible exit for Grenville's assailant was through the cellar, where Rockingham had been when the lights went out. Examining this, he found that Grenville's strategic arrangement of pails and tin trays was undisturbed. It seemed incredible that anyone could have got out that way without making a din which would have echoed throughout the place.

Grenville got to his feet after awhile, and walked round with Rockingham, while the latter, more and more exasperated, hunted in cupboards and shook out curtains which contained spiders and moths in abundance. It was all quite futile, and at last Grenville burst into a shout of laughter at the sight of the immaculate Rockingham, ruining his trousers by kneeling on the filthy floor, make a wild tug at a boot under the camp bed. It was a very old boot, and contained nothing at all but beetles.

"Glad you think it's funny," growled Rockingham. "It's a wash out, so far as our search is concerned. There must be a trap-door or something which we haven't spotted. I'm not going to fool around any more. It's the police after this."

"Well, it's your pigeon," returned Grenville, "though I must admit I'd like to get to grips with the sportsman first. That's twice he's done the dirty on me."

"And there's not going to be a third time if I can help it," retorted Rockingham. "I'm going to take that suitcase away. No object in leaving it here for the devil to pinch it, and make us look bigger fools than we shall look already when a police inspector starts asking us questions."

"Sure it hasn't gone already—from under your very nose?" inquired Grenville sweetly, and Rockingham swore, and dashed off to the stairway, returning shortly, suitcase in hand.

"Weighs about a ton," he grumbled. "I hope to God we find a taxi. Always loathed lugging things round. Come along, Grenville. No object in stopping in this foul place any longer."

They locked the door which Grenville insisted on calling the "vestry door," and when they stood in the porch again, and had switched off the lights in the hall, Grenville called into the darkness:

"All right, Mr. Bloody Debrette! Two tricks to you. You wait, that's all! I'll get my own back before long."

IV

NEIL ROCKINGHAM WAS NOT SLOW TO ACT ONCE HE HAD made up his mind. He had determined to tell the whole story to the police, but being a punctilious and thoughtful man, he did his best to get into touch with Sybilla Attleton before he took any action. Here he was quite unsuccessful, being told by Weller that Mrs. Attleton was out of town, motoring, and had left no address. Miss Leigh was at her club—the Junior Minerva. Having dispensed this information, Weller himself inquired for news of Mr. Attleton. Had Mr. Rockingham seen him in Paris, and could he suggest a date for his return? Mr. Attleton's lawyers were anxious to get into touch with him. Rockingham regretted his inability to give any news, and asked for the address of Todburys—Attleton's lawyers.

This call completed, Rockingham succumbed to an impulse to call up Mr. Thomas Burroughs. He also was out of town, motoring, having left no address.

Rockingham's third call was to the Junior Minerva, where he was put through to Elizabeth Leigh, who talked to him from her bedroom, not being addicted to the vice of early rising.

"I say, I'm terribly pleased with myself. I won the prize for my corpse-disposal do. It was a huge success," she burst out, on learning who was speaking to her. "We had a really lively argument over it. Can you tell me how long it takes for a body to turn to dust if it's buried in a…"

"No, I can't!" shouted Rockingham. "Look here, Elizabeth. Can you tell me where Sybilla is? It's really important."

"Feeling like that? Who'd have believed it? Sorry, my dear, and all that, but I can't tell you. I really can't. I don't know. Sybilla does these rest-cure jaunts. She's probably having her face lifted, but don't say I said so. Can you tell me where Bobby Grenville's got to? It's the frozen mitt for *him* next time we meet. I've rung him up three times, and he wasn't in. That's more than flesh and blood will stand, you know."

Replacing the receiver, Rockingham next attacked the firm of Todbury, Wether & Goodchild in Lincoln's Inn Fields. He had no sooner mentioned his name to Mr. Todbury than that worthy gentleman piped up. "I'm very glad to speak to you, my dear sir, *very* glad. Can you give me the present address of my client, Mr. Bruce Attleton? The matter is really pressing—"

"I'm sure it is," replied Rockingham. "I don't know where he is, and as I'm thinking of asking the police to find out, perhaps I had better come to see you first."

Mr. Todbury, a learned-looking gentleman of seventy, was much put about by Rockingham's tidings in their subsequent interview. He hummed and hawed, being completely out of his depth, but he deprecated calling in the police prematurely. Perhaps there was *some* explanation...

Rockingham cut him short. "Perhaps there is, but after my experience of last night, I don't feel disposed to wait until the explanation is forced on me. By the way, you said that you wanted Attleton yourself."

"Just so." The lawyer fiddled with his pince-nez. "You may have heard of Mr. Adam Marsham—the head of Mr. Attleton's family—his great uncle in short. He is a very old man and his health is precarious. I might say his death is imminent. He has expressed a wish to see Mr. Attleton."

"Well, I'm afraid his wish can't be gratified just at present," said Rockingham impatiently. "In the meantime, can you give me any advice about approaching the police—because, whatever you think, my mind is made up."

Here Mr. Todbury was unexpectedly helpful, so that Rockingham, instead of walking into Vine Street Police Station, as he had intended, went to New Scotland Yard instead, and was shown into a small office overlooking the Embankment, where a long, lean-faced Chief Inspector named Macdonald listened patiently to his tale of woe.

Rockingham made his story fairly clear, though Macdonald stopped him once or twice and advised him to keep to the facts of which he had first-hand knowledge, since other people could add their versions later. Rockingham, accustomed, perhaps, as a successful dramatist, to an audience more easily impressed than this long-jawed Scot, had a curious feeling that he was being stripped, mentally if not physically. He was still in a state of excitement concerning his experience of the evening before, and his narrative was not as direct as it would have been had he felt his usual calm self.

Macdonald, having asked a few cogent questions, summed up as follows:

Mr. Attleton had expressed strong irritation over the com-munications of a man named Debrette, who, in Rockingham's estimation, might be a blackmailer. Having booked a room at the Hotel Bristol, in Paris, Mr. Attleton left his house in London on Wednesday, March 18th, with the avowed intention of going to Paris. He had not arrived at the Bristol according to plan and had not been heard of since, as far as could be ascertained. His suitcase had been found in the Notting Hill studio where Debrette had been tenant until recently. When Mr. Rockingham went to that studio the previous evening, an assault had been made on his companion, the present tenant, by a person unknown.

"That's all straightforward," said Macdonald, as though the history related to him had been the most normal affair. "To get one point quite clear—has anybody in the Attleton family seen Debrette?"

"Not to my knowledge. I saw him just the once, when he spoke to Attleton. Grenville saw him, last Friday evening, and he seems to be quite well known in the neighbourhood of his studio."

"Good. Now what was the reasoning that led you to believe—or imagine—that Mr. Attleton was being blackmailed by Debrette? Why not assume that he was being dunned for a debt which he didn't mean to pay?"

Rockingham mused for a while before he answered.

"Attleton generally pays his bills," he replied. "In any case, if it had been a matter of an ordinary creditor, I believe he'd have told me about it. It struck me that there was fear, as well as anger, behind his agitation."

"In addition to that, were you not aware that there was some point on which Mr. Attleton was susceptible to blackmail, sir? Half truths are no good to us here, you know."

Rockingham moved uncomfortably in his chair. The manner of the Chief Inspector was courteous, his "sir" reassuring, but there was a relentless look in his eye.

"There was something of the kind," he replied uncertainly. "Damn it, this is pretty beastly. What I tell you will be regarded as a confidence, I take it?"

"Certainly, as far as is compatible with the process of the law," replied Macdonald. "The very fact that you are sitting there, informing this department that your friend has disappeared, is an indication that you consider the police have a part to play. We can't do our part with goggles on, nor yet rose-tinted glasses."

"Well, I'll tell you the facts as I see them," replied Rockingham. "When Attleton married, nearly ten years ago, he had made a considerable name over his first two novels. He also made a lot of money over them. His early promise has not borne fruit—and his wife is not over sympathetic concerning failure—or only partial success. As her husband became less prominent in the public eye, Mrs. Attleton became more so—as you probably know. It did not make for domestic felicity." Rockingham's face flushed uncomfortably, and he looked appealingly at Macdonald. "Need I dot all the I's and cross all the T's?" he said. "Attleton's my friend. I like him and trust him. It seems a poor sort of friendship to spread myself over his failings."

"It may be the truest friendship in the long run," replied Macdonald. "What it amounts to is this, I suppose. That Mr. and Mrs. Attleton went their own ways, and he sought elsewhere the sympathy that was not forthcoming at home?"

"That's about it," replied Rockingham, and a gleam of humour showed in his troubled face, "but it's no use asking me for the address of the sympathiser, because I don't know it."

"That must be a comfort to you," said Macdonald dryly, "because I should certainly have asked for it. Next, has Mr. Attleton any private means, apart from his earnings as a writer?"

"None," replied Rockingham. "I know that for a fact."

"And you also probably know that a household which is presumably run by the wife's money is not a very gratifying affair for the husband," went on Macdonald, and Rockingham nodded his head, while one eyebrow twitched an acknowledgment of the other's shrewdness. He was beginning to like Macdonald.

"One can also assume, I take it, that Mr. Attleton had no wish to fall out with his wife to the extent of leaving the mixed joys of their joint household? Quite. Well, I admit that the situation presents possibilities to the blackmailer, assuming that the wife was still sufficiently concerned to be jealous."

"She'd be like a raging fury if she knew that Bruce..." Rockingham stopped abruptly, but Macdonald merely nodded.

"The situation's not exactly a new one," he said. "We'll leave it at that for the moment. Now about Mr. Attleton's relations. Has he parents living, or brothers or sisters?"

"No. His parents both died before the war. He quarrelled with his only brother—Guy. He died in Paris about a year ago. A cousin who recently turned up from Australia also died, only a few days ago. Attleton's singularly badly off for relatives. Barring an ancient uncle, or great uncle, who is senile, he appears to have neither kith nor kin."

"How long have you known him?"

"Ten years—rather more. I met him first at the Authors' Club, just before his marriage. We've been pretty close friends ever since."

"I take it that he hasn't many intimate friends?"

"Why do you assume that?"

"Because you haven't mentioned them. If he had any particular crony, you'd have gone to him before coming to me. The only other man you've mentioned is Mr. Grenville, whom you speak of as considerably junior to you and Mr. Attleton. Where does Mr. Grenville come in?"

"He wants to marry Elizabeth Leigh—Attleton's ward. He's been haunting the house for months."

"Why doesn't he marry her, then?"

The dryness of the tone set Rockingham chuckling and he replied, "Elizabeth's a minor, and can't marry without her guardian's consent—which isn't forthcoming at the moment."

"I see. Any fortune involved?"

"Hardly a fortune. A competence. A few hundred a year, I gather."

Macdonald's next question went off at a tangent.

"Why did you hit on Mr. Grenville to rout out Debrette?"

"First, he'd already heard of Debrette and questioned me about him," replied Rockingham. "I told you the incident of the telephone call. Now, while I very much wanted to find out where Debrette lived, I didn't want to go investigating him myself, because the chap had seen me with Attleton. I thought that if he saw me near his own quarters, or in a pub he frequented, he might get wind up and bolt. Then Grenville is a shrewd fellow. He's done a good deal of inquiry work along journalistic lines, and he's intelligent. Where I went wrong was in trusting him to go so far and no farther—but as things have turned out, I suppose it was all to the good that his curiosity got the better of him."

"It appears so. You and he were the only people present when Attleton was told about that phone call? There weren't any other visitors?"

"Not just then. A man named Burroughs had been there during the evening, but he had just left."

"Another friend of Mr. Attleton's?"

"Of his wife's, more correctly speaking, but he's a pretty frequent visitor."

"And Mrs. Attleton is away?"

"She is—the deuce knows where. It was a pretty problem for me, Inspector. If you'd found out what I did, what the blazes would you have done?"

"Just what you have done. It was the only possible thing to do. Mr. Grenville ought to have informed us as soon as he discovered that suitcase. A man doesn't leave his passport in an empty studio for any normal reason. A suitcase conceivably. A passport, no."

"That's what I felt about it," said Rockingham, "but I'd like to say this. Grenville may not appear to you to have acted with much wisdom, but he's straight enough. I swear to that."

"It's always satisfactory to have a testimonial of good character, sir," replied Macdonald equably. "A little common sense is a desirable asset, also. Can you tell me this? Why did Mr. Attleton object to Mr. Grenville marrying his ward? Anything against his character?"

"No. Nothing. Miss Leigh is only nineteen, and Attleton has theories about marrying in haste and repenting at leisure. The girl's only been out of school a year or less. Attleton likes Grenville all right. I think he'd have agreed to the marriage if he hadn't been preoccupied with this business of Debrette, whatever it is."

"I see. Well, I think I've got all the data that's immediately necessary, sir. I shall find you at The Small House I take it, if I want further information?"

"Yes—or at the Authors' Club. I haven't a resident servant, so if I'm out the phone won't be answered after midday. I shall be in this evening, anyway."

"Good. I may get Mr. Attleton's servant to go through the contents of the suitcase and see if anything's missing. Meantime, I'll have that studio looked into."

Rockingham drew a breath of relief.

"Thank the Lord I've got it off my chest!" he said. "I had the hell of a night wondering what I ought to do. I loathed the idea of handing Attleton's affairs over to a police department."

Macdonald shrugged his shoulders.

"You might have found yourself in a very queer corner if those susceptibilities had guided you," he replied.

When Rockingham had gone, the Chief Inspector made a précis of his notes and considered them for some time. He then spent a short time on certain works of reference which gave a few precise details about Bruce Attleton, his wife, the well-known actress, and about Neil Rockingham, dramatist.

Armed with which information he went and reported the matter to Colonel Wragley, the Assistant Commissioner.

"It's a funny story, Macdonald," grunted the latter. "Open to various interpretations."

"Yes, sir. Possible murder of Attleton by Debrette or Debrette by Attleton. Possible dirty work on the part of the inquiring Mr. Robert Grenville. There's only his own statement to prove that that suitcase was found in the studio cellar. Also possible ingenious work on the part of defaulting guardian, getting away with his ward's money while the going's good. That's an old story."

"Seems a bit elaborate, with Debrette and all—and there's one cogent point against it." He pointed to a sentence in Macdonald's notes, but the latter replied:

"I see a way out of that. However, I think the Belfry Studio and Mr. Robert Grenville are worth interviewing simultaneously."

"What did you make of Mr. Neil Rockingham?"

"Difficult to size a man up when he's on edge, as this chap was. He struck me as intelligent and reasonably straightforward. The only really silly thing he did was to put that journalist on to the track of Debrette. He ought to have turned it over to us if he suspected blackmail, or else have left it alone."

"More men lose their heads over a threat of blackmail than for any other reason on this earth," said Wragley. "Well, get down to it. You'd better find out if Debrette really exists."

"Or existed," corrected Macdonald. "I think that answers itself. He's been seen to drink whisky in a pub. Mr. Grenville wouldn't have dared to invent that. Too many witnesses of the conversation, sir."

Macdonald, after leaving instructions to Inspector Jenkins to carry on with the job which he had been employed on before Rockingham turned up (a series of burglaries in the outer suburbs), got his car out, and, taking Detective Reeves with him, drove up to Park Village South. Here he saw Weller, and inquired about the time when Bruce Attleton had left home on the previous Wednesday.

"Mr. Rockingham is a bit worried because he can't get into touch with your master, and his lawyers are bothered by his absence, so they want us to find him," explained Macdonald cheerfully. "Our lost property department is the most popular section of our organisation."

Weller smiled. "Yes, sir. I shall be glad when you've got into touch with him. Very disturbing, all these inquiries and not being able to give any answer. Mr. Attleton left here on Wednesday morning last, shortly after ten o'clock. I packed his suitcase the previous evening—just a change of clothes and a dinner jacket, etc., seeing he only meant to be away for a week or ten days. He left by taxi—I called one up from the rank myself—and he told the driver to go to Victoria, continental side. Folkestone-Boulogne he was travelling."

"That's just what I wanted to know," said Macdonald. "The only other point is this. Did you call that taxi by phone, or go out and whistle up a crawler?"

"By phone, sir—the Gloucester Gate rank."

"Thanks. I hope I shall soon have some news for you," said Macdonald, and hastened out to instruct Reeves to follow up the taxi report.

"You oughtn't to have any difficulty over finding the taxi-man who took Attleton to Charing Cross—or wherever he did take him," said Macdonald. "Then, if you go to Leon's, in Bond Street, you can get a photograph of him. There was a good one of theirs in the *Writers Who's Who*. Carry on with that. Railway stations are your long suit."

Reeves grinned and departed—a good man at his job, as Macdonald knew well. The Chief Inspector himself drove on to Notting Hill, where he had made an appointment over the phone with Grenville before he left Scotland Yard.

Arrived at the Belfry Studio—as The Morgue was described in the house-agents' registers, Macdonald was admitted by Grenville. Before he gave much attention to the building (and he was so accustomed to queer buildings that Macdonald took this one as all in the day's work) he studied Robert Grenville unobtrusively. A hefty fellow, about five feet ten in height, with powerful square shoulders which showed their muscular development through the loose tweed coat he wore, and a square, cheerful face, comely in a rustic fashion. There was aggressiveness in the tilt of his jaw and humour in his eyes, but in addition Macdonald noted a shrewdness and quickness of glance in those rather wide-set eyes, and a tendency to look all round him as though he were suspicious of the very walls. A young man who could look silly if he chose, and yet had all his wits about him, Macdonald decided, of country stock and rearing, to judge by his physique, and yet city trained—too quick and alert for the countryman.

Grenville in his turn stared at Macdonald and summed him up. "Scot to his finger tips. Pragmatic and prosy may be. A fine upstanding fella', in good training, hard as nails. Reckon he'd enjoy clapping the darbies on anybody."

Aloud, Grenville said, "Well, so old Rockingham's spilled the beans. Probably wasting your time. Here's my choice abode. What d'you think of it?"

He threw open the inner door of the porch with a dramatic gesture, but got no exclamation from Macdonald. His steady grey eyes roaming round the building, he gave no sign of surprise. "J'en ai vu bien d'autres," he said with a shrug.

"I bet you have," grinned Grenville, thereby showing Macdonald that he was not unacquainted with idiomatic French. "Still, this isn't bad for a high-class residential neighbourhood, what?"

"Not at all bad." Macdonald's eyes went afresh over the littered floor and came to rest on the grand piano in the apse. Then his gravity gave way, and he fairly laughed.

"Lord! what a mess!" he exclaimed, and seeing his face then, Grenville saw that the long-legged "Presbyterian of a chap" was not merely a police automaton, but a human being like himself.

"Is that your bed?" inquired Macdonald. "If so, let's sit on it and get down to the story."

Grenville was an excellent witness. He told his story well, keeping events in order, and making the whole thing "come alive," and Macdonald, who sat smoking a pipe, let him go straight on without interruption. At the conclusion of the narrative he said:

"At present the only people connected with this case who have actually *seen* this Debrette are you and Mr. Rockingham, and your view of him was a snapshot affair. Still, give me your impression of him as fully as you can."

Grenville sat forward, his fingers caressing the large bruise on his forehead which was now stained a lively purple hue.

"He was a neatly-built chap, I should say a bit shorter than myself, and several stone lighter. Neat on his feet. Beard and gig-lamps as I told you, and a lot of hair—fuzzy and curly. Look here, I've got a dotty sort of idea. I've kept it to myself so far, but since old Rockingham's lost his nerve and gone pouring out his woes to you, I might as well go all frank and candid, too. I told you how I saw the chap—in silhouette against the light, and only for a second or two at that. Something in his build reminded me of Bruce Attleton—and something in his voice, too. Sounds idiotic, I dare say, but there it is."

"Quite interesting," said Macdonald, "so when you saw that suitcase you weren't so flabbergasted as you might have been? You didn't tell Rockingham this notion?"

"Not I. He'd have gone up in smoke. Stiff old stick is Neil. Reminds me of the Head of my Prep school. Besides, it opens up some nasty avenues."

"Such as?"

"Glory! Don't put on the innocent abroad air to me. Don't suit you. Look here, Neil R. told you he'd seen Debrette *with*

Attleton, didn't he? Well then, they're not one and the same. There *was* a Debrette. Wherefore if the chap I saw was Attleton, it means he'd togged himself up to impersonate Debrette. If that's so, I say again there *was* a Debrette—used to be. Had been. Tense past historic. Perfect."

"I see. If that story's got any punch to it, why did Mr. Attleton leave his suitcase here to give the show away?"

"Well, there's various ways of looking at it. That suitcase is a noticeable affair, opulent, and all that. Got Attleton's name and private brand on it, so that it's nice and easy to pick out in the Customs—Douane—Dogano—Bagaglio Spedito in tran-sito and all that. It's covered with gaudy labels, too, Meurice, Ritz-Astoria and so forth. Not the sort of bag I'd carry about in the street if I didn't want to be noticed—nor yet put in a taxi. Better to come back one evening with a nice large sheet of brown paper and some string, and take it away under cover, No adequate paper here. No string. Lots of bits and pieces, but not suitable."

"Quite. An idea. Now funny stuff apart, Mr. Grenville, can you really imagine Mr. Attleton murdering Debrette and then bolting—in such a manner that he could never hope to show his head in any civilised country again?"

"I don't know." There was a wicked gleam in Grenville's aggressive blue eyes. "I'm not murderous by disposition, but if I ever chose to murder anybody, I'd hit on a blackmailer to start on. Dirty swine! Moreover, if Bruce Attleton did do anything of the kind, he's had bad luck. How was he to know that old Rockingham'd set me sleuthing just when he was getting busy? Another point—most chaps who'd had a glass of whisky chucked on their faces by way of welcome would take care not to ask for another. Stay away, in fact. I'm not like that. I came again, and took on the tenancy of this desirable abode when a man might well have believed it'd stand vacant until the housebreakers took over. I look at this all round, you know." He faced Macdonald truculently. "It's your job to see people don't run amok, and since you're on the job I've got to be straight with you—for my own sake—but there's two points of view."

"I agree with you in part," said Macdonald. "You're wise to recognise that frankness is a synonym for wisdom so far as you're concerned, just now."

"Gosh, I'm not entirely a mug!" protested Grenville. "Old Neil R's eyes nearly blew out of his head when I told him I'd found that suitcase just below there. You promptly ask yourself, 'Did he find it there—or did he plant it?' Nothing like understanding one another, is there?"

"Nothing," agreed Macdonald politely. "Meantime, let's go and have a look in that cellar."

"Right." Grenville sprang to his feet with alacrity. "Not that there's anything interesting to see. I've looked. Concrete floor, not dug up or anything."

"Concrete floors aren't easy to dig up," said Macdonald, "and most men accustomed to good living aren't much of a hand with picks. Hullo! what's that?"

They had reached the "offices," the bathroom and kitchenette annexe when a clatter of ironmongery sounded below them, a prolonged rattle of pails and trays which echoed weirdly in the space below.

Grenville sprang forward with a shout.

"Hell! the blighter's come back and sprung my booby trap. Down here. Lor! what a lark!"

He sprang forward down the stone steps which led from a door in the corner of the room, with Macdonald close at his heels. Daylight filtered in through a little unglazed window in a little area recess, where dank ivy pushed its shoots across bars which had been broken and twisted awry. Pails there were, a tin tray and scattered fire-irons, odd bits of coke and coal, old tins and a variety of other rubbish, but no sign of any living intruder to account for the collapse of the booby-trap.

"Damn and blast!" burst out Robert Grenville, "the blighter's hopped it again. Hi! If we legged it out of the back door we might…" He turned violently and collided with Macdonald, who saved him from collapse on the one-time coal heap by a powerful, but not gentle, arm.

"Too late," said the Chief Inspector calmly. "If there were any one here, he's had lashings of time to get away. You'd like me to be quite frank with you in return for your frankness, I take it?"

"Yes, of course!" Grenville's nose fairly twitched with eagerness.

"Good. The most helpful thing you can do now is to go home and stay there. I shall have this place searched and other matters attended to, but I'm afraid you can't help. Got that?"

"Marching orders? Damn it, you're no sport. There's a lot of things I could show you here—"

"I've no doubt you could, but I promise you I shan't miss much on my own account. The one thing you *can* do is to phone the Yard for me, and tell them to send another man along here to help."

"Ah!" Resentment shone in Grenville's eyes. "You don't fancy being left here alone, Scotty! Cold feet?"

"Definitely," said Macdonald placidly, pulling out a note-book. "Pity there's no phone here, to match the other amenities. Just give this message word for word as I write it." A moment later he tore out the sheet and handed it to Grenville. "Did you bust those bars yourself when you first got in here, Samson?"

Grenville's eyes followed the Yard man's to the broken grating. "More or less," he admitted. "I'm the whale of a chap for moving things. Look here, Lord Trenchard etc., let me stay and help search. I'll look after you, I will really."

"Git!" said Macdonald, pointing to the stairs. "This turn may prove to be funny, or it may not, but you're going to be conspicuous by your absence. Up the stairs, laddie, and quick march!"

Still protesting, Grenville climbed the stone stairs to the "bathroom," and Macdonald saw him to the door of the porch.

"Now go home, and stay there!" he said severely. "No Sherlocking on your own account. If you make yourself a nuisance to me by not being where I want you when I want you, I'll have an all-stations call sent out, and have you in jug by the evening. No smokes. No drinks. It's dull, I tell you straight!"

"Fer—r-r-rightfulness. Thr-r-reats, and me the star turn witness! All right, Mr. Elder of the Meeting but I'll tell you this. If I meet that Debrette round the corner, I'll bash his ugly face in so he'll be past identification for weeks!"

"Do," said Macdonald, and shut the heavy door.

V

THE TELEPHONE CALL WHICH ROBERT GRENVILLE PUT through brought a police-car with four plain-clothes C.I.D. men in it. Of these, two stayed with Macdonald to assist him in searching the studio, and two were despatched on other business, one to The Knight Templar, and one to ensure that Mr. Robert Grenville did what he'd been told to do—or failed to do it, as the case might be. A variety of tools and implements were removed from the car, and the three men went into The Morgue looking equipped for duties of sexton, surveyor and plumber respectively.

Police work is always thorough and orderly, seldom spectacular, and on this occasion three experts in the detection of crime set to work as calmly as but more energetically· than the usual phlegmatic British workman. Under Macdonald's directions, they first went round and investigated all possible exits, ensuring that locked—or blocked doors—were fool-proof. The "plumber" was left to work in the bathroom, while Macdonald and Detective James—a powerful young man in blue dungarees—set to work and rendered the escape through the coal hole useless as entry or exit. After which they cleared a space carefully on the cellar floor, ensuring that not so much as a pin escaped their attention, and then began to move the accumulation on the floor to the space they had cleared. It was no nice job. The past tenants seemed to have fed to a large extent on tinned food, and they had cast old salmon tins, sardine tins, condensed milk tins, and a variety of other malodorous receptacles to mingle with the coal dust in the cellar. Young James twitched an inquiring nose, not in disgust, but in hopefulness and the spirit of pure science.

"Smells high," he observed. "Sulphur dioxide and similar stinks. Nitrogeneous remains somewhere. Definitely organic."

"A dead cat, probably, or cats," said Macdonald. "One chap here liked prawns. Losh! I hope he died of them! There's some left in the pot!"

They were very methodical. One pile in the corner was kept for tins, one for coal and coke, one for sundries (among which was the dead cat Macdonald had expected, exhumed from a grave of coal dust). After nearly two hours of careful work, they had inspected every inch of the cellar floor, whose entire surface they could pronounce intact, disinterred a variety of mouldering canvases ("Masterpieces of the Coal Measures Period," as young James said) and investigated the rusting remains of a one-time furnace connected with a defunct hot-water pipe system. "And that," said Macdonald, "is definitely that. Score nil. Honours easy."

He was clad in a suit of overalls thoughtfully provided in the police car, and looked like some engineering expert, black of face and hands, but serene of countenance. "Now we start upstairs," he said. "I wonder if Davies is through with his job yet. He might go to the pub and get us some food—not of the tinned variety—and beer. Beer! What a good thought."

Davies was busy plumbing, apparently, with a variety of receptacles on the floor beside him. He had been disconnecting the joints of the waste pipe, which owing to the improvised method of setting the bath in an apartment never intended for a bath, had various unusual kinks in it.

"I reckon you've got a true bill, Chief," he said dryly, indicating one of the bottles which stood beside him. "Baths seem so safe—always popular. It was a neatly done job, I reckon. Bath cleaned afterwards and then mucked up a bit with rust and dust and what nots—but every kink tells a story. I reckon there's a straight job for the analysts."

"If that's so, we'd better get busy upstairs, Davies," said Macdonald. "There's a sink in the studio. You can wash under the tap there, and so can we. After that you can go and get some food at the pub nearby. We'll eat it in the car. I don't fancy this place as a dining-room. Come on, James. We shall want some brooms and shovels to get that floor clear, later. We'll give it the once over, first."

Neither the "once over," nor the subsequent thorough moving of everything, including lifting the grating over the old hot-water pipes, brought an enlightenment to those earnest toilers. It must have been years since that studio floor was so well swept as it was by those painstaking members of Scotland Yard. They collected everything—marble chips, clay, plaster of Paris, old paint tubes, brushes, cans, and bottles of oil and turpentine, rotted (once damp-proof) wrappings for clay models, odd tools, pliable piping for the centring of large clay figures, broken palette knives and sticks of charcoal. James it was who crept beneath the old platform and met a large rat, much confused and annoyed by the beam of an electric torch, but apart from the rat and a quantity of illustrated French volumes (mostly pornographic) his gallantry produced no result.

It was a tired, depressed, and incredibly dirty trio of investigators who at last sat upon the platform and consulted together.

"Look here, Davies," grumbled James, "what d'you bet me it's not rust you've got in those precious bottles of yours? Any chance the whole thing's a leg-pull, sir?"

Davies shook his head. "It's not rust. I'll bet you any money that you like to lay that it's blood—or diluted remains of same. I'd better be off to the labs and make sure."

Macdonald nodded. "That's it. I'm puzzled over the whole show. I might have believed the sportsman I had in here this morning would have had the nerve to work a leg-pull, but not Rockingham. He was dead serious. I'm willing to take Davies' word for it that he knows what he's up to, but the point is—what have we missed? If a murder has been committed here, the overpowering probability is that a corpse is on the premises. No one would have risked carting a body outside to dispose of it elsewhere. They'd have had to load it up into a car or van on the pavement, either in daylight, or under the light of a street lamp in a well-patrolled neighbourhood. Doesn't make sense."

He looked around the gaunt building which they had cleared. Everything in the studio—barring the piano—was now stacked in a heap in the centre of the floor, and the bare stained walls were clear for inspection, with every cupboard and press open wide.

"Wait a jiffy, though. I'd forgotten. Debrette was known as a sculptor. It would have been all in keeping for him to have heavy stuff moved, in crates, if he chose. This looks like being a teaser."

"If it was big stuff he moved, he'd have needed help in handling it. Might get a lead that way," said James hopefully.

"Might not," growled Davies. "You bet he did it alone and unassisted. Talking of your sportsman this morning, Chief, what did you make of his little avalanche trick down there? Did he work it, or did some one else?"

"If he did it, he's a conjurer," said Macdonald. "I didn't take my eyes off him. It could have been worked from outside easily enough, but by the same reasoning, a cat might have done it—jumped in from outside on the top pail and brought the rest down together."

"What did the silly jackass think was the good of it?" grumbled Davies. "Can't see the sense of it."

"Oh, his mental process was clear enough," said Macdonald, "assuming that he's speaking the truth, that is. He's had a glass of whisky chucked in his face, and that's enough to put a man's back up. He's a big chap. He hoped Debrette—or Attleton—would come back, and he'd have the chance to use his fists. Human enough."

"But by the time the silly juggins had got downstairs, the quarry would have legged it by the way he came in," complained Davies, but Macdonald shook his head.

"No. You're wrong. It'd take time to climb through that grating in the cellar. It's too small to use your arms properly. That's why I knew there hadn't been anybody inside there this morning. The whole thing's a bit of a mess at present. We'd better concentrate on following up Debrette and the Attleton trail. I'll have another look at those walls before I leave. Meantime, Davies, get on to the lab. with your specimens and report to my office. Come on, James. You take the north and I'll take the south. No, don't start singing Loch Lomond, or I shall brain you."

The walls were in a bad state throughout. Cracks and crumblings were the rule, not the exception. Damp was everywhere, and a good deal of mildew. One patch attracted James's attention in particular—a roughened portion, in which lumps stood out like rough-cast, but Macdonald looked on it with an experienced eye.

"A painter had this place once—for a long time I'd say. He was an extravagant bloke. He scraped his palette clean every evening and put the surplus on the walls with his palette knife. Layer after layer. That's good paint, James, gone to waste, not a pointilliste tour-de-force—though they look alike, I grant you."

Their survey of the walls was as fruitless as their sweeping of the floor. Neither tapping nor visual inspection gave them any satisfaction.

"We shall have to leave it for the time being, James," said Macdonald. "We've done everything we reasonably can. I'm going to lock up and put a man outside. There's no other entry, unless it's by way of the roof—and if any sportsman likes to try getting in that way, let him. He'll give us a lead somewhere. You'll have to stay on the premises until you're relieved. I'll send Wilton along."

James stood and looked upwards at the cross beams of the roof. "A pulley?" he hazarded, "and monkey tricks?"

"Don't believe it. Anyway, you and I aren't going to break our necks that way. I'll get some ladders in to-morrow. As for the tower, no one's been through that door for a couple of years at least. London soot's a fine indicator of passing feet, and it's not been disturbed since the Lord knows when. Cheer up, laddie! You're within bowing distance of a bath. Not that one, though."

Whereupon Macdonald turned his back on the Belfry, bats and all, and returned to Scotland Yard to pick up the reports of the inquiries he had set on foot under the heading of "routine," pertaining to Attleton's movements when he left home, to Debrette's tenancy of the Belfry as known to agents and

neighbours, and recent movements of that enterprising sportsman Robert Grenville.

The latter, when he was so uncompromisingly shown the
door of his own studio by Macdonald, did what he was told to
do, and went straight home, much against his own inclinations.
Grenville had, however, enough common sense to realise that if a
criminal charge eventuated from Macdonald's investigations, he
(Grenville) needed to keep on the right side of the law in every
detail. He had told a story concerning which there was—and
could be—no outside corroboration, and uneasiness grew upon
him as he travelled eastwards towards the city.

Grenville's abode was, in its own way, as remarkable as
Rockingham's, though it boasted none of the architectural beau-
ties of The Small House in Mayfair. In the tangled network of
courts and alleys which lie between Fleet Street and Holborn,
Great Turnstile and Farringdon Street, there still exist certain
small houses which were built not long after the great fire of
1666. It was in one of these that Grenville had been fortunate
enough to find quarters—an absurd little red-tiled house of two
storeys, with a grass plot in front of it and its immediate neighbours. On all sides around this ancient oasis of greenery towered
enormous blocks which reverberated day and night with the roar
and clatter of printing presses, of restaurant activities, with the
incessant whirr of the machinery which maintains the civilisation
of this bewildering epoch of ours, but in a little plot below the
windows of Grenville's sitting-room, daffodils were now bending
their straight buds to unfold their golden perianths, a rose tree
was putting forth brave green shoots, and "gilly flowers" blos-
somed surprisingly, as they might have done in the days of the
Merry Monarch. Furnival's Court was the name of this queer

city survival, and the house where Grenville lived was kept by the widow of a master printer, a severe-faced matron to whom the roar of machinery was a normal accompaniment to life.

Arrived back in his own quarters, whence he had been summoned by Macdonald's telephone call, Grenville decided to put on record the events of the last week, and to make a schedule showing how his evidence was arrived at, but he had not proceeded very far along these lines when the telephone bell rang, and the voice at the farther end banished all rational thoughts from his head.

"Look here, Robert Grenville," began Elizabeth Leigh's comminatory voice. "Don't think I'm ringing you up out of pure friendliness, or anything of that nature. I'm not. You can boil in oil so far as I'm concerned, but will you kindly tell me this. What's all the shemozzle about? Where's Bruce, and what is he up to, what's wrong with Neil Rockingham, and what's it all about?"

"Darling," began Grenville, but she snapped back:

"If you start being familiar I shall ring off. You've ignored my existence for a week—"

"Darling, I haven't. Oh damn! Look here, Liza, it's all too damned complicated for words, and the devil of it is I've been told to stay at home until Scotland Yard tells me I may go out again."

"Whoops!" came from the other end, "and what on earth have *you* been doing to interest Scotland Yard?"

"Nothing, angel, absolutely bally-nix, I swear it. Look here, Liza. Be an angel. I can't come to see you, or ask you out to dinner or anything until that reptile says the word go. Can't you stretch a point and come to see *me*? You've often said you would—"

"Have I? I don't seem to remember it. However, if I come on this occasion, don't imagine it's for your beaux yeux, Mr. Robert Grenville."

"Angel, I won't. Look here, this place is the devil and all to find. You want to come to—"

"Idiot! I'm not an imbecile, nor yet a deaf mute. If there *is* such a place as Furnival's Court I shall find it, and pretty presto, too, so don't go doing a vanishing trick before I come."

Grenville heard the receiver banged down and the line went dead, whereupon he executed a war dance around the room. During the next half-hour he spent the time in a hectic activity of tidying his room, and equally hectic mental searchings to determine just how much he could tell Elizabeth Leigh. He was under no oath of silence, but he realised that it was not going to be easy to avoid indiscretions which he might repent at leisure.

Elizabeth, shown into Grenville's sitting-room by a landlady whose face implied that she was past being surprised by anything anybody did in these days, came straight to the point.

"What's happened to Bruce, Bobby? Don't go walking round in circles. Tell me."

"But I don't know," he began. "Honestly, I don't know. Nobody does. That's the trouble."

She screwed up her face, saying:

"Is it anything to do with this Debrette horror?"

At the end of half an hour, Elizabeth sitting in the arm-chair, and Grenville on the floor at her feet, had threshed out all that was known between them. Grenville did his best to keep his own counsel, but he was in love, and Elizabeth was determined, and he was as wax in her hands. She learnt the actual facts concerning the Belfry Studio, the suitcase, and the excitements of the previous evening which had resulted in the bruise on Grenville's forehead, and Rockingham's decision to go to the police. For herself she supplied the following fact: Some ten days previously, walking home just after dusk to the Attletons' house, where she was staying on a long visit, she had heard a man's voice behind her inquiring if she knew where Mr. Attleton lived. Turning, she had seen a bearded man, wearing large glasses, a wide hat and a long, foreign-looking cloak. Accustomed to odd-looking visitors—for both Bruce and Sybilla had some original-looking acquaintances—she replied that Mr. Attleton lived at Little Park House. The man thanked her and hurried on, walking quickly, but he did not stop at the Attletons' house. When she saw Bruce later in the evening she had described the gentleman in the cloak, with the curious white streak in his beard, and had been astonished to see her guardian look perfectly livid. Her disposition to rag him had passed quickly when she realised the furious temper she had aroused in him. Later, over their coffee, Sybilla had said, "Oh, that's the Debrette man. Goodness alone knows what Bruce's little secret is. He's got to come clean with it sometime or there'll be trouble. I'm not going to have queer foreigners ringing up and uttering cryptic threats over *my* telephone."

Sitting by the fire in the very comfortable little sitting-room, Elizabeth and Robert looked at one another in consternation. The girl went on, with a little shiver:

"It's beastly, Bobby. It's all very well to joke about murders and corpses, but now I feel a bit sick. You know, I believe Sybilla had got to hate Bruce. I've never told you, but I felt uncomfortable whenever I was alone with them, just lately. When I left them and went to stay at my club, I swore to myself I wouldn't go back there again."

"Why, Liza? Just because it was beastly being with two people who scored off one another?"

She lit a cigarette, and blew the smoke towards the ceiling. "Yes, only it was worse than that. They quarrelled—not in front of me, but I've heard their voices—and they both implied, when they were jibing at one another, that they each knew some secret about the other. I think Sybilla wanted to get a divorce from Bruce—and he wouldn't agree. Holy deadlock—and all that."

"Good Lord! How foul for you—to have to know anything about that sort of muckery!"

"Oh, tosh! You can't live among theatrical people and keep the Virginibus Puerisque touch. There's not much I don't know about this wicked world, Robert. I don't mind. Illusions don't help anybody—but I can't help shivering when I remember Sybilla's face after that evening when we were discussing my murder game. 'Build him into the fabric of the establishment.' Ugh! I thought she was just acting when she mimicked Bruce saying that, doing the sinister-female-on-the-stage touch. I didn't think about it again until just now. How horrible."

Grenville jumped to his feet. He couldn't sit there at Elizabeth's feet with that gruesome phrase echoing in his ears, "build him into the fabric of the establishment." Ugh!

"But Liza," he protested, "I don't see that Sybilla fits in anywhere. What about Debrette? It's he who is the crux of the matter."

"Say if Sybilla put him up to blackmailing Bruce—just for a blind? Perhaps he's some out-of-work actor, that's what he looked like. Then there's that odious man, Burroughs. He's crazy over Sybilla, you know. Oh, isn't it all beastly?"

"I should jolly well think it is!" exclaimed Robert. "Look here, darling. I expect we're getting all het-up quite unnecessarily. Old Rockingham got cold feet, and went off to the police in too much of a hurry, and Bruce and Sybilla will be just raving mad with him when they roll up again."

"You don't think so, really," groaned Elizabeth. "You know something awful's happened, and so does Neil Rockingham, and so does the reptile whom you call Macdonald. You all know something grim has happened, and you're just trying to be cheerful over it. Bobby, I do wish you'd never gone near that beastly Belfry place."

"So do I," said Grenville soberly, "and I guess old Neil R. wishes so too."

After Elizabeth had gone, Grenville returned to his "write up" of the case, but he spent more time smoking cigarettes and chewing his pen than in making notes, and when the door of his sitting-room opened, shortly after his tea had been served by the admirably uninquisitive Mrs. Blench (the master-printer's relict) and Macdonald walked in, Grenville was almost thankful to see him.

"Got him?" he inquired idiotically.

"Got who?" inquired Macdonald. "I've got a few facts, but no individuals. I want your finger-prints, if you really want to know the reason of this sociable call, also it might be a good move on your part if you'd like to write a small diary, with particular reference to your doings on the Wednesday, Thursday, Friday, and Saturday of last week. Just for your own good, you know."

Grenville fairly gaped, and Macdonald went on, "In case of misunderstanding, let me assure you that I'm on an eliminating tack. The suitcase which Mr. Rockingham thoughtfully removed from the Belfry is, as you observed, of first-class material, well polished, and presenting a good surface for finger-prints. Presumably yours are on it, since you opened it and moved it. So are Mr. Rockingham's. If Mr. Debrette moved it also, he may have been kind enough to leave a record of his own. He may have done nothing of the kind, being a shy bird—but we might as well decide which prints are yours, if you've no objection?"

"None," said Grenville. "Get on with it. I thought you generally offered suspects a shiny card and asked them if they'd ever seen it before."

"I like detective stories myself, they make me laugh, whereas real crime isn't funny," said Macdonald. "You're probably well up in the procedure, so we won't waste time."

"And about that diary," he continued, when he had filed Grenville's record in a case not unlike a cigarette case. "Attleton left home at ten-five. He reached Victoria at ten-thirty, and he took a taxi to Charing Cross at ten-forty. He was then alive and well. You found his suitcase in the Belfry cellar on Saturday morning. It might be as well to let me have a record of your movements—as complete as possible, with corroboration if obtainable—between those periods, with particular reference to the Wednesday morning. Take your time over it. No hurry."

"Then you think he *has* been murdered?" asked Grenville, the words sticking in his throat a little.

"I don't know. I think a crime of violence may have been committed, but nothing is certain yet. We have collected a certain amount of evidence about your friend Debrette, from the house agents who let him the studio, the pub where he dropped in of an evening, and the tradespeople. I don't think we shall have much difficulty in putting your little theory to the test.

Whatever else a talented impersonator can do, he can't be in two places simultaneously."

"No," said Grenville, "he can't."

Macdonald looked at the young man's square face. Something had happened since that morning to deflate him. He was no longer full of bright ideas and cheerful back chat, but looked a very sobered edition of the Robert Grenville who had chattered away so merrily in the Belfry. On his way to the door, Macdonald came to a halt.

"If you do happen to know anything about this rigmarole, it would be much more sensible to get it off your chest," he said, not unkindly, and Grenville looked up at him quickly.

"I don't know anything, not in the way of facts," he said slowly, "but I've had time to think things out a bit, and I don't like the look of it. I talked a lot of hot air about Bruce this morning, but looking at it in cold blood, I don't find it amusing. It's all very well to talk about murder and corpses and all that, until you begin to think of some one you know corpsing people."

"And then it ceases to be funny," agreed Macdonald. "Who was talking about murder to you recently?"

"Look here, if I get it all off my chest, will you promise to forget about it if it doesn't turn out to mean anything?" inquired Grenville.

Macdonald grinned. He couldn't help it. "I think you can be quite certain of one thing," he replied. "It's far more sensible to lay all your cards on the table than it is to make me and my department pick up items with forceps, so to speak. Every one connected with the Attletons will be interrogated pretty thoroughly, and if there has been any talk of murder, you can bet your last sou we shall hear about it. As for the assurance you want, I can tell you this. If your remarks haven't any bearing on the case, it will be as though they were never uttered. Now what about it? You started the ball rolling when you poked your nose into the Belfry Studio. You might as well roll it in the right direction."

Grenville thereupon told the Chief Inspector about the murder discussion, and Sybilla Attleton's famous brain wave and Bruce's subsequent comment. He did not mention Elizabeth Leigh, but Macdonald was already aware of the girl's visit to Furnival's Court and drew his own conclusions.

When Grenville had finished what was, for him, an exceedingly tame narrative, Macdonald observed:

"If a man—or woman—is contemplating murder, they don't generally advertise their method beforehand. If it is any consolation to you, I can assure you that no one was electrocuted in a bath or wash-hand basin at the Belfry, and no one was concreted into the bath or cellar there. Also, I should say it's very improbable that any woman carried out the crime which we suspect may have been committed there."

Grenville drew a deep breath. "Perhaps Sybilla's having her face lifted after all," he observed, "and Bruce is bird-fancying in Brussels."

"May be," observed Macdonald, "and you, I might point out, have had a nasty knock on the head, and though you don't know it, your wits are wool-gathering in consequence. If I were you, I should take a couple of aspirins and go to bed and forget all about it."

"Thanks, and all that, but I generally go out to my dinner. The old girl here doesn't oblige. Any objection to my feeding at the Golden Cock?"

"Feed where you like," replied Macdonald. "I've done with you for the moment, only don't try butting in, and the less you talk about all this, the better."

Grenville appeared reassured, and his wide grin was more in his old manner as he replied, "All right, uncle."

Macdonald, wending his way out of the devious courts back to Fleet Street, decided that two items of information were worth considering in Grenville's farrago of blether. (1) That Mr. Thomas Burroughs had taken no part in the murder discussion. (2) That that phrase, "concrete him up into the permanent fabric of the establishment" looked as though it might be prophetic.

VI

MACDONALD, HAVING RECOVERED HIS CAR FROM ITS appropriate parking place by the law courts, drove westwards to call on Neil Rockingham again, with the intention of picking up Bruce Attleton's suitcase and taking it to Scotland Yard as exhibit A. Before he entered the car, he got into touch with the indefatigable Reeves and told him to go and find out what he could about Mr. Thomas Burroughs who lived in chambers in Knightsbridge, but was at present away from home.

Reeves had already spent a busy day. Having had a stroke of good luck early in the day in finding the taximan who drove Attleton to Victoria, he had then provided himself with a photograph of that well-known author and tackled the porter on the continental side of the station. Industry and pertinacity had rewarded him by finding one Henry Hobbs, porter, who remembered taking Attleton's suitcase off the taxi, and who had been told to wait with it in the booking hall while its owner telephoned. A few minutes later Attleton came hurrying up, obviously excited and put about, and told Hobbs to get another taxi and put the suitcase on it. This had been done at top speed, and the order Charing Cross given to the driver. Since Hobbs knew the second taximan by sight, Reeves was enabled to catch him at his midday meal at a nearby cabman's shelter, and learnt that he had deposited his fare at Charing Cross Station, that here Attleton had alighted, carrying his own suitcase, and walked into the station—and off the map, so far as Reeves was concerned. No amount of patient questioning got him any further.

Reeves always knew when it was waste of time to belabour a vanished trail. This one had eluded him for the time being (not surprising, as Macdonald observed, considering Charing Cross booking hall was filled with a large party of Czechoslovaks, assembled for their return journey), so Reeves began on another line—that of Sybilla Attleton herself. She also had left home on the Wednesday morning, shortly after Bruce had done, but had driven herself in her own car, a green Hillman Minx, taking two suitcases and a jewel case. Weller had no idea of her destination.

Reeves pursed his mouth up a bit. While he considered it improbable that Mrs. Attleton had driven to a railway station (a taxi would have been simpler for that) it was obvious that she had all England to choose from, and Reeves no indication at all to guide him.

"Elimination" is a byword at the Yard. If you can't find where a man—or woman has gone, you can sometimes find out where they have not gone. Mrs. Attleton might have taken her car abroad; if so, it would be easy to discover the port of embarkation. If she had not taken it abroad, a concentrated all-stations interrogation could do marvels about discovering the abiding place of any car.

Reeves had his lunch and returned to Scotland Yard. The telephone, allied to the system whereby every police station in England received a "lookout" warning, did its work in a marvellously efficacious manner. Reeves spent the afternoon at the phone, but before evening he had learnt that Mrs. Attleton's Hillman Minx was now in a garage in Southampton, the owner having given orders for decarbonisation, as she would not be needing it again until April 1st, when it was to be ready for her.

Having achieved this result, Reeves was quite ready to attack
the trail of Mr. Thomas Burroughs, who, as Macdonald suggested, might also have gone to Southampton—possibly.

When Macdonald arrived at The Small House, he rang
Rockingham's bell several times before he got any answer, and
was just beginning to feel somewhat anxious, when Rockingham
opened the door, consternation written large on his countenance.

"Good Lord! I've made the damnedest fool of myself," he
blurted out. "I've let my own nerves play old Harry, hauling you
in like this. I could kick myself! That was Bruce Attleton on the
phone just now, talking to me, after I've been spending my time
concocting blood-curdling stories about him."

"I'm glad your anxiety is appeased," said Macdonald politely.
"All the same, you'd better let me know what he said."

"Of course. Come in. Holy Moses, old Bruce'll never forgive
me for the song I've raised!" groaned Rockingham. "Look here,
Chief Inspector, if there are any damages to pay over this, let
me have a note of them."

"All in good time," said Macdonald, "accounts aren't in my
department, anyhow. I'll just use that phone if I may." He went
straight to the instrument and called up the operator, giving
instructions that the call which had just come through should
be traced, and then turned to Rockingham.

"What had Mr. Attleton got to say for himself?" he inquired.

"Hardly anything. Just said he was sorry he'd let me down
in Paris, but he'd had unexpected news and had to go up north ✀
in a hurry, and would be writing in a day or two. Then I butted
in, as you may imagine, and wanted to know where he was and
what the devil he'd been up to, and before he answered me we
were cut off. Good Lord! What a crazy story!"

✀ not from Charing Cross

"Sure it *was* Mr. Attleton?" asked Macdonald, and Rockingham stared at him.

"I'm as sure as I can be of a voice I know as well as my own," he retorted, and then stared at the other man. "Oh, hell!" he groaned, "don't tell me it wasn't he! I tell you it was."

"Well, I'm glad to hear it," replied Macdonald. "I've no reason to contradict you. Hullo! there's your phone again. Perhaps he's making another call."

Rockingham fairly bounded across the room, and snatched up the receiver.

"That you, Bruce? Grenville? What the blazes? You've seen *who*?" After a moment or two during which Macdonald could hear the buzz of an excited voice from the receiver, interspersed by violent ejaculations from Rockingham, the latter snapped:

"Tell him? Of course you must tell him. Hold on, he's here! For God's sake don't get cut off before you've finished. Where are you?"

Turning, he held out the receiver to Macdonald.

"It's Grenville. Says he's just seen Debrette in Trafalgar Square and lost him again. He's in a call-box at Charing Cross."

Macdonald caught up the receiver and listened to the excited narrative which followed. Grenville said that he had been about to cross the Strand at Trafalgar Square when the traffic lights changed against him, and just as the buses started moving forward he had seen Debrette standing on the opposite pavement. Grenville had lost his head, plunged into the traffic in an effort to reach the man on the other side, and been knocked over by a motor cyclist. By the time he had disentangled himself from the subsequent confusion, Debrette had naturally vanished—"had time to get miles away," said the wrathful Grenville, "and one

of your damned traffic cops says he's going to summons me
for walking to the public danger, and the chap on the mo-bike's
been taken to Charing Cross Hospital. What a bloody mess."

"Bad luck!" said Macdonald. "Are you sure it was Debrette?"

"Sure, certain, honest to God abso-bally-lutely certain,"
retorted Grenville. "There can't be another beard like that in
London, nor in hell neither, and the chap's as dark as a dago.
Besides, he footed it like knife when he saw me. What shall I
do? I told a mutton-headed copper about it, and he just kept on
saying, 'That's all right, sir, now don't you get excited.' What
shall I do?"

"Go home to bed, and ask your landlady to make you some
Bengers," retorted Macdonald. "I'll come and see you later.
No, you mutton-headed journalist, you can't. The chap's in
Golders Green or Timbuctoo by this time. Go to bed, do, and
stay there."

Replacing the receiver, Macdonald turned to Rockingham,
who had got a bottle and glasses from a cabinet while the Chief
Inspector was admonishing Grenville.

"I apologise," said Rockingham, raising the glass he held,
"but I needed it. I've never felt such an insufferable ass in my
life. Do for pity's sake, have a drink. You must have met plenty
of other idiots in your time, so I'm not unique." His face, when
he began speaking, was a picture of dejection, when, catching
Macdonald's eye he began to laugh, throwing back his fine head
and fairly shouting with mirth.

"Crackbrained fool that I was, letting that blasted belfry get
on my nerves. I'd made up my mind that Bruce was murdered
and Debrette was a fugitive from justice, and now inside ten
minutes I learn that Bruce is right as rain, and Debrette is in

Trafalgar Square. My dear chap, I know the world's full of mugs, but I'm the biggest!"

"Well, it looks as though I'd better go and call my pack off," replied Macdonald. "We're like the London Fire Brigade, accustomed to false alarms. All the same, I'll take that suitcase—Mr. Attleton can take the trouble to call on me when he comes home, and explain why he left it in a cellar in a studio that didn't belong to him."

"He jolly well can. I wash my hands of it," said Rockingham. "Provided Bruce is all right, I'll never butt in to his affairs again. I've had my lesson."

"You've nothing to blame yourself for," said Macdonald. "I told you, I should have done exactly what you did."

"Well, I was out of my depth," said Rockingham, rising to his feet as his visitor showed no signs of staying. "I've never had any truck with melodrama, either on the stage or off, and when Grenville took me to that demented studio, my reaction was police. Not heroic, perhaps, but heroics aren't my long suit."

He was still chuckling when he saw Macdonald out into the mews, and the Chief Inspector heard him laugh again as he closed the front door.

Arrived back at Scotland Yard, Macdonald deposited exhibit A, and inquired for the man who had been sent to the house agents—Messrs. Keyland & Belling—in Notting Hill.

"Got me the chap I want, Raines?"

"Yes, sir. Party named Wetherby. Had the tenancy of the Belfry for three years previous to the chap who hanged himself. He says he'll meet you there at nine."

"Good man!" said Macdonald. "Gives me time for a meal. So Davies was right in his hunch?"

"He's not often wrong, sir. Blood it was, and human blood, too."

At nine o'clock punctually, Macdonald arrived, at the gates of the Belfry, and saw there a short fellow smoking a pipe.

"Mr Wetherby?"

"That's meself. You're not wanting to buy a pre-war concert grand, are you? There's a fine one in there."

"I've seen it," replied Macdonald. "Is it yours?" He opened the gate, and the little man waddled in unconcernedly. "They say possession's nine points of the law, so I suppose it was nine-tenths mine, only I didn't bother to take it away. I found it when I took possession. Some of the treble strings were still good, then. It's the hell-uv-a shame the way they're letting this place fall to pieces. Best studio I ever had—only it rained."

Macdonald produced the key which he had taken from Grenville. "By the way, my name's Macdonald. If you'd like to see my warrant—"

"Streuth, and what for? Some police wallah—a very polite young man—comes along and says you've a fancy to inspect the place with me as guide. I'm not supposing half London's yearnin' to see the Belfry after dark. Think I'm afraid of you, Jock? Think again. I'm from County Cork meself."

Macdonald chuckled. "I'm of a cautious race, and it is always worth while finding out who's leading you into the local Morgue."

"Get along with you. It's the most peaceful spot in London, abode of Beelzebub that it is, but it rained."

Switching on the lights as they entered, Macdonald said—"I want you to tell me if anything fundamental has been altered since you were here. Just have a look round."

"The bastards have swept the floor," said the little man sorrowfully. "Did ye find a number six Rigger, good red sable, Robeson's? No? I liked that brush. Saints and angels! What's the canopy for? Ah, the rain—sculptor wasn't he?" He wandered round burbling inconsequently. "That easel now, young Billy Duveen fell on it once too often, till it wouldn't hold a man up nor a canvas, neither. There was a nice cat used to come here, black, answered to the name of Satan, a rare devil for rats, he was. So you've filled the niche up, Jock. Presbyterian? Statues and images repugnant to the deity, you heathen Lutheran! I liked that niche. I had an Artemis up there myself. Am I drunk, laddie? There *was* a niche there?"

"Show me where it was exactly."

The little man walked up to the wall and peered at it.

"It's the devil himself must have done it—Devil a mark. I tell you there *was* a niche! See you here."

He waddled across to the opposite wall and pointed to some marks on the wall. "That's our base, where Billy and me played darts. At herself, there in the niche, you know, with chalked darts. Ten if you got her amidships and rubber for a right and left in succession. Grand game, Jock!"

"I've no doubt it was. What did you do with the lady when you left? Take her away?"

Wetherby began to laugh, it was a jolly laugh, beginning in a series of chuckles and rising to a roar.

"No, and I didn't! Wasn't she part and parcel of the establishment, like that grand piano up there? We had a party me last night here and we ended up by putting Artemis in the bed there in me bedroom, to comfort the next poor devil. Fine she looked, with a sheet tucked up nicely round her! Man, we painted her like a lady, with rose madder on each cheek and lake on the lips!"

Macdonald's lips twitched.

"I'd as lief had my bed to myself," he replied, and little Wetherby roared, and clapped him on the back.

"And meself, Jock! I didn't sleep in that, I've got me own ideas of comfort, and if Artemis and the piano and the bit of a bed were 'part furnishing,' as the spalpeens called it, it wasn't for me to take 'em away. Have you still got the jolly old gas stove in there? Twas a fine blow up we had with it that day I turned on the oven gas and forgot to light it and all. John Shand went in with his pipe alight and opened the oven door to look for the leak, and he lost his eyebrows and all."

Macdonald got rid of the jovial Irishman at last by walking him round to The Knight Templar and leaving him to the congenial society of Melisande (a name whose origin Macdonald could not fathom) and his native whisky, after which the Chief Inspector rang up reinforcements from the Yard, and strolled back leisurely to the Belfry, looking, with his pipe between his teeth, and his air of placid unconcern, the most untroubled inhabitant of that pleasant neighbourhood.

Once inside the studio, Macdonald walked to the spot indicated by Wetherby and stood and stared at the wall space he had examined that morning. There was nothing to indicate that a niche had ever existed; the smears on the wall ran across the surface unbroken, the plaster felt neither more nor less damp than that of the surrounding walls. A penknife stuck into it caused it to crumble away as might have been expected, save that Macdonald, picking up the dislodged fragments and rubbing them between his fingers, observed them to be whiter in colour, and different in substance from ordinary wall plaster. It crumbled, but did not powder, and his subsequent diagnosis proved correct, "quick-drying plaster of Paris—the chap was a clever workman."

When his men arrived, Macdonald set them to work on the space indicated, warning them to be careful how they worked. A short reconnaissance however, showed how the niche had been concealed. A few inches of plaster were stripped off, and then a wooden boarding displayed itself, fitting closely up to the arch of the niche. The latter was about six feet high by two feet across. When part of this boarding was removed, a cascade of white dust began to come down, which proved to be a mixture of plaster of Paris and quick lime, together with larger fragments which must once have constituted the cast of the Artemis. It was not long after that that the niche revealed its secret in the mummified bundle which was carefully roped on to the wall and kept in place by staples.

Macdonald had seen many gruesome sights, and his nerves were of the steadiest. He regarded human remains as calmly as a dissector might, not confusing the poor clay with the feelings of the living, breathing, sentient being which it had once been, but he was glad to go outside and smoke a cigarette once the main task was over.

"Well, you tumbled to it, Chief," said Jenkins cheerfully, "and a cunning piece of work it was."

"Tumbled to it!" said Macdonald. "Tumbled down on it, you might say. Who is going to identify those remains—a headless and handless corpse? It's the remains of a once healthy man, but who, Jenkins? This morning I should have said, 'It's either Attleton or Debrette,' this evening I've been told that Attleton rang up a man who knows his voice better than I know yours, and Debrette was seen in Trafalgar Square. If some one swears to those remains, how can we tell they're right? It's the very devil of a problem! Assuming—as appears—that deceased has no scar or physical abnormality whereby he can be recognised, how is any pathologist to state who he was?"

Jenkins puffed away at his pipe.

"Yes. It's difficult. You'll have to go on probabilities."

Macdonald nodded. "The probabilities are all in favour of Debrette being the murderer," he said. "Debrette was known as a sculptor, or posed as one. He might have had the skill to plaster up that wall. It was the work of a skilled hand, and it seems unlikely that Attleton could have acquired that skill—but is the argument conclusive? We take it for granted that Debrette lived here, but that's only a surmise. He was here on and off, showing up in the neighbourhood occasionally. Attleton *might* have worked such an impersonation, it's not impossible, and during the hours he spent here have practised the craft of plastering."

"It's not impossible, but it looks to me unlikely," said Jenkins. "Then what about that suitcase? Would he have left it there to prove that he was implicated?"

"That's just what he might have done, if he were clever," replied Macdonald. "He left it there to prove that that corpse was his own. The argument's obvious. One says at once, 'If Attleton were the murderer he'd have taken that case away.' He may have counted on that."

The two men smoked for a while in silence, and then Jenkins went on.

"Well, how do you make sense of that telephone call? Seems to me all wrong."

"Everything sounds all wrong, man! There are two answers. Either Rockingham is lying, and I can't see his point, or else Attleton is alive and beginning to lose his nerve. Knowing Rockingham, he was afraid of him going to the police and starting the hue and cry. He wouldn't have known that friend Neil would have acted so promptly."

"But who was the chap who played poltergeist in this old shanty, when those two were in here yesterday evening, if not the murderer? Grenville got a sock in the jaw, didn't he?"

"No. He got a bang on the nut. I don't believe there was anybody else here at all. There's cats and rats and God knows what else in this barn, and I believe both those chaps were rattled. Grenville hears something upstairs, and comes blinding across the little room and tripped up—on what? On the fuse box and meter which project from the wall there. That shook the contact and the lights went out temporarily, and the fellow crashed his length and hit that straddling easel—the blow on his head was obviously not made by a man's fist, but by a bar or rod of sorts. He was knocked out and confused—semi-concussed, and assumed some one had gone for him. I've barged against an obstacle in the dark myself, and sworn some one had hit me. Then when Rockingham found him, they both assumed there was some one else here. I'm certain that's the explanation—unless Grenville is up to tricks, and put the light out and bashed his head on something for verisimilitude."

"Good enough. We're assuming that Attleton doesn't know Rockingham's come to us, nor that Grenville's found his suitcase, and he—Attleton—rings up to reassure his friend, and get a few days' grace. Where did that call come from?"

"Charing Cross Station. Call box."

Jenkins whistled. "Jumping Jehoshaphat! and the chap rings up ten minutes later from the same spot to say he's seen Debrette. Sounds promising."

"Sounds a long sight *too* promising," said Macdonald. "Even supposing that Grenville's clever enough to imitate Attleton's voice, would he have been such a mutt as to make the second call from the same spot? Besides, he can't have faked that motor-bike accident. That had to be the pukka thing. Too many witnesses, and our chaps at that. A man may run his head against a bar to get a bonny bruise, but it takes a cool nerve to plunge into traffic with the intention of faking an accident. That's more like suicide."

"Where the raving rats are we?" groaned Jenkins. "Do we take it that Attleton's walking about London dressed as Debrette, ringing up his friends and saying oke in a friendly spirit?"

"Maybe. When I heard about that glass of whisky chucked in Grenville's face, I was certain it was done to blind him—*pro tem*. He'd seen just as much as he was to be allowed to see. It did enter my head that Rockingham was the funny bird, but this spills it completely. If Grenville saw Debrette at Charing Cross while I was with Rockingham in Mayfair, it lets the latter out. One comfort is that we ought to be able to get outside evidence this time. If a bloke with a white streak in an otherwise dark beard *did* stand on the pavement at Charing Cross, some one will have seen him."

"It'd be nice to fix on a motive," mused Jenkins, and Macdonald fairly snorted.

"Motive? There's lashings of 'em! Attleton kills Debrette who blackmailed him. Debrette kills Attleton for seducing his daughter or some such. Grenville kills Attleton because he wants to marry his ward. Mrs. Attleton eggs on Thomas Burroughs to kill unwanted husband, and urges virtues of concrete, as in anecdote. That reminds me. We're minus a head and a pair of hands. Was another brainwave adopted? Plagiarism at parties. Do we follow the thread and search in London crypts for missing members, or send out a party to explore dene holes?"

"More likely the English Channel, if you ask me," growled Jenkins, and Macdonald said:

"Oh, that reminds me. Neil Rockingham went to France on Wednesday, the 18th, and returned on Wednesday, the 25th. I managed to look at his passport while I was telephoning. It was stamped as plain as daylight. Exit Neil Rockingham. It wasn't he who chucked whisky at his little friend on Friday night. Excellent thing, our passport system."

Jenkins agreed, absent-mindedly. He was deep in thought.

"By heck, it's a teaser!" was his only other contribution to the conversation.

VII

AFTER THE AMBULANCE HAD DRIVEN AWAY FROM THE Belfry, bearing the poor, mutilated remains which presented the C.I.D. with such a baffling problem, and Macdonald had left with his assistants, one watcher remained in the shadows at the back of the building. This was Detective Fuller, detailed to remain on guard in case any further developments occurred in the premises of The Morgue. Fuller expected nothing more than a boring night, during which he might exchange a cautious word with the point-duty man at given intervals, and long for the first streaks of dawn to lighten the eastern sky. It seemed to him that the focus point of interest had left with the ambulance—the corpse was unearthed and removed, and The Morgue, having yielded up its secret, was but one of those unoccupied premises which occasionally attract the interest of the police, are depicted in the picture papers for a brief season, and then return to their dull obscurity of waiting for a tenant.

Fuller had no faith in the popular adage that a murderer always returns to the scene of his kill. In the cases which he had investigated the murderer always took care to put a good distance between himself and the place to which he had hopefully relegated his victim's body.

Sitting on a ledge in the dark little garden at the back of the studio, Fuller pondered over the cases in which he had been engaged. He knew the importance, from a police point of view, of an early identification of the corpse in a murder case.

This new murderer's "technique" of removing the identifiable portions of their victim was a snag from the viewpoint of the C.I.D. In this case, now, they were likely to have a lot of trouble in sorting things out if they could not identify the remains which had been so skilfully concealed in that niche.

Occupied with his own thoughts, Fuller heard a distant clock boom midnight. Could that be Big Ben, he pondered—three miles away as the crow flies, wind from the south, maybe—He was just about to get up and make another tour of the premises in his charge when he changed his mind, and drew back into the shadow of the bushes. The iron gate which led to the road had creaked on its rusty hinges.

Straining his ears for a footfall, Fuller heard nothing more, but in a moment a shadow appeared on the stone flags at the corner of the building, cast by the lamplight outside the gate, and then a man's figure appeared. He moved quite silently, being shod in shoes with crepe-rubber soles, and he was clad in a long raincoat, with a cap well pulled down over his face. Fuller said "Glory!" this being more than he had hoped for in this lonely vigil, and waited for developments.

This visitor was no tramp, seeking to doss down for the night; even in the uncertain light it was obvious that the coat was a good coat, and the cap of good shape. The visitor came to a halt by the porch, and tentatively turned the handle. ("Poor mutt. That won't work," said Fuller.) Being only a few yards away from him, the detective could see that this was not the famous bearded man whom Macdonald wanted, neither, in Fuller's opinion, was it Attleton. The latter was described as spare and active, about five feet ten in height, with a long, lean face. This party was a heavily-built fellow; the belt around his coat defined a figure inclining to stoutness, and the cheeks visible beneath the cap were full.

Leaving the door, the visitor advanced round the corner of the building to the coal-hole, let himself gingerly down into the little area, and investigated the window with the assistance of a flash lamp. The reflected light enabled Fuller to see the rather highly-coloured face, heavy jowl and fleshy ear of the intruder. He also heard him swear quietly as the realisation of the blocked aperture dawned on him. He proceeded to climb out again, and Fuller decided that time for action was ripe. Switching the beam of his own powerful bull's-eye on to the unknown investigator, he said politely, "Now, sir, what are you doing here?"

"The devil!" exclaimed that gentleman, and turned about in his tracks as though to make a hurried departure, but Fuller blocked his way.

"What the devil's it got to do with you what I'm doing here?" spluttered the other. "When it comes to that, what are *you* doing here? Up to no good, that I'll swear. Clear out of this or I'll give you in charge."

"Won't do, sir. I'm in the police force. I'll have to trouble you to come along to the station and give an account of yourself."

"What the deuce d'you mean? You can't play tricks like that on me. I won't stand any of your nonsense, understand that! Get out of my way!"

"Now, sir, that won't do!"

"Won't it, you damned impostor, you!"

The blow aimed at Fuller had got plenty of weight behind it, but the detective side-stepped. The heavy man recovered himself with a surprising agility for one of his build, and lunged out again. The second blow was a different business, and while it winded Fuller, it also made him see red. A savage blow beneath the belt is enough to try the temper even of a well-disciplined C.I.D. man, accustomed to a rough-and-tumble. Fuller, grunting with pain, let the other chap have it, hot and strong, and having got him on the ground, rammed down a knee amidships without overmuch thought of where it was going, and got the handcuffs on his prostrate victim, having told him what he thought of him in language more forceful than academic.

It was at this stage in the night's proceedings that the point-duty man turned up, running round the flagged path with very audible footfalls.

"Got him?" asked the constable foolishly, being not very intelligent by nature, and not overfond of running.

"I should say I have," replied Fuller. "Now then, get up, *sir*, and reckon you're lucky I didn't serve you with your own sauce. Up you get, and you've no one but yourself to thank for your troubles. You'll have to go along with the point-duty man to the station, and you can explain there what you were doing on these premises, and why you struck a police officer during the execution of his duties."

In the struggle the well-shaped cap worn by the intruder had fallen off (it was now less well-shaped, having been trodden underfoot), and Fuller could see his opponent's dark head, the sleek hair all awry and the heavy, flushed face of a very angry man. Nevertheless, the handcuffed man made an effort to speak reasonably.

"Look here, Inspector," he began. "I apologise. I made a damned fool of myself and lost my head completely, but you haven't the ghost of a reason for running me in. I just felt curious about this queer old place, and thought I'd like to have a look round. I didn't even try to break in, you know that quite well. Look here, let bygones be bygones, and I'll make it worth your while, both of you—"

"You're one of that kind, are you?" said Fuller disgustedly. "You first kick another chap in the middle, and then offer him a bribe to get off. Well, you've made a little mistake this time. Bates" (this to the constable) "I'm detailed to stop here. You'd better whistle up your point-mate at the next corner and tell him to take over your beat till you return. Report to the superintendent that the man you've got in charge was arrested for suspicious behaviour attempting to enter the Belfry, and that he attacked the officer in charge in attempting to escape. And you can keep *your* explanation for my superior officers, sir," he ended up in his best manner.

"Now then, are you coming quietly?" demanded the constable, and marched his man off.

Fuller, composed in mind if still somewhat pained in person, sat down on his ledge and awaited further visitors, but none occurred that night.

Macdonald, getting up, as was his custom, shortly after six, had a phone call from the superintendent of the Belfry neighbourhood just as he had shaved.

"I didn't see any point in waking you up in the middle of the night," explained that official. "Fuller collected a gentleman named Mr. Thomas Burroughs in the Belfry grounds last night. Loitering with suspicious intent—and then used his boots on Fuller in the hope of doing a get-away. Won't give any account of his reasons for being there. Just idle curiosity. He's been cooling his heels here ever since. I find it generally pays to give that sort leisure to think. More likely to come across with it after a night in the cells. Seems a prosperous sort of bird."

"That sounds satisfactory," replied Macdonald. "I'll be along shortly. Kind of Mr. Burroughs to look us up. I rather wanted him."

Mr. Thomas Burroughs was shown into the Chief Inspector's presence in a small office in the local station at the uncomforting hour of eight a.m., and if the stockbroker had ever looked genial and self-confident, he did not look it now. He was a very angry man, but not, so far as Macdonald could see, a frightened one. He spent some time in a blustering exculpation of his own actions before Macdonald interrupted him.

"You don't seem to have grasped the nature of the case into which you have blundered," said the Chief Inspector at last. "The reason that we had a man on duty at the Belfry Studio was that a murder has been committed there. A man's body was removed from the premises only a few hours before you were caught loitering there."

Burrough's face was a study. From being apoplectic in hue it became livid, and the rather prominent eyes fairly bulged.

"Murdered?" he gasped, "not…" He shut his jaw with a snap before another word escaped him, and then made an effort to speak more calmly.

"I'm horrified at what you tell me, Inspector, horrified! I understand now the somewhat violent behaviour of the man you had in charge, but I assure you that I knew nothing about this murder, nothing at all. My visit there was dictated by curiosity, nothing more. I happened to be passing the place, and it struck me that it looked unusual, bizarre, in fact, and I gave way to an impulse to have a look at it. I'm not a burglar, Inspector, nor yet a tramp or vagrant. Here is my card. You have only to send for my solicitor to identify me."

"I'm not doubting your identity. Not in the very least," said Macdonald, and something in his voice made the other blench. "As a matter of fact, I have been wanting to get into touch with you. You are a friend of Mr. Bruce Attleton's?"

Burrough's face became again suffused with red.

"Well, yes. I know him pretty well."

"Have you seen him lately—during the past week?"

"No. Not since—let me think, Tuesday week it'd be, ten days ago."

"Yesterday morning, information was given to my department concerning Mr. Attleton, to the effect that he had disappeared. He did not go to the hotel in Paris where he had engaged rooms, and his friends were uneasy about him. They became still more uneasy when Mr. Attleton's suitcase was found in the untenanted Belfry Studio. On investigation, a man's body was discovered in the building."

Watching Mr. Burrough's face, Macdonald thought that he was going to faint, so livid had his face become, and the Chief Inspector got up and poured out a glass of water for him from the carafe on the superintendent's desk.

"Thanks. Silly of me, but I can't stick horrors," said Burroughs weakly. "Beastly story—You say you found poor Attleton's body."

"No. I didn't say so. I said we found *a* body. It has not yet been identified. Now, sir, I think you will see that it is reasonable to give a full account of the motives which prompted you to visit the Belfry, and to investigate a window by which it was possible, until recently, to make an entry into the premises. An account of the manner in which you have spent the last ten days, will, I hope, enable us to release you without preferring a charge."

Burroughs sat stock still, his face frowning, his jaw set.

"And if I decide to say nothing at all, Inspector? On what grounds do you charge me?"

"I prefer to detain you on suspicion, sir. You can see for yourself the position in which you are placed. Had you not offered violence to the officer who interrogated you, you might be better placed."

"I lost my temper," said Burroughs acidly. "I was doing no harm."

"Then in that case a statement of your actions can do you no harm, either. For instance, why were you in this neighbourhood after midnight? I know you have been away from home for a week or more, because I tried to get into touch with you yesterday, and could get no address."

Burroughs shook his head. "I'm not prepared to make any statement at all," he said obstinately. "Look here. You say you've found a corpse. Either it's Attleton's or it isn't. What about my identifying him for you? I don't like corpses, but I'm willing to waive my feelings over this one."

"I should be very glad if you could identify the remains, sir," said Macdonald, "but it's not going to be easy. The corpse has been mutilated, and the head and hands removed."

"Good God!" Mr. Burroughs looked round the tiny room as though seeking for escape. "Horrible," he groaned. "My God, horrible!"

"Very horrible," agreed Macdonald, and the other sat with his face in his hands. Looking up at the stern-faced man beside him, Mr. Burroughs shuddered weakly. "Is this a nightmare?" he asked.

"No. It's very grim reality," retorted Macdonald. "This is a police station, and I am an officer of the Criminal Investigation Department working on a case of murder. It's better for you to remember it."

Mr. Burroughs was biting his finger nails now—a habit which Macdonald loathed.

"Look here," said the former. "From what you say, this corpse may not be Attleton at all. It may be anybody. You've got no reason to connect me with it."

"You connected yourself with it," replied Macdonald. "You had better answer a few questions. Do you know where Mrs. Attleton is now, or where she has spent the last week or so since she left home?"

"No," replied the stockbroker dourly. "I do not."

("Lie number one," registered Macdonald.)

"Have you ever heard of a man named Debrette?"

Mr. Burroughs continued to bite his finger nails, very thoroughly, and then he said slowly:

"Look here, Inspector. It's no use going on like this. I'm not going to answer any questions until I've seen my solicitor. I'm at liberty to communicate with him. That's common law."

"It is," agreed Macdonald. "You were told so when you arrived here."

"And seeing you're going to keep me here until you've cleared the mess up, I should like some clean clothes," went on Mr. Burroughs. "Any objection to that?"

"None," said Macdonald. "If you have made up your mind not to answer any questions, it is no use my wasting time asking you any. Only remember this. You are under suspicion by your own action in going to the Belfry and making a bee-line for the one spot where you might have obtained access. If you refuse to make any explanation of your action, you remain under suspicion and your recent doings will be subject to routine inquiry. Believe me, you'll save yourself trouble in the long run, as well as me, if you tell me just why you went to the place last night."

"I've told you," replied Mr. Burroughs glumly, and Macdonald got up and went out.

"What d'you make of him?" asked the superintendent, as the C.I.D. man came to his office, and Macdonald shrugged his shoulders. "Nasty fellow. Bites his nails. Got something to hide, and though he's frightened, he's much more afraid of saying his bit than sitting mum and facing the music. He wants his solicitor, you might get that fixed up for him. It's more likely that his own lawyer will make him see sense than that I can. 'Detained, pending inquiries.' I'll take the responsibility. See that he's decently fed, and all that. He looks pretty green at present."

Macdonald's next port of call was The Small House in Mayfair, where he found Rockingham eating his breakfast, with *The Times* propped up in front of him.

"Hullo. Thinking of running me in for misleading the police?" inquired the bald-headed gentleman cheerfully. (He reminded Macdonald of a very prosperous don when he was placid and cheerful, as at present.)

"No, sir," returned the latter. "I'm afraid I've got bad news for you. It's distinctly unpleasant, so be prepared."

"I'm sorry about that," said Rockingham, his cheery face suddenly sobered, "and do, for God's sake, leave off calling me 'sir.' What's the trouble now?"

Macdonald told him, and Rockingham pushed back his plate of toast and marmalade, set his elbow on the table and leaned his face in his hands.

"My Lord!" he groaned. "This fairly puts the lid on it. Who on earth was the poor wretch?"

"That's just the problem," said Macdonald. "I want you to think again—very hard. Are you certain that it was Mr. Attleton's voice over the phone yesterday?"

Rockingham took his time before he answered. He lighted a cigarette, and frowned up at the ceiling.

"I thought so at the time," he said wearily. "It didn't occur to me to question it. Now—God knows! If you were in my place, how would you like to have to answer that question? If I swear that it *was* Bruce's voice which spoke to me, what's the conclusion? Doesn't it stare you in the face? It's as good as sending him to the gallows. It'd be better to believe he was plastered up into that niche—"

"It's no use thinking along those lines," said Macdonald quietly. "It may be difficult—don't think I underestimate it, to be impartial, but it's the only line to follow. Nothing but the whole truth will serve now."

His quiet voice was curiously impressive, and Rockingham flinched a little. Emptying his cup, he refilled it with black coffee from the little cafetiere which bubbled at his elbow, and sipped the scalding liquid as Macdonald went on:

"Tell me the exact circumstances of that call, and exactly what was said."

Rockingham took a deep breath before he replied:

"I had been tuning-in the wireless to a foreign station, and when the phone rang I was still busy with it. I lifted the receiver to stop the bell ringing and said, 'Hold on a minute, whoever you are.' Then I went back to my set and stopped it hooting. I tell you that because it may explain why I was cut off. I wasted a couple of minutes perhaps. Then, after I'd said, 'Hullo, who is it?' I heard Bruce say in that short staccato way he has, 'That you, Neil? Bruce speaking.' I chipped in here, as you may imagine, and he went on in answer to my queries, 'Sorry I let you down over Paris. Had an urgent letter which took me north. I shall be back in a couple of days.' Then I asked him where he was, and what the devil he'd been doing, and then the line went dead. Rather a funny thing, I had the impression it was a long-distance call, because his voice sounded faint, and the line was noisy, as the continental line often is, but I heard no warning from the operator that time was up."

"You wouldn't. It was an automatic exchange. The call came from Charing Cross."

"Charing Cross! Where Grenville spoke from? Good Lord! That's a crazy idea."

"No use having any ideas at all. Stick to the facts," replied Macdonald. "You heard a voice speak a couple of dozen words, in the abrupt manner of Mr. Attleton, after your mind had been prepared for his voice by the announcement of his name. As evidence, it's not too good. However, the intention was undoubtedly to prove that Mr. Attleton was alive. Let us leave that point. The next thing I want to know is this. Did Mr. Attleton ever employ a masseur, or take Turkish baths?"

Rockingham nodded. "Yes, at his club. He always employed the same masseur."

"That's the best hope of identification—or the reverse," said Macdonald. "He had never been operated on, I imagine? No chance of getting a surgeon's opinion?"

"Not to my knowledge. Look here, what on earth was the idea of this ghastly mutilating business?"

"The idea's all too obvious," replied Macdonald. "To prevent identification. It may be successful yet. It won't be easy for a masseur to swear to anything. There weren't any distinguishing marks as far as I could ascertain. You'd better have some brandy in that coffee. You look all in."

He got up and went to the sideboard, realising that Rockingham was not far off fainting point, and finding a bottle of cognac, returned to the table with it and poured a stiff dose into the cooling coffee. Rockingham swallowed it gratefully, saying:

"I can't get away from the horror of it—cutting up—"

"Then try to think of something else," said Macdonald brusquely, adding a moment later, "It's no odds to any man what happens to his corpse. I'd as soon leave mine to a school of dissection as anything else. Don't confuse living and non-living. Do you feel fit to answer a few questions along another tack?"

Rockingham nodded. "All right. Get on with it."

"Where does Mr. Thomas Burroughs come into the picture?"

"Burroughs?" The surprise in Rockingham's voice was patent. "What's he to do with it? I don't like the chap, and Attleton doesn't either. He's one of Sybilla's hangers-on. Rich as Crœsus and mean as muck—except when he's on the pursuit of pleasure. Bites his nails."

"So I observed," said Macdonald. "He was caught in the grounds of the Belfry late last night, trying the coal-hole entry. He won't give any why or wherefore."

"Burroughs? This grows more and more lunatic. I've admitted I don't like him, but I can't see him running amok. He hasn't the nerve of a flea."

"Wasn't he one of the party at your genial -and theoretical murder discussion? I gather that he hadn't any theories to advance on that occasion. Has he ever done anything in the acting line?"

"He fancies himself as an amateur—in one of those West End do-it-for-charity humbugs. Sir Peter Teazle, dolled up in satin breeches. You know the stuff."

"I know it. Did he and Attleton get across one another?"

"More or less. If Attleton had been master in his own house, Burroughs would never have entered it."

"I take it that Mrs. Attleton would have welcomed it if she'd found grounds for divorce?"

"Possibly. She has never mentioned it to me—I don't discuss her husband with her."

"But you knew that Mr. Attleton sought consolation elsewhere. Once again, are you certain that you can't enlarge on that point? It's time no for reticences."

Rockingham shook his head. "No. I don't know a thing about it—beyond assumptions. I took care not to. I've other ideas on the subject of—pleasure, if you like to use the term. Chacun à son gout."

Macdonald nodded. "Well, I'll leave you in peace now. Sorry to have brought you such an unpalatable tale."

Rockingham screwed his face up.

"The devil of it is, I don't know what to wish," he replied.

Macdonald, on his way to Park Village South, pondered over another idea. What if Attleton had fulfilled some private vengeance, and then sent Burroughs a letter which had taken him to the Belfry?—a suggestion that Attleton himself could be caught *in flagrante delicto*? Leave the stockbroker in the lurch— but why that telephone call? Faked? For what purpose? To prove that Attleton was alive.

"I've a hunch he isn't," said Macdonald to himself.

VIII

MACDONALD'S BRAIN-WAVE OVER CONSULTING ATTLETON'S masseur bore fruit in an identification, which, if not absolutely positive, was sufficiently so to weigh the scales of probability almost to a certainty.

The bath-attendant and masseur who had pommelled Attleton regularly after his baths was a man named Jennings, a cool, steady-headed, competent fellow, who undertook the task set him without fuss or protestation. He said frankly that he could not swear to an identification, but was sure of it in his own mind. The very fact that Attleton's body had no scar, or birthmark, or other distinctive mark, made him the more certain he was right. Nearly every one, he found, had some distinguishing mark—but not Mr. Attleton. Jennings it was who suggested consulting the chiropodist who had attended to Attleton's feet, and this man also concurred in Jennings' opinion. Coupled to the evidence of measurements obtained from tailors and shoemakers, these men's evidence convinced Macdonald that there was little or no room for doubt. It was Attleton's body which had been concealed in the Belfry Studio.

Macdonald had had a long talk with Weller, the butler. From him he learnt that Debrette had been ringing up at intervals for the past three months; but—and this struck Macdonald as a curious point—the calls always seemed to have come when Attleton was out. Since, however, his master answered the phone himself very frequently when he was at home, Weller could not say that Debrette had never caught Attleton at home. He could only say

that on the occasions he (Weller) had answered the calls and
heard the foreign-sounding voice, Mr. Attleton was always out.
Debrette had occasionally left a message asking Mr. Attleton to
ring him up, but had never mentioned his own number. It was
only recently, said Weller, that Mr. Attleton had expressed irritation over Debrette's messages, and only on the occasion when
Mr. Rockingham and Mr. Grenville were present that he had
actually lost his temper when told of Debrette's call.

Macdonald asked the butler to tell him, quite frankly, what he
had himself imagined to be the situation with regard to Debrette
and his telephone calls. Sitting in the library, where Macdonald
had told the punctilious butler to sit down and take his ease, the
latter thoughtfully rubbed his wide, well-shaven cheek with a
wide, fat thumb.

"Well, sir, I did ponder over the matter a bit, I admit. Not
that it's any business of mine, but human nature's the same in
all of us, master and man alike. Mr. Attleton's one that likes a
flutter, he'd gamble on anything, and he always goes over to
France to see them classic races over there. Grand Prix and all
that. I reckoned this Debrette might be a foreign bookie he'd
had dealings with, things going well for Mr. Attleton at first, if
you follow me, and then going against him. When this Debrette
began to sound nasty, and Mr. Attleton to get rattled, I says to
meself, things has gone against him as they always do in that
game in the long run—that's my opinion, sir—and the bookie
was pressing for his account to be settled."

"Sounds quite reasonable," agreed Macdonald. "You thought
Debrette sounded of the bookie type?"

"Well, no, sir, I didn't, not at first," admitted Weller. "Seemed
to me a cut above that line of gentry. It's difficult to tell with

a Frenchy, very polished some of them, even the waiters, but I took Debrette for a gentleman. Even when he began to sound 'ectoring, as you might say, he still struck me as a person of education so to speak. Then I did wonder—" He hesitated and broke off, and Macdonald encouraged him.

"Go on, Weller, you needn't be afraid of what you tell me. If it's not relevant, it won't go any further, and if it is relevant, you'd better hand it over to me."

"Very good, sir. Mr. Attleton's way of life—not what you'd call regular, sir—and yet it's all against his interests to have an open break with Mrs. Attleton. He liked his comfort, sir. Good service, good food, a good club, Turkish baths, swimming, fencing, motoring and all. Mr. Attleton's a very pleasant gentleman to work for, appreciates good service, and is generous when he's in funds, but if anything isn't just so, he'll not put up with it. If his linen sheets aren't always the same quality, his bath water as hot as he likes it, his bath salts just so, he mentions it. Likes good living, as I say, sir, but who pays for the linen, and the heating, and the service, in this house, sir? Not Mr. Attleton."

Macdonald nodded his appreciation of this really oratorical effort on the part of Weller, and put in:

"Mrs. Attleton pays the piper, I take it. D'you know if that has always been so, ever since they married?"

Weller shook his head. "No, no, sir. Mr. Attleton made a lot of money at one time—and spent it. His first books brought him in a tidy little pile, and he spent any amount on this house, but when funds ran low with him, Mrs. Attleton took on the paying of the household. You remember she played lead in *When Lovely Woman*. Ran for two years, to packed houses all the time, and Sybilla Attleton was the chief draw, folks said. A lot of money's

made by them at the top of their profession, and the mistress
has got her head screwed on the right way where money's
concerned. Well, I'm very long-winded, sir, but what I mean is
this. Mr. Attleton's been having it both ways, his comfortable
establishment here, and his bit of pleasure elsewhere, I should
say, but it wasn't to his interest for Mrs. A. to know about his
ways. That opens the door to blackmail, sir."

"It does," agreed Macdonald. "But what reason have you for
saying that Mr. Attleton's conduct was irregular?"

Once again Weller rubbed his smooth cheeks, and then said,
"Might I trouble you to step outside, sir, to see Mr. Attleton's
writing-room? You'll appre'end my point more easily, sir, if I
may say so."

They had been sitting in the library—a really beautiful little
room, fitted from floor to frieze with finely-designed bookcases. The carpet on the floor was a Persian one, showing the
famous Tree of Life design, and the chairs and writing-bureau
were perfectly matched, Sheraton rosewood, with ball and claw
feet to finish the graceful turn of their finely-wrought legs. The
entrance hall of the little Regency house was a masterpiece
of architectural ingenuity. Advancing from the door of the
library on the extreme left, Macdonald stood at the head of a
miniature state staircase. Behind him were the folding doors of
the octagon drawing-room, to right and left, at the end of the
little landing on which he stood, the two wings of the staircase
curved elegantly down to the parquet floor of the hall. The front
door was approached through a conservatory, now ablaze with
spring flowers, fragrant with the scent of hyacinths and freesias
whose perfume filled the place. At either end of the hall—whose
breadth was triple its length—were two tall arched recesses, or

niches, designed for statuary. There were no figures in them now, but pots of arum lilies, whose graceful foliage showed up against the creamy walls of the recess behind them.

Seeing the niches, in proportion similar to that which he had uncovered in the Belfry, Macdonald took a prompt dislike to one of the most beautiful pieces of interior planning he had ever seen. Weller led the way to a small door at one end of the conservatory entrance, saying:

"Mr. Attleton had his writing-room built—or adapted—from a little garden house at the end of the garden, sir. He had to have a place where he would not be disturbed, and it is an understood thing in the household that when he is there in the writing-room it is as though he was out. No one may go there to disturb him on any pretext."

The slightly pompous tones of Weller's voice amused Macdonald considerably. He guessed that the last speech had often been produced to overawe new domestics. Leading the way across the small garden, Weller went on:

"Mr. Attleton often works here at night, sir. He begins to write after the household has retired to bed, and many's the time I've seen his light still burning when I've got up of a winter morning."

Having crossed the grass to the rather absurd yet charming little imitation of a Doric Temple which was known as the writing-room, Weller produced a key from his pocket and opened the door.

"You will observe, sir, that there are two entrances. The one at which we stand, to which I have the key for purposes of cleaning, and the other door which gives access to the road. Mr. Attleton alone had the key of that door, and when he works in here, this door is secured from within—" indicating the door at which they stood.

"I see," said Macdonald, his thin, mobile lips twitching with amusement at the butler's prosiness. "For a man of what you termed 'irregular habits,' this place has points."

"Yes, sir." Weller went to the writing-table and rearranged the handlamp on it thoughtfully. "If it's a matter of confidence between me and you. I'll admit that Mr. Attleton's light may burn all night sometimes when he's no need of it." The butler's eyes dwelt on the second doorway. "As you say, sir, the arrangement has 'points.' Who is to know when he's here and when he isn't?"

If Macdonald's ears had been of the mobile variety they would have twitched, but the movement was only in his mind. "And the fact is, Weller, you know that Mr. Attleton occasionally spends his nights abroad, so to speak?"

"I think, sir, trusting you to respect the confidence, that it is not improbable."

"And how much does Mrs. Attleton know about this?"

The butler looked doubtful. "I should say, sir, nothing. When she is acting, Mrs. Attleton retires as soon as she comes in. It is some considerable time, I believe, since she and Mr. Attleton—er—shared the same room. In some respects they follow the adage of live and let live, if you take me. They don't altogether hit it."

"Does Mrs. Attleton ever ask you questions about her husband, Weller?"

"Never, sir. Mrs. Attleton is most punctilious in her dealings with her staff."

"Thanks very much, Weller. I shall be glad when we have found where Mrs. Attleton is staying. I'm afraid she will have a shock to face when she returns."

Weller's face showed an admirable professional concern, lighted as he spoke with a more human curiosity.

"I'm sorry to hear it, sir. You have bad news of Mr. Attleton?"

"I'm afraid so. I can't tell you anything for certain yet, but I think things look bad."

"If you'll pardon my saying so, sir, I had a feeling that trouble was afoot when you first began to make inquiries. There's been a nasty feeling in this house. I was half afraid there'd be another accident."

"Another?" queried Macdonald.

"I'm superstitious, sir. When I saw the new moon through glass I said to myself, 'That'll mean more trouble.' It was only the day before he went away that Mr. Attleton went to young Mr. Anthony's funeral. A sad business, sir. He was one of those rash drivers, and his brakes failed on Porlock Hill. Very melancholy. Then, a matter of a year ago, Mr. Attleton's older brother died in Paris. Gas turned on. Suicide it was."

"And you saw the new moon through glass on both those occasions?"

"No, sir. In the case of Mr. Anthony, he upset the salt at table, and with Mr. Guy Attleton, he sat down as one of thirteen at table. I saw it myself, sir."

"What's that got to do with a 'nasty atmosphere,' Weller?"

The butler looked uncomfortable. "If you'd lived in this house, you'd have felt it yourself, sir. Recriminations. Malice. Not nice at all."

"What do you make of Mr. Thomas Burroughs?" The abrupt question evidently surprised Weller, who raised his hairless brows and then nodded his pontifical head as though in agreement.

"What I should call a nasty piece of work, if you'll pardon the liberty, sir," he replied.

"Not a friend of Mr. Attleton's, I gather?"

"Just so, sir. It's a funny thing," went on Weller, in an outburst of confidence. "They say what's sauce for the goose is sauce for the gander, but it depends on the nature of the individual how you look at it. Now Mr. Attleton has his failings. I've told you so frankly, but I like him for all that. I'd lend him my last fiver and do it gladly—but that Mr. Burroughs. No. No class, sir. Not a gentleman. Very wealthy, I'm told, very wealthy indeed, but not a person I'd like to serve, and that's a fact. Don't know how to treat a servant, that's what it is."

"Anything else, Weller?"

"Not as I'd care to mention, sir. It's one thing to talk about Mr. Attleton's little ways—when all's said and done, most gentlemen are much alike—but I've nothing to say about my mistress, sir."

Macdonald could not help being amused. Weller's carefully-worded abstention had told him as much as a string of innuendoes. However, he saw fit to break off the conversation, and leave it at that.

"I shall have to go through the papers in Mr. Attleton's desk, Weller. I have a warrant, of course, and in Mrs. Attleton's absence, the only thing to do is to carry on and explain the necessity to her later."

The butler looked troubled. "Then you think Mr. Attleton has met with an accident, sir?"

"I'm afraid so," said Macdonald, "but once again, I'm not absolutely certain. I may be mistaken. Put it like this. An accident has occurred and a man has been killed, but he has not yet been identified for certain. He was too badly damaged."

"I'm very sorry, sir. I liked Mr. Attleton."

Macdonald went to the desk, which was a modern one, and tried the drawers. They were all locked, and from the look of the locks would take a good deal of opening, short of doing violence to a very good piece of furniture. Having many other matters to attend to, Macdonald decided to put seals on the doors of the room and return later to investigate the papers. He told Weller so, inquiring if any other keys existed which gave access to the writing-room. The butler said that save for his own key—which he handed over sorrowfully—the only remaining ones were in Mr. Attleton's possession.

"You have those, yourself, sir?"

"No. I haven't."

"Then he was robbed—after the accident?"

"Perhaps. It's not been ascertained."

Weller looked at him queerly, but to Macdonald's surprise, made no inquiry as to the nature of the "accident."

Macdonald finally left Weller with instructions to go to Scotland Yard to examine exhibit A—the suitcase, and to make a note if anything was missing therefrom. After which, having thanked the butler for his assistance, Macdonald proceeded to the offices of Messrs. Todbury, Wether & Goodchild in Lincoln's Inn Fields.

Mr. Todbury received him with urbanity, but with a solemn face, and his solemnity had increased considerably by the time Macdonald had given a résumé of the facts which he had unearthed in the last twenty-four hours. Mr. Todbury had never come within bowing distance of criminal proceedings, his practice being concerned with settlements, wills, leases, mortgages, and a very sound instinct to keep his clients from litigation of any kind.

"Settle it out of court," was his invariable advice to an aggressive client.

"A most shocking story, Chief Inspector. Most shocking. Never in my life have I heard anything so appalling. It's almost unbelievable! Time and again I have said to Mr. Attleton that he would come to no good—but this!" and the dry little man mopped his face in distress.

"It is, indeed, a shocking story," said Macdonald, his grave, sympathetic voice low-pitched, "and I'm sorry to have to distress you with it, but it is my job to ascertain the facts. On the evidence which we have, I think it can be taken for granted that deceased was Mr. Attleton, and the next question which arises is this—Who had a motive to kill him? You must know, as well as I do, sir, that profit is the motive in many murders, quite as much as revenge, hatred, or jealousy. You can answer the question, who profits by Mr. Attleton's death?"

The lawyer spread out his hands in a gesture of helplessness. "Who profits? Nobody, my dear sir, nobody—not even to the extent of life insurance. Bruce Attleton was improvident to a degree. He made money at one time easily. Light come, light go. Instead of investing it, he spent it. I insisted upon his insuring his life on his marriage. He has realised on his policy. To the best of my knowledge he leaves nothing but debts and whatever royalties may accrue to him in future will go to liquidate those debts."

"Had he any expectations in the way of legacies?"

"Not to my knowledge. His family have been singularly unfortunate. They were, I know, folk of some substance two generations ago, but their wealth was all dissipated. Bad management! Bad management!"

"I should be glad to learn something of his people," said Macdonald, and Mr. Todbury went on:

"His relatives, like their fortune, have passed away, Chief Inspector. I was only looking into the matter after young Fell's death. So far as I can ascertain there are only two members of the family living. Alas, no! With poor Bruce's death… Dear me! dear me! It is an almost inconceivable thing. The old man, Mr. Adam Marsham, must be the sole survivor, and he will be a hundred years old if he survives until June of this year—a most remarkable thing!"

Macdonald asked for and got, full particulars of Attleton's family from the prosy old lawyer. Mr. Todbury was admirably precise, and on his own ground, brief and explicit, and the record that he gave was as follows:

There were originally known to his firm (in the days of Mr. Todbury's father) two brothers named Marsham, of whom Adam (still surviving) was the elder and James the younger. There was also a sister named Mary Anne. All these three had inherited good incomes from land on which coal had been discovered in the early nineteenth century. Adam had dissipated his fortune early and gone to live in Australia, whence he returned as a widower at the age of fifty-five, having made a few thousands which he invested (very profitably, as it turned out) in an annuity which brought him an income of about £300 a year. He had one daughter, Alicia, who married an Australian tradesman in a small way of business, and whose grandson, Anthony Fell, had recently come to England and died there. Anthony had inherited an income from his parents (both dead) of £50 a year, which was left to a friend in Melbourne.

James Marsham, born in 1840, had one daughter, Janet, who married Henry Attleton, a stockbroker, in 1890. Henry Attleton had lost his fortune in speculation and shot himself in 1910, his wife dying shortly after him. They left two sons, Guy, born in 1891, and Bruce born in 1892. Guy had done fairly well in a shipping agents' firm, but his health was ruined by after effects of war-time gas, and he had killed himself in 1935.

The sister of the two Marshams, Mary Anne, born in 1841, had made a mésalliance with an Alsatian artist named Brossé, had gone abroad with him, and had died some time in the seventies. Mr. Todbury's father had made inquiry into her estate at the time of her death, and found that her husband ("a scoundrel, my dear sir, undoubtedly a scoundrel!") had realised her fortune and lost it in betting and speculating. Adam Marsham, who had quarrelled with Mary Anne at the time of her marriage, had been bitterly indignant over her squandered fortune.

"They were a curious family," said old Mr. Todbury, his fingers together at the tips, his eyes now beaming quite happily at Macdonald as he gazed at him over the tops of his glasses. "My father told me that they all quarrelled bitterly at the time of their parent's death, each one seeking to claim a larger part of the inheritance than was their due. This bitterness was carried into the second generation, when Alicia and Janet wrote abusive letters to one another over the same old bone of contention. Then Adam did his best to make trouble between Janet and Henry Attleton and their sons—a curious, unbalanced family."

Macdonald had been busy making notes of Mr. Todbury's statement, and put in here, "Then I take it that Bruce Attleton was the only living descendant of these three Marshams, unless

Mary Anne, who became Mme. Brossé, left any issue. Have you any information on that point, sir?"

"Nothing reliable," replied Mr. Todbury. "Mary Anne married early in the sixties—1862, I think. She went to live in Alsace—Grandville, it was, and my father had an idea that a son was born, but after the upheaval of Sedan and the annexation of Alsace, it was difficult to get any reliable news. That section of the family has been lost sight of entirely."

"Well, it looks to me as though it might be coming into the daylight now, and letting me see daylight at the same time," said Macdonald. "How would this do for a possible hypothesis, based on a hypothetical inheritance. *If* old Adam Marsham has any substantial sum to leave behind him, Bruce Attleton, through the death of his cousin, Anthony Fell, and his own older brother, would be the only member of the family to inherit—*unless* Mary Anne Brossé left a son. Assume for one moment that she *did*, leave a son—or daughter—and that the man we know as Debrette is the grandson of Mary Anne Brossé—née Marsham."

The elderly lawyer waved his hands in excited protest.

"My dear sir! This is an unwarrantable stretching of the imagination to suit your fancy. You have no facts to go on, none whatever…"

"Oh, yes, I have," retorted Macdonald imperturbably. "I admit I'm stretching them, and then using my imagination to fill in gaps, but there's some reasoning behind the process. Within a comparatively short time, two lives have been removed from this line of succession, leaving Bruce Attleton as heir—if there is anything in the family to leave. Now he is removed—violently—and a foreigner named Debrette seems to have been involved, to say the least of it, in his passing. Is it stretching the imagination too far to connect this Debrette with the Alsatian family of Brossé? Remember that Debrette would be cousin to Attleton if my idea holds water, and one witness at least has suggested a likeness between Attleton and Debrette."

Mr. Todbury looked bewildered.

"You go too fast, Chief Inspector," he protested, and Macdonald agreed.

"Yes. I'm outrunning my data, but you will have to prove—or disprove—my preposterous suggestions. I take it that you are not in charge of Mr. Adam Marsham's affairs?"

"That is so," announced Mr. Todbury. "He quarrelled with my father—dear me, a great many years ago it would be. I think, however, that he has very few affairs to manage from the legal point of view. His solicitor is Mr. Piddleton of Clifford Inn. I have some communications from him occasionally, as recently when it was considered that the old gentleman—the 'Old Soldier' as Bruce Attleton called him—was about to die. Dear me, he has been going to die a great many times in the last twenty years, and on each occasion has summoned some member of the family to his death bed."

"To hear his testamentary dispositions or last wishes!" said Macdonald cheerfully. "Now, sir, I know that all good lawyers hate giving information concerning probable estates."

"Quite rightly, *quite* rightly!" put in Mr. Todbury, and Macdonald heartily agreed.

"*Most* rightly, but in this case the information is to be given in confidence to you and to Scotland Yard. I want to know just how much the Old Soldier has saved during the forty years he has been in receipt of an annuity."

"Dear me, dear me!" murmured Mr. Todbury. "Now you mention it, there does seem a possibility—not so remote, perhaps. If he had saved £50 per annum for forty-five years, investing the interest."

"—At compound interest," put in Macdonald firmly, and Mr. Todbury scribbled diligently.

"God bless my soul!" he exclaimed. "£50 a year for forty-five years at five per cent.—I make it £9,000 odd at a rough estimate."

"Not a bad little sum," said Macdonald, "and he may have had a little bit of capital in addition to what he sank in the annuity. It probably kept him alive, you know—taking an interest in the interest."

Mr. Todbury wiped his glasses, and looked down at his figures with a speculative eye.

"And you can also inquire, sir," went on Macdonald trenchantly, "if either Mr. Bruce Attleton or his brother, or any gentleman with a foreign accent, has endeavoured to learn anything of Mr. Adam Marsham's affairs within the last few years."

The old lawyer's face, which had become quite enthusiastic as he worked out his figures, fell again like a little child's.

"Dear me! This terrible affair! I still don't quite follow you, Chief Inspector."

"No, sir. I'm finding it a bit hard to follow myself. As you say, all this jumping to conclusions is unwarrantable, but I do see possibilities. Imagine this Debrette, with a certain amount of information at his disposal, getting into touch with Bruce Attleton, and sounding him as to his own knowledge of Mr. Marsham's affairs. You mention Attleton's family as of unstable temper. The father took his own life. The old man is obviously of an erratic and ill-tempered disposition. There may have been a kink in their minds."

Seeing Mr. Todbury's troubled face, Macdonald did not go on with his disquisition. Instead he said, "At least, sir, you will get for me the information I ask? I could get it myself, but I admit that I am working from unsure premises. I do not wish to trouble another kind-hearted lawyer, such as yourself, with the attentions of Scotland Yard."

Mr. Todbury laughed at that. "What you really mean, my dear sir, is that you know you are making unjustifiable guesses, and you put the onus of the inquiry on me, rather than on your own very estimable department. But do not fear! I will get the information for you if it is to be got. Forty-five years! God bless my soul!"

Macdonald, leaving Mr. Todbury with the warmest expression of thanks for his thoughtfulness, allowed his own ingenious mind to get on with the possibilities involved.

"If Attleton and Debrette both knew there was a fortune involved, they may have had an equal determination to become residuary legatee—in which case, it may have been pure chance which of them we found in the Belfry—according to which got his blow in first. As it turned out it was Debrette. But why, in the name of common sense, did Burroughs go butting in? What does *he* know about it? Losh! There are too many whys in this case, but there's something in the idea of £9,000. Quite substantial as a nest egg, anyway."

IX

W HEN MACDONALD RETURNED TO SCOTLAND YARD AFTER
his talk with Mr. Todbury, it was nearly half-past four.
His note-book testified to a good day's work, being entered up
as follows.

8.0–8.15.   Interviewed Burroughs at Station.

9.0–9.45.   With Rockingham at The Small House.

10.0–12.0.   Author's Club. Took Jennings to Mortuary.

12.15–1.15.   Park Village South. Weller.

1.30–2.30.   Lunch. Pagani's.

2.45–4.0.   Lincoln's Inn Fields. Todbury, Wether &
            Goodchild.

Seated drinking his tea, Macdonald listened to Reeves' report
of his day which had also been profitably spent, but Reeves, a
great believer in routine, kept his narrative in strictly chrono-
logical order, so that his *bonne bouche* came last. His morning
had been occupied by "getting a line" on Mrs. Attleton—not
very successfully. After an overnight consultation with Weller,
Reeves knew that Mrs. Attleton had a mother, Mrs. Langtree,
who resided at Brighton. The Southern Electric took Reeves
to that famous resort in exactly an hour—according to schedule—(a trip he had much enjoyed) and by half-past ten he was
interviewing a very unwilling parent in the Riviera Hotel. Mrs.
Langtree described herself as a neurasthenic, under the treatment of a psychoanalyst, and she interviewed Reeves from a

couch, speaking languidly and petulantly by turns. She assured Reeves that she had no idea of her daughter's address, that Mrs. Attleton was taking a rest cure (like herself) and that this fuss over Mr. Attleton's whereabouts was uncalled for. Bruce was the most erratic of men, and it was quite characteristic of him to break engagements, to stay away for days at a time without giving any address, and generally to behave in an inconsiderate manner, and this intrusion on her (Mrs. Langtree's) privacy was quite unjustified. She had already told Mr. Rockingham so, and considered that the latter had lost his head completely to be making such a to-do. Reeves left the scented, over-heated apartment without any information, but a conviction that Mrs. Langtree was frightened—very much frightened.

"She's probably agitated about her daughter and Mr. Thomas Burroughs," said Macdonald. "I expect we shall find that Thomas has spent the last week with the injured wife—that's why he's doing the strong silent man touch. What oddities these people are, Reeves. Mrs. Attleton wants a divorce, but she also wants to be the injured party. Her husband was to supply the evidence while she posed as Julius Cæsar's wife and got the world's sympathy. We'd better turn the B.B.C. on to the job—and if Mesdames Langtree and Attleton get a shock, that's not our fault. We've wasted enough time considering their feelings. I'm glad you liked Brighton. Personally—and professionally—I never want to hear the name of the place again."

"It doesn't bring the department luck, and that's a fact," admitted Reeves, "however, I earned my oats when I got back. Caught the eleven twenty-five. Back at Victoria at twelve-thirty. Not bad. I've been on the run about after Debrette. That chap Grenville wasn't pulling the long-bow. Debrette *was* in Trafalgar

Square yesterday evening, and what's more, he's pretty well known by sight."

Reeves had got his first information from a newspaper vendor close to Charing Cross Post Office. Apparently the man with a white streak in his beard was a not infrequent visitor to Trafalgar Square. He stood and listened to the outpourings of Communists and Fascists, he had been seen by the janitors of the National Gallery, and had on one occasion been moved on by the police for "causing an obstruction" by the peaceful pursuit of drawing on the paving-stones to earn a few pennies. (According to the newspaper man, "Streaky Beaver" was a toff with a bit of chalk.) Continuing his researches (occasionally with the assistance of small largesse) Reeves had talked to the loungers who were always to be found in Trafalgar Square—wrecks of men, unemployed and unemployables, who spent wretched days and nights in streets and doss-houses, scavenging in the very gutters, living on the uncertain charity of passers-by. To them "Streaky Beaver" was not unknown. While he was not, apparently, destitute, inasmuch as he had decent boots and a presentable suit, he yet lived a queer nomadic existence, having no property save what he could carry about with him, and sleeping occasionally in hostels such as those run by the Church Army and the Salvation Army for the flotsam and jetsam of London's manhood. From lodging to lodging Reeves had gone in his search, hearing reports that the man he was after had spent the night there.

"Calls himself all manner of names," said Reeves. "Barbler is one of the most frequent. Talks English all right and puts on a foreign accent or not as the fancy takes him."

"Barbler," ruminated Macdonald, "Barbe Bleu, probably— Bluebeard—Go on."

"Some reckon he's a bit touched," went on Reeves after a good drink of tea, "but they all say he's harmless. One chap—an old actor—said Barbler must have been in the profession at one time. When he's had a drink he'll rant away for hours—old melodrama stuff, and Shakespeare and French and German as well. He's never been in our hands, that's certain. There's no official record of him anywhere. The last place I heard of him was a doss-house behind King's Cross. He stayed there a month or so ago, and the funny part was he seemed in funds. He'd got a clean shirt and collar and cooked himself a chop in the kitchen. He seems to've been off the map for weeks, most of the reports I've got went back to before Christmas."

"And for the moment he's still off the map?"

"Yes, sir—but we're sure to cop him before long."

"It's a queer story, Reeves. Sounds all wrong to my mind. Now listen to my bit."

Macdonald produced a résumé of the facts he had gleaned from Mr. Todbury, and when he had concluded, Reeves said:

"Well, I grant you it's a rum story, but it seems to fit. This Debrette—or Barbler or Brossé or whatever his name is—gets a line on old Marsham somehow, and rings up Attleton to sound him. They compare notes, and between them clear the ground of other claimants. Probably Debrette presses Attleton for funds to keep him going, and Attleton gets tired of stumping up. Finally Attleton goes to the Belfry intending to put a stop to Mr. Debrette, and gets put a stop to himself. That's all right. Seems quite clear. It was Attleton who supplied the funds in the first place for Debrette to take the studio. If what you guess is any-where near the truth, Attleton would have *had* to pay up—and go on paying up."

Macdonald frowned down into his cup, deep in thought, and Reeves went on cheerfully:

"Debrette's been quite smart, really. He made himself known as a harmless, half batty, down-and-out in some of the London doss-houses, so that he had got a background he could sink into if ever the time came for playing possum. Probably got an alibi, too, if he needed one. With a few coppers to spare you could buy as many alibis as you want from some of those poor devils, as you know well enough. He's a cunning old fox, is Streaky Beaver."

"Then why the dickens hasn't he had the elementary common sense to shave his beard off?" demanded Macdonald. "Tell me that. Does it make sense to you, because it doesn't to me."

Reeves cocked his chin up as this great thought percolated to his policeman's brain, and Macdonald went on:

"Go back to the beginning again, assuming Debrette is Brossé. Debrette approaches Bruce Attleton, and the two charmers—both hard up according to their different standards—put their heads together over the possibility of raking in a few odd thousands. I'm convinced that there must be something of the kind in the offing, because there have been too many sudden deaths in the family just lately. Attleton, as you say, provides funds, and probably provided that reference for the agents which led to a dead-end. Debrette took a fancy to the Belfry, envisaging further possibilities, and lived there, more or less, occasionally putting in an appearance at his old haunts. He gave out at The Knight Templar that he was a sculptor, he needed to be, if he wanted plaster of Paris in bulk. That's all believable. Very cunning, as you say—*but*, and it's a large but, why did he show himself to two different people whom Attleton knew? He went out of his way to draw Rockingham's attention to himself, and likewise Elizabeth Leigh's. What's the point? To show himself was simply to ask for trouble. It was silly—and the rest of the story isn't silly, it's infernally clever."

"I can't see his point," admitted Reeves.

"Nor any one else either. Now remember that Grenville had a chance of looking at him, too—not much of a look, admittedly, but enough. That's three different people had seen Debrette and he knew it. He next contrives a murder, mutilates the corpse, conceals it, and bolts. Yet a week later he is wandering round the Strand with his silly beard like a Belisha beacon, plain for all the world to see, when he must know that Grenville would tell the police sometime about that little do with the whisky glass."

"Yes, but isn't he being just a shade *too* clever," argued Reeves. "It's not easy to identify a corpse like that one. First, Debrette reckoned that his hidey hole wouldn't be discovered until the housebreakers get going at Michaelmas. Then he argued that the corpse would be taken for his own—with Attleton as the murderer."

"More fool he not to have shaved his beard," said Macdonald. "For a man who's done an uncommonly skilful bit of murder, he seems to have got some blind spots. I wonder…"

He went off into a blue study over his empty teacup, and at last said:

"I've got it! He took the risk of showing himself to that blithe young ass Grenville just to fix it in the chap's mind that Streaky Beaver's still going strong, and then hopped into some suitable spot and shaved himself, took off his blinkers, and reappeared as commonplace looking as you—or me. Now can you tell me how we're going to find him—until the Old Soldier dies, and he rolls up to claim the boodle. If that boodle's not in existence,

Reeves, I shall retire and grow mushrooms. I've simply put my money on it."

"Doesn't look a certainty to me," replied Reeves cautiously. "One of the points I froze on to was that about Debrette being an old actor. Seemed to fit in with what Miss Leigh suggested. Ever seen Sybilla Attleton on the stage, sir?"

Macdonald shook his head. "Not I. Modern comedy gives me what Jenkins calls the proper pip."

"Well, I've seen her, and I'd say she's a hard-faced jane," said Reeves darkly. "I rather fancy Mr. Burroughs as number one, with the funny stuff supplied by the wits of the leading lady. You look into it for yourself, sir. This Streaky Beaver sounds the goods to me—a real balmy penniless gutter-crawler who's come down from touring companies to street crawling. Say if Mrs. A. employed him to show up and draw suspicion, while her gentleman friend got on with the job."

"Who taught him to plaster like an expert?" asked Macdonald, "and what did he go back to the Belfry for last night?"

"Why, the suitcase, sir."

"He hadn't a nice large piece of brown paper and string on him," complained Macdonald. "I rather like that chap Grenville. He's got a constructive mind. Answer that phone for me."

Reeves grinned as he put down the receiver.

"Park Village South speaking, sir. Mrs. Attleton's come home, and would be pleased to see you. What did I say? She's come to bail out Mr. Thomas Burroughs—Faithful and all that."

"Wind-up, more likely, Reeves. You might do a little more combing out after Streaky Beaver."

"If your hunch is right and his beaver's gone west, it doesn't look too good," groaned Reeves. "We shall have to publish

to-morrow morning and get the papers to find him for us. Did
you hear how much money Mr. Attleton had on him when he
left home, sir?"

"About £20, in treasury notes," replied Macdonald. "Enough
to give Beaver a run for his money but you're going back on
yourself; ten minutes ago you were arguing a brief in favour
of Streaky Beaver as a harmless and much maligned innocent."

"When I have a hunch and you have a different one, sir, it's
mine goes to the wall every time," said Reeves.

Macdonald set out for Park Village South with feelings of
very lively curiosity, human as well as professional. It was Sybilla
Attleton's dramatic reappearance which interested him most.
What was the reason that she had thus suddenly come back
from her retreat? An appeal from Mr. Thomas Burroughs, or a
natural sense of the dramatic?

The door of the Attletons' house was opened to him, not
by the friendly faced Weller, but by an exceedingly smart maid
in the smartest of organdie aprons over her black taffeta frock.
One glance at her face and immaculately neat hair prepared
Macdonald for her speech.

"Monsieur désire?"

No one but a Frenchwoman ever looked quite so perfect in
a maid's uniform.

"Mrs. Bruce Attleton." He produced a card, and the
Frenchwoman motioned to him to enter, closed the door
behind him and led him through the fragrant conservatory,
up the little state staircase, to a door on the extreme left
which corresponded to the library door on the right. Having
picked up a salver, the maid preceded him into the room, and
Macdonald stood at the doorway and looked in. The room

was papered in dull silver; candelabra of some silvery metal were on the walls, and silver bowls held tall purple irises. The floor was covered with a silvery-grey carpet, very light and silky in texture. The curtains and upholstery were of the same intense violet as the irises. Macdonald, standing at the door, felt that the whole scheme of "decor" was unreal, as though he were looking at some costly ballet set. Outside, the grey light of a March evening was closing in. Here the violet silk curtains were drawn across the long windows, their shot texture reflecting the pearly light which shone through nacre shades on the sconces.

The maid returned to the door, saying "Entrez, Monsieur," and Macdonald advanced across the silken carpet, and bowed to the lady who sat on the couch before the cedar-wood fire.

A striking apparition was Sybilla Attleton, as thousands of playgoers testified. Her skin was dead white, like a powdered camellia. Her hair, intensely black and smooth as silk, was parted above the centre of the low, broad forehead, drawn behind the small ears, and dressed in a great knot low on the nape of the neck.

She looked up at Macdonald with grey eyes as expressionless as stone, surprisingly large and round beneath the pencilled arches of her black brows. Dressed in a tea gown of dead white satin, she lay back against her violet cushions, and stared at her visitor.

"Mrs. Attleton?"

"Yes, Chief Inspector. I am anxious to have an explanation of your visits to my household."

("So that's going to be her line, is it?" said Macdonald to himself.)

With a wave of her hand she indicated a chair on her right, and turned her head to watch him as he sat. Macdonald had a feeling that he was acting a part in a carefully-staged production.—The curtain is raised to discover leading lady, *c.*, detective, *r.*, french windows up-stage. ("Tilburina, stark mad in white satin, her confidant, stark sane in blue suiting," ran idiotically through his mind.)

"I can surely take it for granted that you have heard something of the reason of my investigations, madam," he replied.

"I take nothing for granted at all," she replied coldly. "When, on returning home after a much needed holiday, I find that Scotland Yard has been taking possession of my household, I do not expect my servants to supply adequate explanations. I look to the Inspector who has undertaken the inquiries."

"Very good." Macdonald returned stare for stare, trying to formulate an estimate of the personality behind that powdered mask. "Acting on information received" (he produced the good old tag with a certain satisfaction), "my department investigated premises known as The Belfry Studio in Notting Hill. A suitcase of Mr. Attleton's was discovered in a cellar there, containing his passport and the usual luggage for a short holiday. Mr. Attleton, we learnt, was not at home, and he had not been to the hotel in Paris where he had booked rooms."

He paused here, and watched for any sign of anxiety or emotion on the face of the woman beside him, but could read none. Almost expressionless, save for the slightest aspect of insolent scorn, she sat as still as a graven image, hardly breathing, it appeared, beneath the matt white draperies of her trailing gown.

"I regret that my narrative must be of a distressing character," he continued formally, but because he was a very humane man

Macdonald's voice altered a little in pitch. This was the wife of the man whose poor remains had been taken from the boarded-up niche last night, and Macdonald felt a very human distaste from telling that story to his wife.

"Further investigation," he continued, "resulted in a very ghastly discovery. A man's body had been concealed in a niche in the walls of the Belfry Studio. I am sorry to say that we have every reason to believe that the remains are those of Mr. Bruce Attleton."

As he ceased speaking, a crystal clock which stood upon the mantelpiece began to chime, tinkling out an intolerably long preamble of lucid notes, and then striking six with maddening leisureliness.

Still perfectly motionless, Sybilla Attleton raised her grey eyes to the clock face and stared at it. Macdonald realised that she was too good an actress to show any expression on her face against her will, and his eyes dropped to her hands. Half concealed by the long open sleeves of her gown, the white fists were clenched, the scarlet nails driven into her palms.

"What do you mean by telling me that you have every reason to believe that the body was Mr. Attleton's? Could you not find anybody to identify him? Has he no friends, no servants, who could enlighten you?"

The deliberate voice, devoid of any feeling at all, took away from Macdonald the sense of discomfort which humanity had aroused in him. This woman, it seemed to him, was as devoid of feelings as the clear-speaking clock.

"Neither friends nor servants were able to enlighten us," he replied quietly. "The only hope of identification was in the physique of torso and limbs. I got the masseur who had treated

Mr. Attleton to assist us. In this man's opinion—and I think his opinion is to be relied upon—the remains are those of Mr. Attleton. Other opinions, and measurements, reinforce this judgment. I am sorry, but I do not think there is any reasonable doubt about the identification."

"You assume, then, that my husband was murdered?"

"I do not think that any other assumption is tenable for a moment."

Quite suddenly Sybilla Attleton sat erect, her back quite straight, her magnificent shoulders squared, and she looked Macdonald full in the face.

"You have been very straight with me, Chief Inspector. I asked you for a clear statement, and you gave it, without beating about the bush. I will be straight with you in turn. Any murder is horrible and revolting. You have told me this horrible story with a minimum of horror—and I appreciate it. Understand this. I am shocked as I might be shocked if I had read such a story in a paper. It is a long time since I had any feelings of affection for Bruce. He killed all that. I am not complaining, nor posing as the injured wife, but don't expect me to cry. Any tears I had to shed on his account were shed a long time ago—a very long time ago."

She got up, and began to walk to and fro over the silken carpet, the train of her dress gliding soundlessly over it, like a snake in its ripples and undulations. Macdonald rose, too, and watched her, an almost unreasonable dislike overcoming him. Something of the Calvinism of his ancestors rose to the surface in him, and tried to condemn this marble-faced woman for every trait she showed, her lovely powdered face and exquisitely clad body, her red-tipped fingers and cruel blood-red mouth. He pulled himself up, and realised that he had let personal antipathy colour his outlook, and tried once again to be impartial.

"As the officer in charge of this investigation, madam, it is my duty to question you."

She came to a halt in front of the fire, ceasing her restless pacing, much to Macdonald's relief, and threw herself back into her corner of the sofa. "All right. Get on with it—but do, for heaven's sake, get me a drink. I need it."

It was not, as Macdonald said to himself, an unreasonable request, given the tension of the last few minutes, but the voice in which it was uttered, and the gesture of her hand to a cabinet by the wall, reinforced that feeling of acting in a drama. He went to the cabinet—an object of some ivory-like substance, edged and handled with some silvery metal, and found therein the usual bottles and shaker for cocktails. Mixing gin and bitter he thought to himself disgustedly "Gin! That about puts the lid on it," and carried the glass to the lady on the sofa. Taking it from him, she swallowed it down and said:

"What do you want me to tell you? I don't know one single thing that can help you."

"You know the name Debrette, I think."

The grey eyes met his own. "Yes, I know the name, but that is all. I don't know the individual who answers to the name."

"Will you tell me, please, how you know the name?"

Turning away from him she stared up at the clock.

"Some man calling himself Debrette rang up and asked for my husband once or twice. He was a foreigner, apparently, but would never give me any idea of his business. Then—he wrote to me."

She paused and Macdonald waited without a word until she chose to continue.

"I told you, just now, that there was no longer any affection between my husband and myself. He has long ceased to care for me, and bestowed his attentions elsewhere. I knew that quite well. I am not a long-suffering woman, Chief Inspector. I intended to divorce my husband when I could get the evidence— but he was clever. I did not care to submit to the degradation of employing a private agent. I waited for an opportunity. One day this man, Debrette, wrote to me. He said that he could obtain for me evidence of my husband's infidelity if I made it worth his while. The sum he asked was £50, to be paid after he had delivered the evidence. I replied that I would pay the sum he asked when I received that evidence."

"Where did you write?"

"To an address in Charing Cross Place. I have his letter. You can see it. Then, when I was away, I received a letter that astonished me. I had given my address to no one, and had taken trouble that no one should have any idea where I was going, and yet this man Debrette wrote to me where I was staying in the New Forest. He said this time that if I sent a trustworthy agent to the Belfry Studio in Notting Hill on the night of March 26th—last night—I should get the evidence I wanted."

"And now we're coming to Mr. Thomas Burroughs," said Macdonald to himself.

"I told you that I was astonished. I had no idea how the creature got my address, but one thing seemed evident. His agency—or whatever it is—was obviously competent in finding out what he wanted to know, else he would not have discovered my address. I assumed that he knew what he was talking about. I did ask a friend to go to the Belfry last night."

Her eyes met Macdonald's again, and this time there was some expression in them. Macdonald, of all men the least susceptible to a charm like Sybilla Attleton's, thought her eyes were like the big grey marbles he had played with at school, but what was the look in them now? Inquiry—to see how he was taking the story?

"And your friend's name?" he inquired stolidly. She shook her head. "No. I won't tell you that, not until I have seen him."

Macdonald sat and stared at her in his turn, quite calmly, pondering over his next move. At last he decided, and went on, "It is probable that I need not trouble you for it. A Mr. Thomas Burroughs was arrested in the grounds of the Belfry last night."

She clapped her hand over her mouth, but the consternation on her face struck Macdonald as a cleverly assumed mask. ("From the theatrical point of view, she knows her stuff," he admitted to himself.)

"Arrested—but why?"

"For various reasons. In the first place Mr. Burroughs was apparently seeking to enter a building in which a murder had recently been committed, and he sought to enter by the one place at which it was possible to break in. When challenged by the man on duty, Mr. Burroughs violently attacked the man who challenged him. Arrest was inevitable after that. Asked by the superintendent to give an account of his reasons for visiting the Belfry premises, Mr. Burroughs refused any explanation at all, and has persisted in that refusal."

"His reason for doing so is now obvious to you," rejoined Mrs. Attleton calmly. "He would not let me down. He could not give you any explanation without involving me in it."

"The explanation which you have given involves a good deal in addition to yourself," said Macdonald dryly. "I think your wisest course would be to give me an account of your own movements since you left home last Wednesday week."

Mrs. Attleton studied him once again with eyes that were now not only inquiring, but slightly pathetic. Macdonald's immobile face gave nothing away, but in his mind he said to himself, "And if you think you can put that sort of stuff across me, you've got a lot to learn, Sybilla Attleton."

X

SYBILLA ATTLETON'S STORY, WHICH SHE PRODUCED AFTER a certain amount of protestation, and at one stage a flood of tears, was, as Macdonald said, such an obvious story that he could have made it up for himself to suit the occasion.

Following Weller's dictum, that what is sauce for the goose is also sauce for the gander, Mrs. Attleton made no inquiries about what her husband proposed to do in Paris during his holiday, but made arrangements for her own "rest cure" in a characteristically efficient manner.

Leaving London in her own car, she drove to Southampton, (corroborated by Reeves) left her suitcases at the railway station while she garaged her car, returned to the station and met the admirably punctual Mr. Thomas Burroughs, retrieved her luggage, and drove with him to a cottage mid-way between Lyndhurst and Brockenhurst.

This retreat was, as Macdonald discovered later, an ideal habitation for two people who wished to escape observation, but to live luxuriously. While it was secluded from the main road in a forest clearing, and so set about by tall hedges of Thuya as to be almost invisible from the track which led to it, it yet had all the amenities which modern electrical engineering and plumbing can supply to the wealthy. In due time Macdonald regarded the marble bathroom with a sardonic eye, observing the glamorous greenery of the sunk bath, the mirror set in the ceiling, and the showers and heating arrangements, with detached interest. He saw also the "sun parlour" on the flat roof, its glass panels and

electric heating rods calculated to enable the sun worshipper
to obtain the maximum benefit from ultra violet rays, whether
the sun shone or not. But when Sybilla mentioned the place
(Antibes was the name given to it) she spoke of "the cottage,"
and Macdonald envisaged some Tudor imitation, with half-
timbering safely nailed on. The nature of the building did not
at first interest him, what he wanted was some corroboration
of the fact that Mrs. Attleton and Mr. Burroughs had spent ten
days together at Antibes. Guessing that housework was hardly
likely to be numbered among Sybilla's activities, he inquired
how service was arranged. Her answer was quite explicit. A
man and wife named Jobson who lived nearby, were retained
by Mr. Burroughs to look after house and garden. When the
owner was in residence, the cleaning of the place was all done
in the afternoon—during which period the two residents either
went for a drive or retired to the seclusion of the sun-parlour.
Food was supplied by a relay of hampers and cases from Messrs.
Fortnum & Mason, whose service was of a nature to supply even
the exigent requirements of epicures such as the two residents
at Antibes.

Macdonald, listening patiently to the lady's narrative, at last
put in a blunt question. "By your own showing it appears that
no one can corroborate your statement concerning the past ten
days. Neither Jobson, nor his wife, nor any other person actually
saw you while you were staying at the cottage? Presumably Mr.
Burroughs saw Jobson occasionally to give him orders, but there
can be no outside proof that you and Mr. Burroughs were there
during the whole period?"

"Of course not." The marble-grey eyes looked scornful. "I
should not have dreamt of going there if there were any risk of

anybody knowing that I was there. The Jobsons are very competent. They understand what is required of them and they do it. There is no need to give them any orders. They clean, they fetch and carry, and they are well paid. They do not interfere in what is not their business."

"From the point of view of Mr. Burroughs' interest, it is perhaps to be hoped that they are not so immune from human curiosity as they appear to be," replied Macdonald dryly.

A very real shadow of fear appeared for the first time on that well-drilled countenance facing him.

"I fail to see what you mean. You cannot suggest—"

"I am not suggesting anything, madam. It is obvious that Mr. Burroughs' actions will be subjected to very close inquiry. His actions at the Belfry last night inevitably cause him to come under suspicion. Meanwhile, I should be glad if you would let me have the letters of Debrette's that are in your possession."

It was then that Sybilla Attleton began to cry, and Macdonald could not for the life of him decide if he were witnessing a performance of surpassing virtuosity by a finished actress, or whether the lady was so agitated that her tears were a spontaneous outburst of emotion.

After a moment during which her sobs (not too loud or uncouth) were the only sound in the room, Macdonald got up and went over to the bell.

"I am afraid that this has been too great a strain on your fortitude, madam," he said politely, but not quite without malice. He had not forgotten her surprising fortitude when she heard of her husband's death. "I will ring for your maid."

Sybilla sat up, a handkerchief still to her eyes, and said brokenly, "No. Do not do that. I am sorry. I am only just beginning to realise it all. I will get you the letters you want. They are in my safe upstairs."

She got up, still busy with her handkerchief, and trailed softly out of the room. Macdonald, while he waited, went to the window, pulled aside the curtains, and opened the glass door which gave on to a low balcony surrounded by a balustrade. The heat of the room, and the scentedness of it, were both unpleasant to him, and he took in a deep breath of the cold moist air outside. Standing by the window, holding the curtains aside with one hand, he suddenly realised that some one had been moving in the garden just below him. In a trice he had an electric torch out of his pocket and turned its beam downwards—to light up the perplexed face of Weller, the butler.

"Sir?" inquired Weller politely.

"What do you think you're doing?" demanded Macdonald, and Weller replied:

"I thought that I heard some one in the garden, sir. I was just looking to ascertain that those seals which you affixed were still secure. I think it would be advisable for you to inspect them, sir."

"Very good. I will—and I think it would be advisable for you, Weller, to stay in your own quarters," retorted Macdonald.

Drawing back into the "silver boudoir" again, Macdonald pulled the curtains across the windows. If those seals had been meddled with, it must mean that somebody possessed the keys of the writing-room. He had not more than a few seconds in which to follow up this line of thought before Sybilla Attleton re-entered the room.

"This is the letter you wanted," she said.

Macdonald took the sheet and considered it. It was written on thin grey paper, certainly foreign in origin, and the handwriting immediately suggested a German origin. The long spidery script with its curious f's, g's and s's was characteristically German. It was dated January 25th, and headed with the address "c/o Blanco, 509 Charing Cross Place."

"Madame," it ran. "I think that it has come to your knowledge that your husband, Mr. Bruce Attleton, has been unfaithful to you. If you wish for unassailable evidence of his infidelity I can supply it to you in the course of time. For such a service I would ask a reward of £50 (fifty pounds) to be paid to me in English treasury notes when my service has been completed to your satisfaction. I will advise you of the manner in which this sum is to be remitted to me if you agree to these terms, trusting to your honour, madame, to liquidate the debt thus incurred. As an instance of my ability to obtain for you the information I suggest, I offer this example. Your husband habitually carries a small wallet. In the inner pocket of this you will find a replica of the photograph enclosed with this letter.

"Receive, madame, the expression of my most distinguished sentiments.—

"LOUIS DE VALLON DE BRETTE"

"Have you kept the photograph, and the envelope in which this letter arrived?" inquired Macdonald.

She nodded and held out to him an envelope of similar paper to that on which the letter was written.

"I have kept both—but I did not realise that the snapshot enclosed was an unfixed proof. I let it rest in the sunshine on my desk for no more than a few minutes, and it blackened completely."

From the envelope Macdonald drew out what had once been a print of a small photograph. It was, as Sybilla Attleton had said, completely blackened, nothing but a shiny purplish surface showing a few finger-prints where it had been touched before the fading was final.

"And you looked in Mr. Attleton's wallet to see if the photographs corresponded—as the letter said?"

"Yes. I did." Sybilla Attleton's little white teeth bit into the scarlet of her lips. "Debrette was right. It was a photograph of a young girl, a fair round-faced little country miss with eyes like saucers. Are you married, Inspector?"

Macdonald almost jumped at the unexpected question.

"No, madam, I am not," he replied stiffly.

"Then you cannot understand what I felt like when I saw that picture. I put it back into Bruce's case. Not for the world would I have had him know that I knew. I wrote to Louis de Vallon de Brette, and I told him that if he would carry out his part of the compact I would pay him the £50 he asked. In reply I received this letter."

She handed another sheet to Macdonald, similar to the first, on which was written:

"Madame, you may rely on me to earn the reward.

LOUIS DE VALLON DE BRETTE."

"And after this, you received no other letter until the one came posted to you at Antibes? Have you got that with you here?"

"No, I gave it to Mr. Burroughs."

"I shall need to see that one, too," said Macdonald. "Now, madam, one very important point emerges from this statement of yours. Who could have known that you were going to stay at the cottage—and by what means did they obtain the information?"

"I can't imagine," she replied. "I told nobody—nobody at all. You can surely take that for granted. I told Louise, my maid, that I was going to have a ten days' cure with Annette Kampf, for skin treatment and slimming. I sent Louise home to her people in Boulogne while I was away, as I don't like her staying in the house when I'm not there. She makes mischief among the other servants. I can assure you that I told no one," she concluded earnestly.

"But since you received that letter, it stands to reason that some one knew your destination before you went away, or else followed you when you left London, since you are so certain that no one saw you while you were at the cottage," replied Macdonald, and she shrugged her shoulders.

"I don't know. I can't imagine how it happened. If any one followed me they were very cunning about it. I kept a look-out. You see I had no intention of letting Bruce get to know, and I didn't trust him," she ended coolly. "He said that he was going to Paris. Perhaps he was—but I took care to see that no car followed me while I was driving to Southampton."

"The cottage at which you stayed belongs, I suppose, to Mr. Burroughs?" inquired Macdonald. She nodded. "Yes. He built it."

"And you have stayed there before?"

She took a long time before she made up her mind to answer that simple question, but at last replied:

"Yes. Once or twice before."

"Then it seems to me that some one must have known that you had stayed there, and when you went away again leaving no address, they concluded you were at Antibes. It would not have been difficult to put the matter to the proof. You say that you went driving. Any one could have seen you in the car going to or leaving the house."

"But why should any one have done that?" Sybilla had by this time entirely abandoned her air of dramatic aloofness and allowed anxiety to percolate into her voice. Macdonald found it difficult to assess her, because he could never be certain when she was acting and when she wasn't, and he was willing to admit that as an actress she was certainly an accomplished one. Her last question irritated him, because it seemed foolish—unsophisticated. Whatever else Sybilla Attleton was, he did not believe her to be dense.

Leaning forward in her place, she looked at him again with that unfathomable stare.

"I told you to start with that I know nothing at all which can have any bearing on my husband's death. This man, Debrette, was simply out to make money from other people's misfortunes."

Macdonald could have laughed. The word "misfortune" struck him as almost comical.

"It is not my business to point a moral from any one's behaviour," he retorted, "but did it not occur to you that if Debrette approached you along such lines, it is not inconceivable that he approached your husband along similar ones? If he found the means to learn what your husband carried about in his pocket book, it is not inconceivable that he found means to learn where you stayed when you went away and left no address. To employ such a tool is to ask for trouble. On what business did you imagine that Debrette telephoned to your husband?"

"Not to give him information about me," she flashed back. "Why? Because his attentions infuriated Bruce. My husband would have been only too delighted to learn anything that could discredit me. Debrette probably tried to get money out of him. I can tell you he wouldn't have got much. Bruce spent all that he made on his own enjoyment. Understand this, too. Bruce had no intention of quarrelling with me to the extent of leaving this house. He was much too comfortable here."

If Macdonald had spoke aloud the thought in his mind, he would have said:

"What a perfectly loathsome pair you seem to have been." Instead he rose to his feet, saying formally:

"I must take these letters with me for further investigation. As you probably know, I have put a seal on the entrance to Mr. Attleton's writing-room. Have you a key of that room, or of the desk within it?"

She shook her head. "No. I never went there. Weller has a key."

"I must thank you for the frankness with which you have answered my questions. It will be advisable for you to stay here, at home, during our investigation. I take it that you have no intention of going away again in the near future?"

Sybilla Attleton stared at him, apparently seeking to fathom the meaning behind that formal voice. Macdonald had spoken with no satiric impulse, but he saw quickly enough the construction which could have been read into his words.

"No. I shall stay here—until you have found the answer to this mystery. You think Debrette killed him?"

"I do not know."

"And the inquest?"

"It will be held to-morrow. You will be served with a notice of it, and I should advise you to have your lawyer at hand, as is customary."

He bowed to her politely and walked out of the room, conscious that he was glad to leave the scented warmth of it.

Going down the charming little staircase, Macdonald saw Weller standing in the conservatory, and the butler came to meet him with a troubled frown on his face.

"I am afraid you thought that I was exceeding my instructions, sir, being out there in the garden," he began. "I thought I heard footsteps and went out to look. The fact is, that French maid of madam's is always poking her nose where it's no need to be."

"You can tell her that she can keep her nose to herself for the time being," said Macdonald. "I will go and have a look at those seals."

He went out of the conservatory into the little garden, deciding that he had better have a man sent down to remove the contents of the desk wholesale to Scotland Yard. For a moment he blamed himself that he had not stayed to examine it earlier, and then reflected that his day had not been unprofitably spent. Nevertheless, he breathed a sigh of relief when he saw that the seals had not been broken. With his torchlight directed on them, he perceived that some one had meddled a little—the seal was chipped at one side, but not broken.

"Of course it would be," he said to himself. "If Weller's telling lies, he had to have some corroboration."

Going back to the house, he telephoned to the Regent's Park police station to have a man sent immediately to Park Village South, to stand guard over the garden house until the

Yard man should arrive to relieve him. Macdonald did not for a moment believe that anything relevant to his case would be found in Bruce Attleton's desk. Presumably the dead man had had his keys on him when he left home, and the murderer would be in possession of them all—the keys of the writing-room, of the desk, and of the house. During the past week he would have had plenty of time to remove anything which he wished to remove.

Waiting for the man from the station to arrive, Macdonald went into the hall again and called to Weller.

"Has the house been left empty any time since your master went away?" he asked.

"No, sir. I have been most particular on that point. There have never been less than two of the staff in. The maids are nervous and do not like being left here by themselves."

"Have you bolted the front door at night?"

"Yes, sir. Mr. and Mrs. Attleton both said that they would not be back before the first of the month, and I locked up myself every night."

"Then you can be quite sure that no intruder has got into the house during the week?"

"I would say, quite sure, sir. The windows and doors have all been in order."

"Did you bolt the further door of the writing-room when Mr. Attleton went away?"

"No, sir. I had instructions not to bolt it."

"Well, be sure that you bolt the front door to-night, Weller. It's quite probable that a latchkey has gone astray."

It was only a few minutes before the constable turned up to take charge, and with him Macdonald left the key of the writing-room to be handed over to the C.I.D. man when he arrived. Whereupon Macdonald left the Attletons' house with the intention of interviewing Mr. Thomas Burroughs, the owner of Antibes.

While driving his car the Chief Inspector had leisure to think over the story told him by Sybilla Attleton. The maddening part of it was that there were two ways of looking at it, both quite logical, but both leading to totally different conclusions. If the story were true, and Debrette had really written those letters, the inference was obvious—Mr. Burroughs was to be induced to go to the Belfry while the police were on guard there, to provide the scapegoat. That hasty-tempered gentleman had obliged by his useless and impetuous show of violence and landed himself in very strong suspicion. But what if the story were not true? There was, at present, no proof at all that the letters had been written by Debrette. To Macdonald's mind their phraseology was not at all the work of a foreigner. Mr. Burroughs, with his businesslike mind, and Sybilla Attleton with her actress's sense of the dramatic, might well have concocted such a composition, and prepared the whole story lest their plans went awry. They might well have taken it for granted that the Belfry would not reveal its secret until its demolition. In which case, argued Macdonald, ever trying to penetrate the criminal's mind, the suitcase was left in the cellar as an indication of the murderer. Attleton's body was not to be recognised, and the police were to assume that he had killed Debrette.

"I suppose we rushed them by finding the body too quickly," said Macdonald to himself. "Losh keeps! How many solutions is that? One: Debrette killed Attleton. Two: Attleton killed Debrette (disproved by identification). Three: Burroughs killed

Attleton. Four: Grenville killed Attleton. And if number one is correct, old Streaky Beaver, known to his fellows as a bit balmy, double-crossed everybody, handed a stout stockbroker the baby to hold, and is capable of the criminal carelessness of omitting to shave his beard. What a story!"

XI

WHILE MACDONALD WAS AT THE HOUSE IN PARK VILLAGE South, Robert Grenville sat hunched up over his fire in Furnival's Court, smoking furiously, and trying to puzzle out some reasoning for the sequence of events in which he had been involved. During the day he had had visits both from the C.I.D. (plain clothes) and Metropolitan Police (uniformed branch) and his landlady was beginning to look anxious. The C.I.D. had informed him of the discovery of a corpse in the Belfry Studio, and warned him that his presence would be required at the inquest, though it was not certain if any evidence would be taken except that of the officers who had discovered the body. Grenville's immediate inquiry as to the identity of the dead man had brought him no satisfaction. The matter was not beyond doubt, to use the phrase of the polite young detective who had called ("to give me the once over again," as Grenville believed).

"Well, you must surely know if it's Attleton or not," burst out Grenville.

"It's uncertain, sir. Deceased was shockingly injured," was the reply.

"Look here, you might jolly well tell me what you mean," persisted Grenville, but the officer refused to be drawn, adding:

"The Chief Inspector told me to warn you, sir, that it would be unwise for you to attempt any further investigation of the man Debrette, whom you saw at Charing Cross. The matter is being looked into."

The uniformed branch wished for further details concerning Grenville's collision with a motorcyclist in the Strand, as the unfortunate rider, who had got mixed up with a taxi, owing to Grenville's intrusion into his front wheel, was lying in hospital with concussion and a broken leg.

"He'll probably bring a case against you for damages, sir," said the genial and portly sergeant. "You'd no business to barge through the traffic with the lights against you."

"Look here, if there's a law prohibiting His Majesty's subjects from walking on the King's highway, tell me when it was put on the statute book," said Grenville indignantly. "If my arms aren't broken it's only because they're unbreakable. I tell you I'm damaged all over, and I've ruined a new pair of bags and my second best hat."

"You should have thought of that first, sir," replied the other. "The other gentleman's got a wife—very strong-minded lady, sir, and she says she's going to take out a summons against you."

"Be damned to her!" groaned Robert. "I shall plead I was assisting the law, and look here, sergeant, I shall be in to tea all right, and if any of you chaps like to look in for a cup, don't stand on ceremony, but I'd be awfully obliged if you didn't come in uniform. My landlady's beginning to get suspicious. She's a very high-minded woman."

"Very good, sir," grinned the sergeant.

Grenville was sorely perplexed, in spite of his back-chat to the police. He wanted to see Elizabeth, or to telephone to her, but with this grim news about the corpse in the Belfry, he hadn't the heart to do so. Sucking away at his pipe, he realised that there wasn't any glamour about a murder case in which you knew the

parties involved. Moreover, it was so difficult to know what to wish. If Bruce Attleton were not identified as the "shockingly-injured corpse" of the Belfry, he would almost certainly be a fugitive from justice, branded as a murderer who had carried out a crime in a particularly ghastly manner.

Even his professional enthusiasm failed him. He had begun a write-up of the Belfry Studio, and he knew that he was in a position to become *persona grata* with Fleet Street, but the fact that Bruce Attleton was Elizabeth's guardian, and that Elizabeth had lived in the Attletons' house, robbed even this situation of its piquancy. Grenville guessed what certain editors would pay him for a description of that evening's conversation in Sybilla's drawing-room—Elizabeth's brainwave about committing a murder and concealing the body, and Bruce's prophetic phrase about "plastering him up."—Very nasty indeed, when turned into actual fact. Going to the telephone, Grenville got through to Rockingham.

"Look here, who is it they've found at the Belfry?" he demanded eagerly, and Rockingham snapped back:

"For God's sake don't go spreading yourself over the tele-phone. It's bad enough without having exchange listening in. I'll come round and see you after tea. It's no use asking me questions. I don't know, neither does Macdonald, yet. Sorry to be surly, old chap, but I've had about as much as I can stand to-day. Good-bye."

Baulked in this direction, Grenville set out to do just what he had been told not to do—to see if he could get a line on the bearded man, whose queer countenance he had glimpsed the evening before. Having a journalist's sense of how to set about things, he covered a certain amount of the ground traversed by

Detective Reeves before him, and consequently his activities were reported to Scotland Yard before the day was up.

Returning to Furnival's Court at tea time, having got much less far in his researches than Reeves had got, but with a much larger expenditure of money and energy, Grenville sat and drank large quantities of strong tea, and then sat over the fire to ponder, when his long-suffering landlady opened the door, saying, "A young person to see you, sir," in accents of obvious disapproval. The entrance of Elizabeth Leigh brought Grenville to his feet with a whoop of joy.

"Angel!" he exclaimed fervently, but Elizabeth only made a face at him.

"I don't approve of coming to see comparatively young men in their own rooms," she announced haughtily. "Not on moral grounds, but because it gives them swelled head. However, my club's no place for a good talk. There's always some long-chinned spinster listening in from behind a pillar, and restaurants are the same, so I just came here. Bobby, where on earth is every one now? Sybilla's back—I just rang up and Weller told me, and Neil Rockingham rang me up last night and said that Bruce was all right. It's all really rather comic, with old Neil R. tearing out what hair he's got left because he went barging to the police when he needn't have, and Sybilla rolling up to look superior just when we were making up the most ghastly stories about her. Why, what's the matter with you, goop-face?" she ended up, looking at Grenville's amazed countenance.

"Rockingham said Bruce was all right!" gasped Grenville, "darling, are you certain? You're not feverish, or having hallucinations or something, are you?"

"No, and I'm not half-seas-over, if that's what you mean," she responded severely. "I mean what I say. Neil rang me up last night to say that Bruce had phoned him, and the whole thing was a mistake."

"Jiminy Jenkins!" Grenville threw up his arms in an astonishment which left him speechless. "Bruce is all right, and... Darling, it's the most incredible business. I was simply sitting here saying funeral services and misereres... oh, confound old Neil R. What the blooming deuce does he mean, leaving me stewing in my own miseries."

"—And imagining corpses and all that," said Elizabeth. "Give me a gasper, Robert, and let's think it all out. I was certain they'd find a corpse in that baleful Belfry."

"But they have found one!" cried Grenville. "That's the whole point, and they don't know who it is. It's not Bruce, angel head, and it's not Debrette. I know, because I saw him in Trafalgar Square last night, and got biffed by a blasted motorbike trying to hare after him."

Elizabeth's eyes grew as round as saucers; with her hat in her hand, and her red curls rumpled up like a baby's, she looked as angelic as a modern young woman could look, with her lips pursed like a Raphael cherub.

"A corpse, in the Belfry? But Bobbie, who corpsed him?"

"I don't know, bambina, and the cops don't know either. Old Neil rang me up just now, simply bleating... I know, the blighter!" A light of comprehension dawned in his eyes. "That blinking Macdonald told Neil R. not to let me know anything. Confound him! He'll be trying to tie the beastly unknown round my neck, like an albatross. He took my finger-prints, and now he'll say he found 'em plastered all over the Belfry, and run me in for doing an anonymous murder. I always said the chap looked too much like Cassius, lean and hungry, and all that."

Elizabeth looked appalled. "Bobbie, he can't!"

Robert Grenville had never seen the girl's eyes look concerned before on his account, and he forgot his own misgivings in the triumph of the moment.

"Can't he!" he said darkly. "He's out for a sensational arrest. All these chaps are."

He got no further with slandering one of the most upright men in the English police, for the door opened and a much-tried voice said:

"A gentleman to see you, and there's this letter."

Grenville wheeled round with an exclamation, ready to curse Rockingham to his face for interfering in such an ill-timed manner, but indignation over the way his friend had treated him got the better of his annoyance at being interrupted.

"You old blackguard, you!" he said severely. "You're a nice one, you are! I wonder you've got the nerve to look at me, let alone come to see me. You and your private corpses, and obliging that tombstone of a Scotsman by telling me the exchange might listen in! Next time you want any dirty work done, you can damn well do it yourself!"

Rockingham came into the room and put his hat and gloves on the table very deliberately. It was the expression of his face that brought Grenville's cheerful tirade to a stop.

"Oh! for God's sake leave off trying to be funny," said Rockingham wearily. "I beg your pardon, Miss Leigh. I came in for a talk with Grenville. The fact that it's a serious matter must condone my ill-manners. Can I reverse your car for you?"

"No, you can't," said Elizabeth, very decidedly. "I don't know what you're crying wolf over next, Neil Rockingham, but did you or did you not ring me up last night and tell me that Bruce was all right?"

"Yes. I did," said Rockingham, and then added, slowly and painfully, "It seems that I was mistaken. I'm sorry. I acted in good faith."

The trio stood and looked at one another, Elizabeth and Grenville aghast, Rockingham with a face bereft of all its normal cheerful colour, his eyes as miserable as a man's could well be. It was Elizabeth who broke the silence. Slipping her hand into Rockingham's arm with the confiding gesture of a child, she said:

"You poor old thing. Come and sit down, Neil R, and tell us about it. After all, I've got to know some time, haven't I? You'd far better tell us both now."

Rockingham patted her shoulder.

"It's no sort of story to tell to a child like you," he said gently, but Robert Grenville burst out:

"Then it was Bruce after all—the dead man in the Belfry?"

"I'm afraid so." Rockingham sat down by the fireside, with Elizabeth perched on the arm of his chair, and related the sequence of events since he had last spoken to Robert over the telephone at the time the latter rang up from Charing Cross. "I did try to get you on the 'phone after Macdonald had left, to tell you about Bruce's call," said Rockingham to Grenville, "but you were either out all the evening or your line was out of order. I rang Elizabeth here—and then when I was having breakfast this morning Macdonald came in with his story about the discovery at the Belfry, and from what he said it was obvious that he believed I'd been spoofed by that phone call of Bruce's. I felt too sick to want to ring you up then."

"Are they certain yet—about the identity?" asked Grenville, his voice very low and flat-sounding.

Rockingham nodded. "Yes. They got on to Jennings, Bruce's masseur. There doesn't seem to be any room left for doubt."

He turned to Elizabeth. "Look here, my child, this is a beastly story for you to hear. I'm more sorry than I can say."

"I'd got to hear it some time," said Elizabeth. "Never mind about me. The point is—who rang you up and pretended to be Bruce?"

"There can only be one answer to that," replied Rockingham. "It means that the murderer knows Bruce well enough to simulate his voice."

"It must be Debrette, it can't be any one else," said Grenville excitedly. "After all, he probably talked to Bruce quite a lot and got to know his voice, and just imitated it to you over the phone, Rockingham. Look here! I've found out quite a lot about the blighter. I went routing round about Charing Cross way this afternoon and found the chap who runs an all-night café in Villiers Street. He knows Debrette by sight, and says he believes he's been an actor. That'd explain it, you know—being able to imitate Bruce's voice. It's just what an actor could do quite easily."

Elizabeth gave a little cry. "Oh, Bobbie, how beastly! Don't you remember what I said about Sybilla getting some old actor on to pretending to blackmail Bruce? Mr. Rockingham, have you seen Sybilla?"

"No. Of course I haven't. If you know where she is, Elizabeth, you ought to say so."

"Know? She's at home! She came back this afternoon. I phoned Weller and he told me."

Neil Rockingham took out his handkerchief, and mopped his broad forehead unashamedly.

"If only I could see some sense in this ghastly mix-up," he groaned. "Didn't Sybilla say she wouldn't be back in town before the 1st? What made her come back? Did I tell you they'd arrested Burroughs in the grounds of the Belfry last night?"

Once again there was a horror-stricken silence, and then Elizabeth cried, "I'd believe anything of that man! I always loathed him! I never disliked Sybilla so much until she took to trailing round with her Thomas. I know he's batty over her, I've seen him pawing her. Beasts, both of them!"

"Well, I'd never have believed it," said Grenville, in slow tones of astonishment. "Why on earth did they do it? They could have—oh, Lord, what a beastly business!"

He got up from his seat and started wandering about the room, while Rockingham was suggesting to Elizabeth that it might be a good thing for her to go away, to those friends in Juan les Pins for instance, until the whole grisly business was settled. Seeing the letter which his landlady had brought in when Rockingham entered, Grenville picked it up and opened it. A moment later his exclamation of astonishment caused the other two to look round with a jump.

"It's from Debrette!" yelled Grenville. "The beggar's had the nerve to write to me!"

Rockingham jumped up and almost snatched the sheet from Grenville's hand. Holding it in fingers which shook with excitement he read it while Elizabeth leaned across to catch a glimpse of it.

"Monsieur," it ran. "I am in great trouble, being put under a cloud of suspicion in the matter of the Belfry murder. I am innocent. I dare not go to the police, for they would not believe my story, but I can prove to you that I took no part in this terrible crime. I beg of you, Monsieur, in the cause of justice, to meet me, and learn my story. I will await you on the steps of Dowgate Wharf, close to Cannon Street Bridge, at seven o'clock on the evening of Sunday next. Do not, I implore you, fail to meet me there. I am but the unhappy tool of malevolent persons. Monsieur, I put myself in your hands. I trust you. Do not, I beg, betray an innocent man.

"LOUIS DE VALLON DE BRETTE."

Elizabeth made a snatch at the paper in her impatience to see the letter more clearly, but Rockingham held it above his head, out of her reach.

"No! no!" he cried. "This letter must go to the police, to the Chief Inspector, and it must go at once. Don't touch it again, either of you. There may be finger-prints on it."

"There certainly are. There are mine, all over it, and some of yours as well," put in Grenville. "Lay it on the table, Rockingham. We won't touch it. Damn it, you can't expect us not to read it."

Rockingham laid the thin grey sheet on the table, then, "fussing like an old hen," as Grenville complained, he kept guard over it, anxiously insisting that neither of the others must touch it.

Elizabeth bent eagerly over the table, rereading the spidery, foreign-looking writing, and Grenville leant forward too, his square, brown head pleasantly near her red curls. Rockingham, excited though he was, was almost moved to chuckle at Grenville's quickness to take his opportunity.

"Look here, my dear young idiots," said the older man. "Realise this. Whether this letter is a leg-pull, or a transparent effort to nab Grenville, I can tell you one thing. It goes to Scotland Yard. And Robert, don't go doing anything idiotic. You've had one knock over the head and a collision in which you might well have lost your life already. Don't go making an ass of yourself over this."

"Keep your wool on, old sermon-face," growled Robert Grenville. "It's my letter, anyway. I say, I wish the blighter hadn't said he trusted me. If Liza's idea's anywhere near right, and this blighter's been employed as cat's paw—"

"Don't be such a damned young fool!" roared Rockingham, in a voice which fairly made both the others jump. "If this chap is innocent, as he protests, the police will be the first to recognise it. Do you think your addled pate is a superior reasoning instrument to Macdonald's, you crass donkey? If this chap were honest, he wouldn't write asking you to meet him alone God knows where—"

"Yes, just where?" put in Elizabeth. "If God knows, I don't. Where is Dowgate Wharf?"

"In Limehouse, I expect," said Rockingham disgustedly. "Some filthy cut-throat waterside hole in the docks. What a fool the chap must be! That letter wouldn't take in a child of ten."

"It's not in Limehouse," said Robert. "He says it's near Cannon Street Bridge. That'd be the railway bridge. Dowgate? Isn't there a Dowgate Hill somewhere near that Wren church—the Walbrook one. St. Stephens, that's it."

"Has it a crypt?" asked Elizabeth weakly, but Rockingham interposed:

"No matter where it is. Grenville's not going there—and don't you go trying to be funny," he added severely to Elizabeth. "I've had enough horrors the past few days. It'd be the last straw if you went poking your pretty nose into criminal haunts. Do, for heaven's sake, go away, as I suggested, my child. At least, promise you won't go being silly over this disgusting piece of effrontery."

He pointed again to the letter, and Elizabeth replied with dignity:

"I'm not such a goop as you think. I don't want to be chucked in the river, thank you very much. Nothing heroic about me. Bobby, you won't go, either, will you? Promise?"

"It wouldn't be much good if I did, not with the old Dominie over there running us all in leading strings," grumbled Robert. "I'm puzzled over this Debrette chap, all the same, Rockingham. The café bloke, who'd seen him mooching around, said he was a bit balmy. Didn't sound like a desperate criminal to me."

"He's not your business," urged Rockingham. "Leave it alone. Now look here. Let me put this letter in an envelope and seal it up and take it to Scotland Yard. You can come, too, if you want to, and then both of us can explain how it arrived."

"Said he magnanimously," retorted Grenville. "I'm not at your prep. school, thanks very much, my dear chap, although you do remind me of the dear old head. I'm quite capable of finding my own way to Cannon Row police station, and presenting the authorities with this valuable piece of evidence, but I want to think it over a bit first. There's more in this than meets the eye at a casual perusal."

He made a face at Rockingham, and Elizabeth exclaimed, "Cannon Row? Is that where your Dowgate place is?" and Robert explained in superior tones:

"Cannon Row police station is the headquarters of the C.I.D. Amateurs with a taste for the dramatic refer to it as 'the Yard'— just like that."

Rockingham ignored the jibe. "I don't care two hoots what you call it. This letter's got to be sent to the proper authorities."

"It shall be, all in good time," replied Grenville. "Don't be in such a feverish haste, my dear chap. It betokens panic and lacks dignity. I wonder if you observed one interesting point in it—the writer refers to the murder at the Belfry. How does he know there's been a murder there? I only knew myself this morning."

"Because he committed the murder," said Rockingham, and his voice sounded a little terse as though his temper were giving way. "It's no time for clowning, Grenville. The thing's deadly serious."

Hearing the weary note in his voice, Grenville promptly relented, saying, "Sorry, old chap. Don't you worry. I'll see this bright little production goes to the proper quarter long before Sunday."

Elizabeth gave a little exclamation of dismay.

"Goodness, how awful! It's nearly six o'clock, and I've promised to dine with the Morton female and go on to *Lady Precious Stream*. I think I shall cut it. I don't feel like theatres and eating."

"Don't you be so foolish, my child," said Rockingham. "A good dinner and a play are the very things you need. Off with you! Go and get into your most frivolous frock and forget all about these grisly topics. It won't do anybody any good for you to stay here and get more and more morbid—Besides, it's not done to cut appointments. Off you go, Liza. I saw you'd left your little runabout in Fetter Alley. The City Police will be summonsing you to-morrow morning if you leave it there much longer."

"Well, if I'm going, I'd better go," said Elizabeth. "Bye-bye, Bobbie. Ring me in the morning and don't go doing heroics on lonely wharves. You'll look after him, won't you, Neil R?"

"I will," said Rockingham heartily, and Elizabeth was out of the door in a flash.

"Call yourself a friend!" exclaimed Grenville wrathfully. "You're a damned old wet-blankety-mollycoddle of a moth-eaten schoolmaster. Damn it, Rockingham, I could understand it if some one batted *you* over the head!"

"Sorry, old chap! I'm too fed up to be tactful," replied Rockingham. "You'll have plenty of time for courting when all this is over, and do, for God's sake, try to avoid entangling that nice child in this very nasty story. About that letter of Debrette's—are you sure you won't let me take it along?"

"No. I won't, and that's flat," retorted Grenville. "I'm quite old enough to manage my own affairs. I know you'll go rushing to the nearest phone, I can see it written all over your virtuous face, but that letter's mine. See?"

"Oh, all right, all right. They say confidence men make their fortunes because the world's full of mugs," replied Rockingham. "I expect Bruce was a mug—and he paid for it. If I have to attend an inquest on you I shall say you asked for all you got. Good-bye."

He strode out with his chin in the air, and Grenville returned to the table and leant over the Gothic-looking script of Louis de Vallon de Brette.

XII

WHEN MACDONALD LEFT PARK VILLAGE SOUTH IT WAS shortly before seven o'clock—a raw, nasty evening, with a fine drizzle beginning to turn to steady rain intermixed with sleet. He drove back to Scotland Yard, intending to give instructions concerning the removal of Attleton's papers before he went on to see Mr. Burroughs, and, if possible, to startle a little truth out of him.

When he reached his own department, Detective James came running up the stairs after him.

"Phone call come through from B division, sir. There's been an explosion in the Belfry and the whole place is burning."

Macdonald turned a wary eye on him.

"Certain it's not another of these bogus calls?"

"Quite certain, sir. Fuller rang up himself and I've got corroboration from the fire brigade. They can see the place burning all over the district. It began in the roof. Fuller heard a detonation and went inside, and the roof beams were burning like fun."

"Good thing too," said Macdonald. "It's all it's fit for. I suppose this is the climax of the great idea. Burn the place out and leave the remains for us to ponder over. You wanted to have a look at that roof, too. I'm glad you didn't."

"Why, sir? I might have found the plant."

"And got blown sky-high, or come down and broken your neck on that filthy floor," said Macdonald severely. "Not my idea of good work. However, the point just now is this. Is it worth while going along there to gape at the spectacle, or do we leave it to the fire brigade? Not much object in interfering until they've got the fire under control. You can go if you like, James, and take Jenkins with you. He loves fires. Then the pair of you can stand by, and I'll come along later. Meantime, I'll stay on here and write up my report, and you can phone me as soon as you get to the Belfry, and report progress. The Knight Templar's the nearest phone. If there's any object in my going to the Belfry, I'll go, but I don't want to stand and gape."

"Very good, sir."

Fuller departed with enthusiasm. Like Jenkins, he was partial to fires, and from what he had heard this promised to be a good one.

Macdonald lighted his pipe and sat smoking furiously, pondering over his case. A whole lot of possibilities had occurred to him, based on the evidence which he had collected, and he tried to fit in a reason for this latest development.

The murderer, who, for purposes of argument, it was simplest to call Debrette, must have schemed out an exceedingly elaborate programme. There was no actual proof that Attleton had been killed in the Belfry. No one had seen him arrive there with his suitcase, but to Macdonald's mind it seemed safe to assume that he had gone there alive. It would have been no easy matter to carry a man's body—or a crate containing it—across that open space of pavement which led to the doorway in the porch. Once inside the building, violence would have been fairly safe. Debrette, therefore, had probably killed Attleton in the building, perhaps by a blow on the head—some method not involving bloodshed, since there had been no bloodstains on floor or walls, and obviously no cleansing had taken place. The body had been then partially dismembered in the bath, and later concealed in the niche. There had been no need to conceal traces of plaster on the floor, for the sculptor's work which had been carried on there provided an explanation of such remains. Barring that inexplicable matter of the suitcase left in the cellar, there was nothing left to arouse suspicion. Macdonald's mind worried round over that suitcase. There was no evidence save Grenville's that the suitcase had been found in the cellar, and Grenville's evidence must of necessity be considered questionable. It almost looked, argued Macdonald, as though two people had been concerned in the crime, both working against one another. One had endeavoured to conceal every trace of the murder, and further to ensure that the body, if found, should be unrecognisable; the other had endeavoured to leave evidence which could not be missed, and had put the final coup-de-théâtre on proceedings by an explosion and a fire. Even though the niche were not made evident by the fire, it was obvious that demolition would be expedited—and no fire would account for the presence of a mutilated corpse. Then again, what was the object of Debrette giving up the keys of the place, and yet leaving that suitcase where it was? Either retain the keys, or else move the suitcase, argued Macdonald, and pulled out the time-table which Grenville had supplied him with according to instructions.

Wednesday. Breakfast at eight-thirty. Left home at ten. Went to London *Mail* offices in Fleet Street to look up back files for information re Cycle accidents in Central London. Stayed there till midday. *(Corroboration of hours quite uncertain,* ran the note of Inspector Jenkins.) Walked to Piccadilly and met Bill Trevor at the Regent Palace. He was late, and didn't turn up till one o'clock. *(No corroboration before one o'clock. Lounge of R.P.H. too full for the staff to remember individuals a week ago.)* Went to a lecture at the

Scientist's Association at two-thirty to get material for article on Biology of the Future. (*Corroborated.*) Returned home at four-thirty. Wrote till seven. Dined at Golden Cock. (*No corroboration between four-thirty and six.*) Returned home at eight-thirty. Wrote. Went to bed at eleven. (*Landlady out from eight to ten. Grenville was in at ten, but may have gone out later, as was his custom.*)

On the Thursday, Grenville's doings were traceable during the day, and in the evening he had been present at *Poison by Post* at the Duchess of Kent's, his critique of which play had been one more nail in its hastily-constructed coffin. On Friday, from ten o'clock till four his doings were again uncorroborated, as he had been on the wander collecting material for an article on London's open-air markets, including the Caledonian Market, the Berwick Market, the Titchfield Market, Petticoat Lane, Artillery Row and the Portman Market. In fact, had he wished to remain obscure, Grenville could not have chosen a better way of occupying his time, since he had indulged in no bargaining, and had simply played an observer's part. In the evening he had gone to the Belfry, and had been found outside the porch by Constable Bell, his head and shoulders soused in whisky. Thereafter, his doings were quite frankly involved with the Belfry, whose keys he had obtained quite openly from the agents, on payment of a quarter's rent.

Rockingham's "dossier" in the case was brief and to the point. His passport (boasting an excellent photograph of his fine, domed head) was stamped with entry into France on Wednesday, March 18th, and departure from that country on Wednesday a week later.

There remained Mr. Thomas Burroughs, whose residence at the cottage named Antibes was still a problematical matter, and the butler, Weller, to whom Macdonald felt less benevolently disposed than he had originally done, and (a very large "and") Debrette, the latter still at large.

Writing up the salient points of Sybilla Attleton's statement, Macdonald was interrupted by a call put through to him from below, and picked up the receiver expecting to hear Fuller's report. It was, however, Rockingham's voice which spoke. The latter proceeded to inform Macdonald of the letter received by Grenville, and expressed considerable perturbation concerning the discretion of the recipient.

"You never know how a man will react to unusual circumstances," said Rockingham's slightly pedantic voice. "I used to think that Grenville had got his head screwed on pretty well, but lately he's shown a disposition to foolhardiness. I thought I'd let you know about the letter immediately, though if he sends it to you, I should be obliged if you wouldn't tell him that I informed you. He resents my advising him."

Macdonald chuckled a little over that, and went on to ask for a description of the paper the letter was written upon and the handwriting thereof—a matter in which Rockingham proved himself a very competent observer, even to having noticed the cancellation time and place—E.C.4., twelve noon.

"You say the landlady took the letter out of the box in your presence?" inquired Macdonald. "Was there any other witness present, in addition to yourself, when Grenville opened it?"

"Yes. Elizabeth Leigh was there. Look here, Inspector, don't bring her into this if you can help it. I loathe the idea of the kid being put into the witness-box, and all the rest of it."

"Quite. I'll do what I can. Thanks very much for phoning me. Are you at home?"

"At the moment. I'm dining at my club—Whelptons—but I shall come straight back here. You can't dine with me, I suppose?"

Macdonald chuckled again. "Thanks. I'm afraid not. I've just heard the Belfry's on fire, and is blazing away like a beacon."

"The Belfry—burning? Well, I don't see the point from the criminal's point of view, but my own reaction is, Thank God for that. Foul place."

"Amen," agreed Macdonald, and hung up the receiver. After a moment, however, he put through another call, this time to Grenville, but only got the satisfaction of hearing a much-tried female voice saying that Mr. Grenville was out, that he always was out at this time of an evening, and she didn't know when he'd be in.

"Oh, what the blazes is the silly ass up to now?" queried Macdonald as he hung up again. "Having dinner somewhere, or—Just the sort of tom-fool thing he would do."

He paused just as he was going to relift the receiver and call the City Police. Dowgate Wharf—five minutes along the Embankment to Blackfriars, five more up Queen Victoria Street to Cannon Street Station. No traffic in the city at this time in the evening. Macdonald knew London—not only the West End and the City, but the waterside as well. He knew all about Dowgate Wharf, and for once he gave way to impulse, hastened out of the room and went downstairs and out to his car.

It was a beastly evening; a mixture of snow and sleet was heralding the approach of spring, and cars on the Embankment threw up a greasy mixture of slush, while sodden drifts of sleet blew across the bare plane trees, and blurred the lighting of the

County Hall opposite. Macdonald had just got a new car—a Vauxhall—and he made something more than legal speed as he drove eastwards along the Embankment and went across the complicated traffic lanes at Blackfriars, with a signal to the man directing the traffic. No cars about here in the evening, no traffic problem in the city, after seven o'clock: up Queen Victoria Street he sped and slowed down as he approached Cannon Street Station. To the right here. What a wild-goose chase that young fool was leading him—probably nothing in it. "Make certain, and give him what-for afterwards," said Macdonald, alighting from his car where the roadway narrowed to a lane, running between lofty warehouses.

Alert to hear any footfall, his electric torch showing up the drift of sleet in front of him, Macdonald kept close into the wall, all his wits about him. He could see the river now, and the edge of the ancient wharf; a few seconds later he could see more—the dark shape of a man's body lying sack-like on the steps, just above the swelling rush of the Thames approaching flood-tide.

Macdonald's police whistle shrilled out as he bent over the inert form, and lifted it up on to the stones of the wharf.

"Grenville! Fool that he was!" grumbled Macdonald, "coming to such a place, alone, on such a night. Hullo there! Police boat? There have been some fine goings on here this evening. Who is it? Bainton? Come and stand by while I have a look at the fellow. Hullo—had a catch yourself?"

Macdonald stood looking into the body of the police launch, while it was manoeuvred alongside and made fast, with a queer feeling of chagrin. Was his case being settled for him by the arch settler, Death?

"Who have you got there?"

"Your quarry, sir, or I'm a Chinaman. Funny you being here. It's the chap with the white streak in his beard. His body fouled the piles there, just up by Blackfriars. Dead as a stone. His head was right under the piles."

Bainton pulled back the tarpaulin which covered the body, and Macdonald looked down at a peaceful, drowned face, with the wet beard showing the odd streak of white. Streaky Beaver. Well, his account was settled, whatever it was.

Bainton and Macdonald, both skilled in ambulance work, busied themselves with Grenville's prostrate body. Just as Macdonald said "This chap's still alive," a constable came hurrying down the lane.

"Ambulance—and don't waste time," was all that Macdonald vouchsafed to him. The uniformed man turned and went, at the double, after one glance in which he took in the sight of the two bodies, and the police launch bobbing up and down beside that ancient dock.

"Might as well get them both aboard. The doctors will tell us how long that one's been dead the more accurately if we hand him over quickly," said Macdonald. "I hope this other chap doesn't pass out before we get him to hospital. I should like to know the truth about this little performance."

Waiting for the ambulance, they covered Grenville with the rugs from Macdonald's car and put a compress round his head. There was no sign of blood, nor of any wound, but Macdonald's fingers found the bump at the base of his skull.

"Coshed," said Bainton. "Would this be about it?"

He lifted an object like a heavy, curved piece of garden hose from the cockpit of the police boat. Both police officers knew what it was—rubber loaded with lead, a deadly weapon for a silent killing.

"The loop was still round Debrette's arm when we fished him out. It was that that hitched on to the piles," said Bainton. "Looks as though Debrette coshed Grenville, and then lost his balance and fell in. I've known many a good swimmer drown in the Thames at full tide, and this Debrette's a poor, thin little rat. Half starved. No stamina."

"Might have been," said Macdonald, "in which case Debrette went to his death through being too much of a practical psychologist. Another instance of the dog it was that died. Here are the ambulance men. St. Joseph's is about nearest, isn't it? I'll carry on with this. You might give my department a call, and tell them I shall be at the hospital. We seem to be having a busy evening. Explosion, fire, assault, and the chief actor fished out of the river too late for him to be helpful. Steady on, there. The chap's got his skull bashed in. You're not lifting coals for your living!"

The last remark was to the ambulance man, doing his best to demonstrate a marked degree of skill in the eyes of two "police swells," but the wharf was treacherous with its coating of sleet, and the ambulance man had slipped a little. He and his mate were trained and experienced men, and he felt hurt in his feelings when Macdonald stood over him with a hand ready to give assistance in case of need. When the stretchers were safely run into their places, Macdonald turned to the two men with a more kindly eye.

"Good enough, but keep her running as smoothly as you can, and don't risk any jerks. The one man's alive, but only just, and he matters a lot."

Sitting beside Grenville in the ambulance, ready to steady him at the least jerk in the smoothly-running vehicle, Macdonald puzzled exceedingly. Bainton's suggestion seemed a not unreasonable explanation of what might have happened. The wharf was very slippery, and it was quite conceivable that Debrette had lost his footing. He might even have been trying to haul Grenville's unconscious body into the river, and have fallen in himself—but what was the object of trying to murder Grenville? What was it that the now unconscious journalist had known which made him so dangerous? True, he knew Debrette by sight, but then so did Rockingham and Elizabeth Leigh.

The drowned man who was being carried in the same vehicle as his presumed victim wiped out some of the more fantastic guesses which Macdonald had conjured up. He had even gone so far as to hazard a theory challenging the identity of the corpse found in the Belfry. This involved the supposition of a victim (a cousin of the Brossé line) of similar physique to Bruce Attleton's, while the latter, having committed a murder, masqueraded in beard and large glasses to impersonate the Debrette of Belfry fame. But a glance at the drowned man's face routed this theory. The beard was real, the man was real—and the man was dead, still and inscrutable, having taken his secrets with him into the cold flood of London's river.

Arrived at the hospital, Macdonald saw the house surgeon before Grenville was moved and entreated him earnestly to do his best for his patient.

"All right, we will, since you make such a point of it," retorted the surgeon. "We generally kill 'em in the lift, to save trouble, especially when we're over full, as we always are. Never met any one like you cops. You always come along with the suicides saying they're special cases, and will we be particularly careful."

Macdonald grinned. "Sorry. I deserved that, but I feel it'll be the last straw if this chap peters out on me. I suppose the policeman grows to resemble the famous parent at school—their kids are always unusual kids, and want careful handling."

While one surgeon examined Grenville, Macdonald was allowed to assist a colleague in the examination of the drowned man. That he died by drowning was patent. His lungs were full of water, and his body showed no signs of violence. He was thin, but not to the point of starvation, or even semi-starvation, and he was much cleaner and better cared for than most of the poor waifs who haunt the sleeping places where he had been known. Macdonald looked down at the lean, bearded face, noting its length, the height of the brow and the well-shaped nose. A good type of head, the face already settled into the half-smiling lines of death, waxen, untroubled, inscrutable.

"Found drowned—favourite line with the coroners," said the surgeon who had examined Debrette. "Particular pet of yours?"

"Well, I wanted him," said Macdonald. "I suppose he committed a murder, amputated the head and hands of his subject—very carefully—and plastered up the remainder into a wall so that you'd never have believed it'd been done."

"Capable beggar," commented the surgeon. "Funny, he looks positively devout now. Found the missing members?"

"No. Probably somewhere in the Thames," said Macdonald. "This is where I examine his effects, as the lawyers say."

"Well, I wish you luck. Rather you than me. Thames mud isn't too savoury."

The garments taken off the drowned man were not in a bad state of repair, and they had certainly been made by a good tailor, once. The tailor's tabs were all carefully cut away. The collar was celluloid, and the flannel shirt showed signs of rough laundering. There was a handkerchief marked with a B—fine linen with a hand-worked initial, not at all the sort of thing a poor man might be expected to possess, let alone a down and out. There was five shillings in small change in the trouser pockets, and in an inner pocket of the waistcoat, obviously constructed by an amateur tailor, were four one-pound notes. In another of the waistcoat pockets was a sodden letter, written on the familiar thin grey paper, the blurred superscription on whose envelope was still faintly legible. It was addressed to Mr. Neil Rockingham. Finally, in the same pocket, was a thin and ancient little volume—a devotional book of Belgian origin, containing the canon of the Mass. On its flyleaf was a name written in thin characters in Indian ink, "Marie Antoinette Brossé."

Macdonald put down the still soaking little book with a sense almost of apprehension. He had the feeling—not uncommon to many people—that came over him in a conversation when some other man mentioned the very topic which it had been on the tip of his tongue to utter. He had guessed aright then. This Louis de Vallon de Brette, with his fine long head and well-shaped hands, had been cousin to Bruce Attleton, resembling him in his spare physique and long featured face. That was what Robert Grenville had noticed, in the flash of time when he had seen Debrette outlined against the light. So does a long shot occasionally hit the mark.

Macdonald took the letter, the book, the handkerchief and the pound notes, and left the clothes to be dried in the drying-room a little before they were taken to Scotland Yard. The letter, though soaked and ready to fall to pieces, opened out in his careful hands, and was spread out on a piece of dry blotting paper. It was a replica, apparently, of that sent to Robert Grenville, save that the rendezvous suggested was Regent's Park tube station (a frequently lonely spot, as Macdonald knew), and the date for the Sunday following that suggested to Grenville.

"If he was clever in some ways, he was an optimist in others," said Macdonald to himself.

A few minutes later he was interviewing the surgeon who had examined Robert Grenville.

"He'll survive—with luck," commented the doctor, "always assuming that he doesn't get pneumonia, which he probably will, after lying out in the sleet with a cracked skull, and provided there aren't any fragments of loose bone lacerating his brain. If he hadn't had the world's thickest skull he wouldn't be alive now."

"If he hadn't had the world's thickest skull in another sense he wouldn't be where he is now," said Macdonald. "Now then, looking at this, and speaking as one optimist to another, do you think he could have cracked his own skull by being over-enthusiastic in staging an accident?"

The doctor took the "cosh" with an amused smile. "Want me to try it out on myself? Speaking as one fool to another, which is what you were thinking of saying, I should say not. More in your line than mine, this. Oh, I see. Rubber loops. Quite a nice rebound. Of course, you *could* hit yourself, if you were a fakir or a contortionist. Try it on yourself, laddie. I'm here to attend to the lesions. You won't get pneumonia, otherwise, ceteris paribus... Come along, put some spunk into it! Scotland for ever. I've met your scrum half, and he wasn't half so careful of himself as you're being."

"Deuce take it," said Macdonald, "if I really try to hit the back of my own head—so," and he bent his long head well forward, "I can't regulate the blow. I don't want to be laid out just now—but there is a possibility."

The surgeon had succumbed to mirth. He laughed till he shook.

"Pity there isn't a movie merchant at hand," he spluttered. "Nothing Charlie Chaplin ever did is so funny as the sight of a Scots detective trying to hit the base of his own skull with a loaded rubber cosh. Man, ye're a grand sicht!"

XIII

AFTER HIS ACTIVITIES AT DOWGATE WHARF AND AT THE hospital, Macdonald decided to leave Mr. Thomas Burroughs in suspense for one more night, and to spend the rest of the evening writing up a report of his case. The Belfry, he heard, had burnt out as thoroughly as a building can, the roof beams having collapsed and set light to the floor. Only the walls and the burnt-out tower remained, with the gargoyles grinning at the angles, the owls having circled round their abode with mournful hoots, and the starlings who had nested in the roof of the hall having sat on adjacent trees and twittered in excited consternation. *What about the bats?*

A clean sweep, meditated Macdonald; Attleton and Debrette dead, the Belfry nothing but an evil-smelling, gaunt skeleton. Only the supernumeraries remained—Grenville, precariously alive. Burroughs keeping up his obstinate silence in a police cell, Sybilla Attleton brooding over the fire in her silver boudoir, Rockingham lamenting the absence of common sense in the world at large. Macdonald rang him up and told him what had happened at Dowgate Wharf, and heard him clucking like a hen in horrified consternation, saying:

"I ought to have come to you earlier."

When Macdonald woke up on the Saturday morning, he was conscious of a vast sense of dissatisfaction. On the borderland of sleeping and waking he remembered reiterating his previous question, "Why didn't he shave his beard off?" in the idiotic manner of the half-asleep. Sitting up and looking out at the greyness of a cold March morning, and the leaden waters of the Thames rising to the flood-tide opposite his windows in the Grosvenor Road, he knew that he did not feel at all as though he had completed a successful case. The whole thing seemed too chancy, his own conclusions too apt.

His first activity was to telephone to the hospital for news of Grenville. Dr. Thessaby (he who had jeered at Macdonald's experiments with the cosh the previous evening) came to the phone to report progress.

"You remind me of the 'child she-bear'," said the surgeon. "Hymns A. and M. Can a woman's tender care? No one would ever believe the solicitude of the C.I.D. Widowed mother's also ran in comparison. Well, your 'child she-bear' is progressing as per programme. Lungs busy with a pneumo-coccus. Shock plus exposure. If it's any comfort to you, he's got the physique of a bull and the resistance of an ostrich. Still, I'm afraid it's not too good."

"No hopes of his being compos mentis? Do you recommend that I come and sit by the bedside?"

"To record the last words? Not a hope. If the pneumo-coccus gets him, there won't be any. Don't you come interfering here. I've put on a special, she'll make a note if he utters—which he won't—not yet. He's in a coma. It's simply a matter of patience. He may pull through, but it'll be a long time before he'll be capable of answering the questions you're yearning to ask him. Do you still think he coshed himself?"

"No. I don't. If he had, we should have found the cosh on him, or by him. As it was, we found it on the other chap. Thanks very much for all your tender sympathy. I need it."

As soon as it was reasonably possible, Macdonald rang up Mr. Todbury, not at his office, but at his home. In a cascade of

"dear me's" and similar unoffending ejaculations, the lawyer gave
the information that "your remarkable acumen, my dear sir, hit
the mark, hit the mark every time." In other words, Mr. Adam
Marsham, now (as usual) at death's door, was a dark horse. Far
from merely owning the beggarly ten thousand or so suggested
by Mr. Todbury, that long-lived gentleman was estimated by his
lawyer to have accumulated a fortune of close on quarter of a
million. The qualities of shrewdness, secrecy and miserliness
innate in the remarkable old man were well known to his own
lawyer, Mr. Piddleton. The latter gentleman had been in charge
of the estate for over fifteen years now. When Adam Marsham
realised that his own powers were failing, he gave explicit instructions to Mr. Piddleton to re-invest all moneys accruing as divi-
dends in government securities, at the conservative rate of 3 1/2
per cent. Mr. Marsham, meanwhile, continued to live on the £300
annual yield of his annuity, tended by a housekeeper whom he
called "young Alice," now a dame of sixty-five, who had been
in Mr. Marsham's service since he returned to England in 1891.

"The old gentleman started his speculations with a comparatively small sum, only a few thousands," went on Mr. Todbury,
all a-twitter at his remarkable story. "He seems to have had
an almost uncanny power of anticipating the movements of
markets. Such shares as the Ashanti gold fields, the earliest
Woolworth issues…"

"Yes," agreed Macdonald firmly. "Remarkably interesting. I
hope you will tell me all about it later. The point which is really
pressing at the moment is this. Have you been able to ascertain if
Mr. Bruce Attleton made any inquiries about his uncle's estate?"

"I'm afraid that he did. I'm very much afraid so," lamented
Mr. Todbury. "Not only of Piddleton—Piddleton was much too

wise to give any information at all, but I am afraid young Alice may have been less discreet. Naturally, the old gentleman rambles in his speech nowadays, and I fear it is only too probable that the housekeeper may have confided in Mr. Attleton, the latter having made a point of being very courteous to her."

"Well, that seems to be that," said Macdonald, after he had bidden good-morning to Mr. Todbury, having made an appointment to meet him on the coming Monday. "As a jig-saw pattern it fits, but the resulting picture looks highly suspicious to me. Let's see what the p.t.b.'s think about it."

Before interviewing the P.T.B.'s—the Powers That Be— Macdonald saw Jenkins, the latter looking very rubicund and cheerful after his activities connected with the fire at the Belfry.

"Good fire?" inquired Macdonald.

"First rate," replied Jenkins. "Quite what you'd call a spectacle. I was sorry my young nipper couldn't see it. He wants to join the fire brigade. Always something satisfactory about a good blaze when there's no question of any one being burnt up in it. The brigade got it under control fairly soon. Very pleased with 'emselves for saving the tower. They thought it'd fall at one time, and do damage next door so to speak. I've been raking round in the embers—nasty, smelly business—and I found these bits and pieces. What do you make of them?"

The "bits and pieces" consisted of fragments of a very thick glass vessel, a sort of bell jar as far as could be guessed from the portions which Jenkins had recovered. One piece had a portion of metal adhering to it, actually welded into the glass. Macdonald examined the discoloured metal and scratched its tarnished surface with his penknife.

"Copper," he observed, and Jenkins replied:

"Some sort of electrical gadget for sparking?"

Macdonald shook his head.

"No. I don't think so. The edges of the copper are all cor-
roded, eaten away with acid, like an etching plate would be
if you left it in an acid bath. This reminds me of something.
I know. Do you remember that dirty trick the special branch
discovered during the war—apparatus for firing ships at sea
some days after they'd left port? They used a cylinder, divided
into two by a metal plate. There were acids in both ends of
the cylinder which in time ate through the dividing wall of
metal, and the two acids when they met formed an explosive
mixture which flared and set light to the stuff packed in the crate
around them. Dozens of ships were burnt out at sea before we
tumbled to the dodge. I should say that this was something of
the same kind."

"I remember," said Jenkins. "They could regulate the time
when the fire occurred according to the thickness of the metal
dividing the acids. Well, well. Your Debrette appears to have
been full of resource and ingenuity. He ought to have known
better than to go and get himself drowned like that. However,
he laughs best who laughs last."

"Yes—and I've got a hunch the beggar's laughing at me still,"
growled Macdonald.

Jenkins looked pained. "According to what I was taught
when young, he won't be," he replied. "Nothing to laugh at
down there."

"Surprising that an amiable bloke like you should enjoy
contemplating hell fires as well as mundane ones," retorted
Macdonald. "Go, get thee to an analyst with your bits and pieces,
and tell me if I was right or wrong."

The contents of Bruce Attleton's desk had been spread out for the Chief Inspector's consideration. Quantities of MS., old galley proofs, typescripts—Macdonald looked at it with disfavour. He had never read Attleton's books and didn't want to begin. Bills—masses of them—mostly unpaid. The accountant could do that for him. Letters—"Fan mail." "Dear Mr. Attleton. Your exquisite book enthralled me from the first line to the last…" and so forth and so on. "Conceited ass, keeping the stuff. It'll take me a week to plough through it," said Macdonald. "What's this?"

"This" was an address book, an elaborate affair of green morocco, edged and cornered with silver, having a lock (considerately opened for Macdonald by the experts who had dealt with the desk). It had an elaborate silver monogram, with the initials S.Y.A. intertwined—Sybilla Yvonne Attleton, and Macdonald's eyes brightened. "Pinched his wife's address book. Now I wonder…" Research quickly put him in possession of the following entry. "Tommy. Antibes. Forest Stanway. Hants." "So he knew all about that, did he?" murmured Macdonald. "This gets more incomprehensible every moment. Still, he didn't want to bowl her out. Just kept the information for contingencies. Query, is Tommy much brighter—and badder—than seems indicated at a first glance, or was he hauled in just to pay him out? Debrette seems to have been a thorough merchant. Tied the whole affair up into knots with the message, 'This is an easy one' written on top of it. So this is a note of Weller's evidence. Samuel Weller. He would be. 'Nothing was missing from Mr. Attleton's suitcase, but the packing was slightly disarranged.' Another careful chap. Now for my old man. He'll be pleased over all this. Nice tidy lot of evidence."

Colonel Wragley, the Assistant Commissioner, heard
Macdonald's report with much satisfaction. While agreeing
that a few details needed clearing up, Colonel Wragley expressed
himself as completely satisfied with Macdonald's reading of
the case. It was a pity, of course, for the credit of the department, that Debrette's hiding place had not been discovered and
Debrette arrested "in Bristol fashion" instead of being fished
out of the Thames when he was no longer of any use to anybody. "He would probably have given away the whole story,"
mused Colonel Wragley. "Still, there doesn't seem to me to be
any reasonable room for doubt that you have apprehended the
whole matter, Macdonald. I can't say you look very cheerful
about it."

"No, sir. I have never felt such an utter fool in my life," replied
Macdonald. "I have just put all the evidence before you, as well
as some of my own guesses. As you say, the evidence makes a
convincing whole. Much too convincing. It convinces me that
we've been led by the nose by an exceedingly astute mind. The
evidence was there for us to pick up. It seems to me to have been
laid by some one who gave us credit for good routine work.
Nothing was too obvious. It was simply laid out in proper order,
like footsteps nicely super-imposed, for us to read at leisure."

Colonel Wragley looked over his glasses in the manner of
one about to rebuke.

"Don't you think you're growing over sceptical, Macdonald?
You're so hardened by the wiles of criminals that you won't
accept a nice, straightforward explanation when it's offered
to you."

"But why didn't Debrette shave his beard off?" asked
Macdonald, quite gravely, and Wragley looked at his most

competent Chief Inspector as though he suspected him of
being feverish.

"Assume that all our deductions are reasonable, sir," said
Macdonald. "Debrette was the grandson of Mary Anne Brossé,
the great nephew of old Adam Marsham. Having heard hints
from his mother and grandmother of Marsham's miserliness,
Debrette set inquiries afoot and eventually approached Attleton
in order to use him as a cat's-paw. Attleton, of course, was senior
in succession to the Brossé line, assuming that old Marsham has
not made a will. Attleton got the information which Debrette
could not have hoped to get by himself, and he and Debrette
set to work to wipe out intervening inheritors. Debrette also
indulged in the side line of approaching Mrs. Attleton and getting
Burroughs involved in the Belfry mix-up. All very ingenious—
but can you see the sense in this? Debrette, having committed
a murder, knowing that he has drawn the attention of a man
like Grenville on to him, continues to wander about those parts
of London where he is known by sight with that preposterous
beard to single him out. He had only got to shave it off and adopt
different spectacles for him to have been perfectly safe. It's not
as though the man was an idiot. Judging by his other actions he
was exceedingly astute."

"Astute? He was a most accomplished criminal," said Wragley.
"There must have been some reasoning behind his behaviour
over that beard."

"Perhaps he had a Samson complex," murmured Macdonald,
and then went on more respectfully, "Can you reconcile the
criminal accomplishment with the description given of his
character by those who knew Debrette when he was destitute? 'Balmy' was the word applied. 'A poor, harmless, balmy

beggar.' Yet he proves to have been capable of carrying out this elaborate plot, of taking a tenancy of a place like the Belfry, of amputating the head and hands of a corpse with a measure of skill, of plastering up a wall very skilfully indeed, and of involving other people in his plot with great ingenuity. Finally, his corpse is recovered from the Thames and on it is found a handkerchief which was probably Attleton's, and a Missal belonging to Marie Antoinette Brossé, and pound notes whose numbers were probably in the sequence of those Attleton drew from the bank the day before he disappeared. It's enough to make any man sceptical, sir. It's much too apropos, too nicely constructed for real life."

"Well, what's your alternative?" demanded Wragley.

Macdonald did not say "Search me," though it would have relieved his feelings to do so.

"There are several, but none of them really satisfactory," he began, and the Assistant Commissioner barked out:

"Not convincing enough, this time, I suppose. Really, you're getting very nice minded, Macdonald."

"Yes, sir," admitted Macdonald, with a grin which he could not help. "There's this man, Grenville, who looks as though he's going to die in spite of all the trouble we've taken over him. It was Grenville who found that suitcase—another perplexing bit of evidence—like Debrette's beard. We have nobody's word for it *but* Grenville's that the suitcase was found where he said it was. Then I'm tired of the way he's always getting himself knocked out (though he seems to have overdone it this time). He got a knock over the head in the Belfry, when, according to their own statements, Rockingham was in the cellar and Grenville himself in the studio. I never believed in Grenville's story of some intruder who got in and got out through locked and bolted doors. In addition, Grenville seems to have gone out of his way to collide with that motor-cycle at Charing Cross. Any journalist who lives off Fleet Street, and is accustomed to dodging the traffic for his daily bread, ought to be able to get across the Strand without being knocked down. If he'd used his head he could have caught Debrette that time—and he didn't catch him."

"Hm. I always thought he sounded a bit odd. The thing I didn't like about him was the way he kept that suitcase up his sleeve for best part of a week. Not straightforward at all. About this man Burroughs. Are you satisfied that his story—or the lady's—rings true?"

"About as true as a lead sixpence," said Macdonald. "The only thing I'm certain about Mr. Thomas Burroughs is that he didn't hit Grenville over the head, or throw Debrette in the Thames last night. Otherwise I'm prepared to believe anything of him and of the lady as well. It's worth bearing in mind that they would both have been delighted to see Attleton out of the way, and if Burroughs hadn't many brains I should say Sybilla Attleton has plenty. In addition to them, there's Weller, the butler. I liked him at first, but I wasn't too pleased to see him out in the garden last evening."

"I'm still of the opinion you're splitting hairs," said Colonel Wragley. "However, you have plenty of loose ends to clear up, so perhaps you'll manage to satisfy yourself in due time. There's the matter of Debrette's hiding place during the past week."

"Yes, sir. That is in hand. It can only be a matter of time before that information comes in. Also, I should like to make the acquaintance of 'young Alice.' She sounds interesting to my mind."

"I'm afraid you suffer from the defects of your qualities, my dear chap. Over much subtlety, hair-splitting in short," said Colonel Wragley.

The interview ended on this note. Colonel Wragley was plainly under the impression that Macdonald had got a bee in his bonnet ("bats in the belfry" as the Chief Inspector said to himself), over a nice, straightforward case. Macdonald found himself suspicious of everybody. If there was one thing he disliked it was having evidence planted on him and no means beyond intuition of proving the plant. "Hoist with his own petard" about expressed it. His good, logical deduction about the Marsham inheritance and the Brossé family had recoiled on him like a boomerang.

Having already set on foot the necessary inquiries for Debrette's place of residence during the past week, as well as researches into the origins of Grenville, Weller, Rockingham, and the matter of Elizabeth Leigh's guardianship, Macdonald felt free to carry on his investigation in his own way. Before he interviewed Mr. Thomas Burroughs again, he had determined to see Weller.

Arrived at Park Village South, the door was opened to him by the butler. Once in the library, Macdonald went straight to the point.

"I want to know if you were at home all yesterday evening, Weller, or if you went out at all?"

A shade of uneasiness crossed the man's face.

"I went out, sir, shortly after you left. Mrs. Attleton sent me on a—a private errand, sir."

"What was it, and where did you go?"

"Well, sir, I'd much rather not say, having had instructions from madam to that effect."

"I'm afraid the instructions must be disregarded, Weller. It's your business to answer questions put to you by the police in a criminal investigation."

Weller looked still more uneasy.

"It wasn't anything criminal, sir—more like a wild goose chase. I've nothing to conceal myself, but it goes against the grain to talk about my mistress. However, you know best. Mrs. Attleton sent for me, sir, when you left, and told me to go to an address in Hampstead, Heatherleigh Mansions it was. I was to go to a flat there where a Miss Lessiter resides, and if the lady wasn't at home I was to let myself in with a key which madam gave me, and to look in a book trough on the desk in the drawing-room for an address book of Mrs. Attleton's which she'd left there. I didn't quite like it, sir, but the way madam put it I didn't like to refuse."

"And you found the address book?"

"No, sir. There wasn't no such thing there. I looked around a little, on the bookcase and so forth, but I wasn't very comfortable about it. To tell the truth, I didn't like being in the place, having let myself in with Mrs. Attleton's key. I shouldn't have liked it at all if the owner had come in and found me there. Might have been very awkward, sir."

"Very awkward," agreed Macdonald dryly. "What time did you go out, and what time did you return?"

"It was about half-past six when I went out and after eight when I returned. I don't know that part at all well. I went by tube from Mornington Crescent to Hampstead Heath, and then I fairly lost myself. Very quiet the streets are in that quarter. Madam complained of the time I'd been, but I thought to myself, she could have told me to take a taxi if she was in a hurry, so I took my time, sir."

The man's face and manner were quite calm as he told his story, as though he were glad to have recounted what he regarded as an odd errand, and Macdonald made no comment beyond, "Very good, Weller. I should like to see your mistress."

The butler cocked an eyebrow.

"Madam is in her bath, sir. I'm afraid you may have to wait some time."

This was a facer. To wait while Mrs. Attleton completed her toilet was no part of Macdonald's programme. Still with the same air of respectful helpfulness the butler added:

"If you would step into the telephone cabinet, sir, I could put you through to her. There is a phone in her bathroom."

"Live and learn," thought Macdonald. After all, he could check up on Weller's story later, but he would very much like to know that Mrs. Attleton was still safely in the house. He racked his brains rapidly for a suitable gambit, and when left alone in the telephone cabinet he shot out the following question:

"Chief Inspector Macdonald speaking. I wish to know if the address book for which you sent Weller to Hampstead yesterday contained the address of the cottage, Antibes."

A pause ensued, then Sybilla Attleton's voice, clear and unmistakable, replied:

"Yes, it did, and the book had disappeared. It must have been stolen."

"Thank you," replied Macdonald. "That is all I wanted to know."

Coming out of the telephone cabinet he reflected that the possibilities of this case were by no means exhausted.

XIV

B Y THE TIME MACDONALD REACHED HIM, MR. THOMAS Burroughs had about reached the end of his tether. Neither obstinacy (and he was by nature obstinate), nor devotion (and he was very devoted indeed), were proof against the undermining effects of two nights spent in detention in a police station. He had had plenty of time to reflect on the exceedingly nasty nature of the hole in which he was placed, and his solicitor had done nothing to comfort him. That exceedingly competent legal luminary had indeed betrayed a consternation which had made Burroughs feel cold in the pit of his stomach. To have been caught investigating premises in which a murder had occurred, and, in addition, "to have resisted the police in the execution of their duties," was, he was given to understand, as nasty a position as a man could be placed in. Nothing but the whole truth would assist him out of it. Mr. Burroughs temporised. He had his own reasons for not wishing to tell the whole truth, and apart from asking his lawyer to have a brief message telephoned to "his country place," relating the nature of his predicament, Mr. Burroughs had sourly said that he would stop where he was and see every one at the devil.

By the time Macdonald arrived, however, Mr. Burroughs had begun to realise that something must be done about it. He was feeling too near the dock to be able to sustain the heroic attitude any longer.

Macdonald, imperturbably polite, bade him good-morning, and inquired if he wished to make any statement. It was more

than ever essential that he should give an explanation of his presence in the Belfry premises, since the body concealed there had
now been identified as a friend of Mr. Burroughs!

The stockbroker visibly paled.

"Well, I didn't have anything to do with it. The whole thing's
a plant," he protested. Macdonald waited.

"I've been staying down in the country for the past week,"
went on Mr. Burroughs. "I had a guest with me—a lady. She
had been troubled a lot by the behaviour of her husband, and
I, well, I have a deep regard for her, and wanted to help her in
any way I could. A letter came for her while she was staying at
my place, saying that her husband was up to some games at this
Belfry place. To cut a long story short, she asked me to look into
it, and I went up to town for that purpose."

He looked at Macdonald appealingly.

"Damned awkward position for me. I couldn't answer your
questions or make any statement without involving my guest.
I didn't know what to do, and that's a fact. I still don't—but I
can't stay here until you charge me with murder. Think of it
for yourself, Chief Inspector. Damned difficult, whichever way
you look at it."

"Very difficult indeed," agreed Macdonald, "but since you
assure me that you had no hand in the murder, I can assure you
in my turn that your only sensible course is complete frankness.
Let me make myself quite clear," he added. "Your actions have
brought you under suspicion, and you have got to remove that
suspicion. If I had any clear grounds for charging you, it would
be my business to warn you that anything you say would be
used in evidence against you. I have at present no grounds for
such a charge, and it is to the interest of the police, as well as to

your own interest, to clear away the suspicion aroused by your behaviour at the Belfry. But, to do that, a general statement without corroboration is of no value."

Mr. Burroughs sweated freely.

"You've got me in a cleft stick," he growled.

"No," replied Macdonald, "you've got yourself into one, and you've got to get yourself out of it."

"What exactly do you want?" asked the stockbroker feebly.

"A statement of your whereabouts since last Wednesday week, and the letter advising you to go to the Belfry. That for your own interest. For that of justice I want you to answer questions concerning the man Debrette, whose name I previously mentioned to you, and concerning Mr. Bruce Attleton, whose body has been identified as that found in the Belfry."

"My God!" said the stockbroker faintly. "I've fairly put my own neck into a halter."

"With outside assistance, so you assure me," replied Macdonald. "It's up to you to get yourself out of it—and believe me, the police system in this country does not aim at charging a man if it is possible to prove he is innocent."

"Seems to me that whatever I say I shall only make things worse," said Mr. Burroughs, "however, here's the facts. On last Wednesday week, the day Bruce Attleton left for Paris, I drove down to Southampton. I got there about one o'clock and garaged my car at the Royal. It's a Rolls Royce two-seater, number AAA 8181; you can check up on that," he added eagerly, and Macdonald agreed politely. "I lunched at the Royal and then I went to meet my guest Mrs. Attleton." He studied Macdonald's face, as though looking for some sign of excitement in that saturnine visage, but got no satisfaction.

"I picked up the car again about three o'clock, and we drove out to my place in the Forest. It's about six miles from Lyndhurst, in the parish of Forest Stanway, and the house is called Antibes. We got there just after four."

"Your servants can corroborate that?"

Mr. Burroughs shook his head. "No. Unfortunately they can't. I haven't any resident servants, the place is only a cottage—not much room. There's a married couple named Jobson living nearby. The man used to valet me before he was married—very competent servant. I put them into their cottage as a matter of fact. They keep chickens. Jobson and his wife look after Antibes for me, and if ever I want to go down there I just send them a wire and they see the place is habitable. I don't think I saw the Jobson's at all that day—in fact I'm damn certain I didn't," he added gloomily.

"That, of course, is a pity," said Macdonald.

"Well, as things were, what'd you expect?" growled Mr. Burroughs. "Mrs. Attleton honoured me by coming down to stay with me as a friend. She was very done up—under the weather—after that long run of her play and then rehearsing. She didn't want to see visitors—and well, there you are," he ended lamely.

"Quite," said Macdonald. "I can assume that you were only seen by your servants on a few occasions during that week, and that Mrs. Attleton was seen by nobody. Is that correct?"

Mr. Burroughs nodded, more gloomily than ever.

"And now for the letter which led to your visit to the Belfry."

"Yes. That damned letter. Sybilla—Mrs. Attleton—had had reason to suspect her husband of not playing the game. Frankly, she intended to divorce him when she got the evidence. If he'd had any decent feelings at all he'd have supplied the evidence himself, months ago. The chap was a sponger, simply living on his wife's earnings. Made my blood boil many a time, I can tell you."

"For your own sake, I shouldn't advise you to let it boil now," said Macdonald. "I fail to see what prevented Mrs. Attleton from leaving her husband, if she found him so unsatisfactory, and letting him take proceedings."

"He wouldn't have. Knew a game worth two of that," grumbled Mr. Burroughs. "Besides, why should the onus be on her—dragging her name through the muck? Mrs. Attleton has very fine feelings, I'd have you know. A very high-minded woman."

"About the letter?" Macdonald reminded him, and Mr. Burroughs glowered.

"Yes, and wouldn't I like to get hold of the swine that wrote it—I'd teach him. Well, as I was saying, Mrs. Attleton was on the qui-vive, when some chap signing himself de Brette wrote to her saying he could get the evidence she wanted if she'd pay for it."

"Can you make any suggestion as to how this man Debrette knew that Mrs. Attleton wished to divorce her husband?"

Burroughs desisted from biting a nail.

"Well, Debrette knew Attleton. I reckon he blackmailed him. In fact I know it."

"How?"

"Attleton as good as told me. He tried to touch me for five hundred one day after the blighter had been phoning him. Said it was a gaming debt. I.D.T. If Sybilla'd asked my advice in the first place, she'd never have had any dealings with Debrette at all. Double-edged tool. However, she answered his first letter, saying she'd pay up if the evidence was produced. I went and had a look from the address he wrote from—a shop called Blanco's in Charing Cross Place. Pretty dirty shop, too, I tell you. Accommodation address, of course. Gone bust now. The chap who ran it—and a nasty bit of goods he was—coughed up a certain amount of information after I'd paid through the nose for it. Debrette, according to Blanco, was a spectacled chap with a beard with a white streak in it. Frenchman or German. Alsatian perhaps, or a Belgian, by his accent. Always spoke French to Blanco. I couldn't find out any more. That's up to you." (Macdonald did not tell Mr. Burroughs that "Blanco" had been repatriated some two months ago, sent out of England as an undesirable alien, and landed in Ostend at His Majesty's expense.)

"Well, when Debrette wrote this other letter to Mrs. Attleton while she was at Antibes, we put our heads together over it," continued Burroughs. "Debrette wrote that if Mrs. Attleton—or an agent of hers—went to the Belfry Studio in Lime Tree Avenue sometime on Friday night, they'd get the evidence required. He added that Mr. Attleton would probably not return there until late, but it was possible to enter the place by a broken cellar window, just round the corner from the porch. I tell you I wasn't keen on it, but I wanted that evidence as much as Mrs. Attleton did—more, by a long chalk. I thought it all over. It was plain that Debrette had a good information service, he'd given proof of that already," (here Burroughs described the photograph incident) "besides, how'd the chap got hold of the address of my cottage? Tell me that!" he added truculently.

"Perhaps Mr. Attleton told him," replied Macdonald pleasantly. "The address of Antibes was written in Mrs. Attleton's private address book which was found locked up in husband's desk."

Mr. Burroughs' face was a study. His naturally robust colour heightened until Macdonald wondered whether an apoplexy would put an end to his overtaxed cerebral processes. The stock-broker's next remark, however, was not illuminating.

"Dirty dog!" he said feelingly. "Lifting his own wife's private address book. That shows you!"

"It shows me nothing," replied Macdonald. "From what I have heard of Mr. and Mrs. Attleton there was not much to choose between them."

Most surprisingly the big man got to his feet with surprising agility and struck out at Macdonald's face.

"Take that!" he shouted.

The blow did not reach its aim, but Macdonald's counter landed true, well on the point, and Mr. Thomas Burroughs went back on the floor, mixing himself up with a very hard wooden chair, amid an outburst of profanity which demonstrated that just the right amount of force had been used. The door opened and an anxious-faced constable appeared, asking if any help were required.

"Yes," said Macdonald. "Pick the gentleman up—he's fallen off his chair—and then get him a glass of water."

To Burroughs he said, as soon as the constable had with-drawn, "If you get over excited like that and lash out at people without thinking of the consequences, you're simply asking for trouble. If you'd cracked my skull, how much better off would you have been? Have a little common sense."

Mr. Burroughs blew his nose, and uttered a series of grunts which appeared to mean that he would like to knock Macdonald's qualified head off, and the latter went on, after the glass of water had made its appearance.

"It is time you looked at all this in a reasonable perspective. Knocking my head off will not alter the fact that Mr. Attleton had, seemingly, as much ground for complaint against his wife as his wife had against him, nor that many a jury would credit you with a motive for desiring Mr. Attleton's decease. Now listen to this question and answer it if you can. Where can I obtain any corroboration of any part of the story you have told me, except that your car was garaged in Southampton shortly after one o'clock on Wednesday, the 12th of March? Since it is, admittedly, a fast car, I don't imagine that it would be beyond the bounds of possibility for it to have covered the road from London to Southampton in a little over three hours in the hands of a skilful driver. You can offer me no corroboration for your residence at the cottage, Antibes, and the matter of the letters is equally not susceptible to corroboration. I saw Mrs. Attleton yesterday evening, and her story coincides with yours, but the letter and the faded out photograph which she handed to me show no finger-prints save her own and yours. It's not too easy a position, Mr. Burroughs, and the readiness to use violence which you have shown on two occasions is not much of an argument in your favour."

Mr. Burroughs' temper had evaporated by now. He sat on his hard chair looking a picture of surly dejection, biting his nails furiously.

"I've told you the truth," he mumbled thickly. "I can't do more. That fella Debrette must have killed Attleton. I always said he was a scoundrel. Stands to reason. He knew too much."

"What is your opinion of Weller, the Attletons' butler?"

The abrupt question made Burroughs look up, but he was slow in answering the question. He looked at Macdonald suspiciously.

"Weller's all right, so far as I know. Decent chap. How can I tell? In a mess-up like this you don't know what to believe. Why the hell should Weller have wanted Attleton done in?"

"When Mr. Attleton tried to borrow money from you, did he ever suggest that he expected money to be left to him, or to come his way for any reason?"

"Left to him? No. He always complained that there wasn't a bean in his family. He'd only got one relation left, hadn't he? The old beggar with the annuity whom they called the 'Old Soldier.' Attleton talked of making money getting his books filmed—only it never came off."

"When you say that Attleton was unfaithful to his wife, what evidence have you to that effect?"

"I've seen him in some funny company myself, before I knew his wife, that is. Some fella told me Attleton kept an establishment in Maida Vale when he'd got the money to do it. I tried to get the story traced, but bless you, you might as well look for a snowball in midsummer. Half his time he didn't sleep at home, but as for where he went, deuce knows."

"As evidence, not very convincing. I shall want that letter of Debrette's which took you to the Belfry."

"You can have it. I left it at my bank on Friday when I came up to town. Didn't want to lose it, and you never know with gentry like that. It might have been some dirty game leading up to a blackmail threat. I didn't like to leave the letter at my flat. Always a possibility of burglary. Look here, how long are you going to keep me here?"

"Now that you have made a statement explaining your movements, I have no further reason to detain you when my interrogation is over. You will, however, have to undertake to remain at your own home, or be within reach, in case your further evidence is needed."

Macdonald had been looking down at his notebook, speaking leisurely, but thinking furiously. He glanced up and met the eyes of the man facing him. Mr. Burroughs had brown eyes, lustrous and a little disposed to protrude, under strongly marked black brows. For a second Macdonald thought that he read their expression, half furtive, half questioning. If ever a man's eyes said "Am I getting away with it?" it was the eyes of Mr. Burroughs at that moment. Even as their glances met, the dark brown eyes altered in expression, as quickly as an actor's might. Jumping to his feet the dark man said:

"Oh, I shan't try to bolt. I'm not such a fool as that. Let's get out of this damned place. I'm about fed-up. If you like to come along to the bank with me, I'll give you that letter of Debrette's—and you can get on with trailing *him*. He's the chap you want."

"You needn't worry about Debrette. He's quite safe," replied Macdonald. "Sit down again for a minute. I'm not quite through."

"Lord, if I took as long over my business as you do, I'd miss all the markets," retorted Burroughs, and Macdonald went on:

"I want a note of your parent's names and the place of your own birth, also your grandparent's names."

An extraordinary change came over the fleshy face of Mr. Thomas Burroughs. It was not only that his colour altered, and a flush spread over his full cheeks and high forehead so that even the whites of his eyes seemed suffused, but the eyes glared in a way that expressed almost animal fury.

"What the devil for?" he spluttered. "What the blooming deuce has it got to do with you who my parents and grandparents were? I'm about sick of you and your silly questions."

"That question has got to be answered," replied Macdonald. "It will be put to every one who can be classed as a suspect in this case. Surely it is a very simple question. In any case, a visit to Somerset House will put me in possession of the facts I want."

"Then go and find out," spluttered Mr. Burroughs. "I've never heard such a damned piece of impertinence. My solicitor and my banker will answer for who I am, and for my integrity as a business man. That should be good enough for you, Mr. Chief Inspector."

"I asked the question because I require an answer to it," replied Macdonald. "To refuse an answer seems merely childish. Whatever facts you give will be treated as confidential once you have been eliminated from the case."

"Well, I've told you everything that could have any bearing on your case and a damned lot that couldn't," retorted Mr. Burroughs, "and I've just about reached the limit of my patience and that's flat. When it comes to asking my pedigree, I tell you frankly, it's nothing but a bloody inquisition and I won't stand for it."

Macdonald let him go on talking. In his own mind he was wondering if he had arrived at an explanation of the past week's happenings. If, in addition to winning Sybilla Attleton as his wife, Mr. Thomas Burroughs (descendant of Mary Anne Brossé, nee Marsham) had seen the opportunity of inheriting a fortune of a quarter of a million, he might have deemed it worth while to work out that extraordinarily complicated plot involving the use of Streaky Beaver as a tool or accomplice. Sybilla Attleton, with her knowledge of actors, past and present, might well have planned out the part that Debrette had played, and seen to it that Weller finished off Debrette before the police got him. In which case Robert Grenville had put in an appearance just at the wrong moment and suffered for his curiosity with a blow from the weighted "cosh."

"Logical reconstruction number three," said Macdonald to himself, his eyes still on his note-book, conscious of the man opposite to him sitting biting his finger nails.

"It's Debrette that you want, not my great grandparents," put in the indignant voice of Mr. Burroughs.

Macdonald looked across at him after a quick decision.

"We have got Debrette," he said quietly. "His body was recovered from the Thames yesterday evening. At the same time another man was found on a wharf close by, but he was not dead, although seriously injured. The second man was Mr. Grenville, who was present, I understand, at a cheerful little discussion on murders which you heard at the Attletons' house."

Mr. Burroughs' eyes bulged more than ever, and his face was frankly horror-stricken.

"Grenville?" he cried. "Grenville? You say he's dead, too?"

"No, that was just what I did not say," said Macdonald. "He is still alive, and will, I hope, be able to answer questions shortly. Now, while I do not pretend that your statement was entirely convincing, I do not wish to detain you here indefinitely. You are free to go to your own home on the understanding that you will be at hand when called upon. I will send an officer to accompany you to your bank to obtain the letter from Debrette. After that I caution you to use discretion in your movements. We shall expect to find you when we need you."

A few minutes later Mr. Burroughs left his temporary lodging, and Macdonald at the telephone was saying:

"Lande's Bank. City branch—and freeze on to him, Reeves. Freeze on to him."

XV

ELIZABETH LEIGH WOKE UP IN THE MORNING AFTER SHE had talked to Grenville and Rockingham at Furnival's Court and stretched herself luxuriously in bed, and then wondered why she had awoken with such a sense of disquiet.

Memory awoke, too, and she remembered the grim story of Bruce Attleton's death, and shivered. Sitting with her hands round her knees, bare-armed, and childish-looking, with her short red curls rumpled up all over her head, she wished that the memory could be relegated to the realm of nightmare.

"What ought I to do?" she asked herself. "I know Sybilla hates me, really, and I hate her, but I can't just behave as though nothing's happened. I shall have to go to see her and say I'm sorry, and watch her crying beautifully, when I know she doesn't care a blue hoot. Oh, how simply horrible!"

As Elizabeth dressed she decided not to telephone. She would just go and do her best to say the right thing. Busy with face-cream, another thought crossed her mind. Now that Bruce Attleton was dead she had no guardian. What was to prevent her marrying Bobbie Grenville straight away? She could never go back to live with Sybilla—and Sybilla wouldn't want her in any case. The only child of an only child, Elizabeth was very much alone in the world, and she suddenly became aware of her loneliness—one of those odd girls living in clubs—and clubs weren't very satisfactory once the novelty had worn off. Chambers in the Temple, or Gray's Inn, as Bobbie had suggested—some nice old panelled room of her own where she could entertain their friends. It might be much nicer than this club business, she meditated.

After breakfast she went round to the club garage and got out her little Morris Saloon named "Dinah." Elizabeth had taken to driving as a duck takes to water; she had a natural "traffic sense" and drove fearlessly through the London streets, enjoying the complexity of steering, and judging distances, and sliding skilfully into the right traffic lanes in the big roundabouts. But while she managed steering and gear-changing, reversing and parking, with the natural facility of a true child of a mechanised age, she knew next to nothing about the working of the engine which she controlled so gaily. It either went or it didn't go. In the latter case the nearest garage mechanic was requested to see to things and rouse "Dinah" to complacent mobility again.

On her drive to Park Village South she became aware that the engine was giving off undesirable fumes, and wrinkled up her small nose in disgust. The hand-brake was off (she had once driven for some miles with it on), the radiator bonnet was rolled up in front, all was as it should be.

"Too much oil or too little," she meditated. "There's always something in the way of a snag."

Arrived at the Attletons' house, she was admitted by Weller. His large pale face looked very melancholy, and she said to him, "Oh, Weller, isn't it all ghastly? I feel as though it's all a nightmare."

"Yes, miss. I woke with that feeling myself," he replied. "Most distressing, miss, and I've never been in a house with the police in and out, so to speak."

"Beastly!" agreed Elizabeth. "I say, Weller, could you look at Dinah for me? She's smoking, and I don't know what's the matter with her. You're so good at engines. You always find what's the matter."

"I'll look with pleasure, miss, if I can make an opportunity. Things is a bit difficult, you understand. Mrs. Attleton all on edge, as one might expect. You'll be wanting to see her, miss?"

"Yes, Weller. I had to come, but it's awfully difficult to know what to say."

"It is indeed, miss." Weller's answer was heartfelt, and just at that moment Louise, the French maid, came tripping downstairs.

"Is Mrs. Attleton in her room, Louise?"

"Yes, mademoiselle, but Madame does not wish to be disturbed. I will tell her that you are here when I have taken her petit déjeuner. Mademoiselle will wait?"

"Of course I'll wait, Louise. Don't be so absurd. I'm not a visitor."

Elizabeth ran up the right-hand branch of the little stairway and went into the library. It looked forlorn, somehow, like a room in a very good hotel, with everything so neat and no papers or books lying about. Elizabeth felt a sudden disposition to cry. She had not had any affection for Bruce Attleton; had, in fact, resented the whim which had made her father put her into Attleton's charge, but now she began to remember the way in which he had been kind to her. It was Bruce who had insisted on Elizabeth coming to live with himself and his wife, instead of living in a club or hostel as she had suggested, and he had done his best in many ways to see that she had had a good time, and even done what he could to teach her to read, to appreciate literature and despise trash, to listen to music as well as to jazz, and to speak English instead of schoolgirl slang. Alone in the room which had been peculiarly his, Elizabeth visualised his tall figure and dark head, with the black forelock he tossed back from his high forehead, and was sorry that she had disliked him.

Walking about restlessly, she lighted a cigarette and then put it out, because the aroma of the Turkish tobacco Bruce had always smoked reminded her of him too strongly. Her thoughts turned to Robert Grenville, and she decided to go and telephone to him and ask him to meet her later in the day.

Going to the telephone cabinet, she dialled Grenville's number and waited impatiently while she listened to the steady brr-brr of the bell at his end. At last a woman's voice answered— the worried, complaining voice of Grenville's landlady.

"He's not here. He's had an accident and been taken to hospital, so the police say. I don't know, I'm sure. I don't know what to think. They say he's in hospital, but you'll have to ask them yourself."

Before Elizabeth could formulate another question, she heard a crash and a shout, then a thud which seemed to shake the walls of the little cabinet, followed by a woman's scream. Slamming down the receiver, Elizabeth dashed out on to the landing of the staircase, and then ran down to the service stairway which was approached by a door at one end of the odd-shaped hall. It was from below that a woman's voice was screaming for help. The electric light was burning on the service stairway, as it always had to be on that dark, steep, awkward flight. At the bottom, past the nasty angle which made the carrying of trays such a tiresome business, Weller was half-sitting, half-lying, in a hunched-up heap, the remains of a heavy cut-glass jug scattered about him. Mrs. Hillman, the cook, was wailing above him, wringing her hands, with blood staining her white apron, and Elizabeth saw, with a qualm of horror, that blood was gushing out from a cut on the butler's wrist—not merely flowing, but pumping out in an ominous scarlet gush.

Elizabeth knew little about first-aid, but she knew enough to realise that bleeding of such a nature must mean a severed artery. If she had little skill, she had plenty of courage. Tearing off the silk scarf round her neck, she ran downstairs crying out, "Telephone for a doctor, quickly, and leave off making that idiotic row, Hillman. Amy," (this to the parlour-maid) "go outside, and get a policeman or somebody. Policemen always know what to do."

Bending over the butler, whose tallowy, frightened face was lolling on his shoulders, she wound her scarf round his wrist and pulled it tight with all her strength. While she struggled, she glanced up and saw Sybilla Attleton at the head of the stairs, her face white and set.

"Oh, do come and help!" cried Elizabeth. "He'll die if you don't do something. I can't stop it. Sybilla, how do you put on a tourniquet?"

A moment later, when Elizabeth, sickened and despairing, was thinking that she could never staunch that dreadful flow, a man came running in from the lower entrance ahead of Amy, the parlour-maid.

"All right, miss, I'll see to him. You go and find some strips for bandaging—anything strong—and find me a skewer, or something like that to twist the bandage with. Have you rung for a doctor?"

Elizabeth dashed to the kitchen, and with the help of Amy, tore some clean linen cloths into strips and returned with them, and a bunch of metal skewers to her unknown helper. Apparently he knew all about tourniquets. He had bound a small metal tube above the cut, and with the assistance of the skewers he twisted the bandage tighter and tighter until the flow of blood ceased. Then, with remarkable strength and dexterity he lifted the large, unwieldy form of the butler down on to the floor of the passage, and laid him flat.

"That was a nasty go, and no mistake," he observed. "Got on to the doctor, ma'am?" (This to the stout and trembling cook.) "That's right. Now we shall want to know how all this happened, so don't go having high strikes. If you take my advice you'll go and change that apron, and make yourself a nice cup of tea."

Elizabeth had sat down on the stairs. She felt sick and giddy, and put her head between her knees, as she had been taught to do at school when she felt faint. Mrs. Hillman broke out into a flow of excited speech.

"And if I've said it once, I've said it a dozen times, that those stairs'd be the death of somebody. Not fit for 'uman beings to carry things on, and that's a fact, and I hope they'll be satisfied now, half killing a good man like Mr. Weller and him so devoted to his duty as I never saw, and that hard-faced wretch upstairs never moving a finger to save him. Chivvy you from morning to night she would…"

"Hold your tongue, Hillman, and go into the kitchen and get on with your work. Amy, go and get a pail and cloth and swab the stairs up," said Elizabeth sharply.

"Beg pardon, miss, but I'd think you'd better leave things as they are until we see how the accident happened."

The voice of the first-aid expert was pleasant and respectful, but Elizabeth turned on him in some surprise.

"It's obvious how it happened," she replied. "There's a slit in the matting at the top of the stairs. He must have caught his foot while he'd got the jug in his hand." She looked at the unknown assistant and added, "I'm awfully grateful to you for helping. Won't you tell me your name?"

"That's all right, miss. I'm in the police—plain-clothes branch. I'll just wait here until the doctor comes, and then make a report. Very nasty accident, it was. I've got to keep an eye on the patient—mustn't stop his circulation altogether."

The doctor appeared before Elizabeth had had time to wonder why a plain-clothes policeman should have been at hand so conveniently, and the girl went straight upstairs to Sybilla's room, and entered, after drumming on the door, without waiting for an answer.

"Really, Sybilla, I think you're the absolute limit, going away like that and not helping at all. The man might have died."

Mrs. Attleton was sitting before her dressing-table. At the sight of Elizabeth's blood-stained clothes she shuddered and closed her eyes.

"Get Miss Leigh one of my skirts and a coat, Louise," she said to the maid, who was standing beside her, and then turned back to Elizabeth.

"I can't stand the sight of blood—you know that. It sickens me. I don't know what you've come for, Elizabeth, but I don't want you here. Please go away. You can change in the bathroom."

"Really, Sybilla!"

"Go away! I've got quite enough to distract me without having you here, too."

Elizabeth caught up the coat and skirt which the maid was holding out to her and said:

"Very well. I came to say I was sorry—about everything. If you feel like that I'll go at once."

.C.R. LORAC

She changed her things in Sybilla's bathroom, and ran down-stairs again. The doctor and the plain-clothes man were talking in the conservatory, and Elizabeth addressed the latter.

"I am leaving here now. My name is Elizabeth Leigh, and my address is the Junior Minerva Club in Grosvenor Street, if you want to find me. I don't know anything about Weller's accident. I was in the telephone cabinet when I heard him fall." Then an idea struck her, and she asked, "Can you tell me where I can find Chief Inspector Macdonald? I want to speak to him."

"You can try the Yard, miss. They'll tell you when he'll be in."

"Thanks. I'll go there now," said Elizabeth. The doctor looked at her with an amusement which he felt but did not show—anything looking less like a visitor for Scotland Yard than Elizabeth Leigh he had never seen. He murmured a few words congratulating her on her efforts to tie up Weller, added that he was sending an ambulance as the butler was in a very shaky state from haemorrhage and shock, and retired back into the hall, leaving Elizabeth by the front door with the friendly-faced policeman.

"If you'd just answer a question or two before you go, miss, it'll save you being bothered later. When you came out of the cabinet did you see any one about on the landing, or in here, or in the hall?"

"No. I saw nobody—I ran straight down to the service stairs when I heard Hillman yelling."

"Did you see Mrs. Attleton later?"

"Yes. I saw her at the head of the stairs, and called to her to come and help. She wouldn't, she hates blood. Then you came. I suppose Amy fetched you?"

"The maid? Yes, miss. I was just nearby. When you spoke to the butler when you came in, did he say anything to suggest there had been trouble of any kind? Words with his mistress, so to speak?"

Elizabeth's round eyes stared.

"No. Nothing at all."

"Very good, miss."

The man stood aside, and Elizabeth opened the door and ran down to her car. She had made up her mind that she was going to see the Chief Inspector and find out what had happened to Robert Grenville. Driving round the Outer Circle, to avoid the traffic of the Marylebone Road, she became aware that "Dinah" was smoking more badly than ever. Impatiently she thrust down the accelerator, and then realised in a flash that the fumes were thickening, and a smell of burning was growing stronger. She pulled up with a jerk, and saw a tiny tongue of flame licking round the clutch, and made a grab at the door handle beside her. It stuck. For a few seconds she wrestled with it in a panic, and then had the presence of mind to get clear of the wheel and try the other door, and tumbled out on to the pavement with smoke pouring out after her.

Her eyes streaming and heart pounding, Elizabeth saw another car draw up behind her, and a tall man running with a fire extinguisher in his hand towards the unhappy Dinah. In a trice a crowd had collected—errand boys, a few startled pedestrians, an amiable looking parson, and a peculiar gentleman in singlet and shorts, who had been taking his morning run. Before Elizabeth had had time to collect her scattered wits, a taximan (with another fire extinguisher) and a policeman had appeared. There was a lot of excitement and questions. Dinah, still smoking, had apparently decided not to burst into flames, and the assistants with the fire extinguishers had opened her bonnet and were giving expert opinions.

"It was the flex from the horn—fused, you know, and the rubber insulating caught fire," declared the gentleman first on the scene, while the constable got his note-book out, and Elizabeth Leigh gave her name and address for the second time that morning, and assured the constable that nothing would induce her to get inside Dinah again, and that there Dinah could stay until the garage people removed her.

"And if you summons me I can't help it," she retorted. "I'd rather be summonsed than frizzled. It was simply beastly, you know!" she assured him. "I couldn't get out. The door stuck."

She extricated herself at last, and was seen into a taxi by the friendly constable, who undertook to keep an eye on "Dinah" until she was salvaged.

When Elizabeth directed the taxi-driver to go to Scotland Yard he fairly goggled at her, and the constable took out his note-book again.

"I meant what I said," snapped Elizabeth. "Get on—and step on it!"

Arrived at Scotland Yard, feeling very conspicuous and more than a bit of a fool, Elizabeth asked the uniformed man at the entrance how she should set about finding Chief Inspector Macdonald, and was surprised to find herself led, without further question, through corridors and up stairs in a building which reminded her of a tax-collector's office which had got confused with the County Hall. Nothing sensational, she decided, and policemen without their lids looked rather like lambs. She had not a notion what "that reptile Macdonald" would look like, picturing something stout and red haired in a flat-topped cap. Characteristically she tried to hitch her skirt straight (Sybilla, though slim, was broader in the beam than herself), went through a door after a pleasant smile from the "lamb," and found herself facing a tall man with grey eyes, in a well-cut blue suit and dark tie.

"I wanted Chief Inspector Macdonald," she began, and the tall man smiled.

"All right, Miss Leigh—you've found him," he replied. "I was expecting you. I'm afraid you've had rather a morning of it."

He drew forward a chair for her, and she sat down in it gratefully.

"Woof! I should say I had!" she replied. "Dinah caught fire— my car, you know, and the door stuck, and I thought I should grill, oh, and then poor Weller—"

"I've heard about poor Weller," he replied, "and I've also heard that you did some very valuable first aid. Tell me about Dinah."

Elizabeth found him easy to talk to, and she poured out a flood of information, finally ending up, "but what I came here for was to ask you about Mr. Grenville. Is it really true he's had an accident?"

"I'm afraid it is," said Macdonald, "and a pretty nasty one, but he's in good hands. They'll do all that can be done at St. Joseph's. He has got a special nurse, and they are taking every possible care of him."

Looking at her, he saw her round eyes—as candid as a child's—fill with tears.

"But he won't die? It's not as bad as that?"

"I hope not," said Macdonald quietly. "Now listen. You have had a bad time of it this morning. I'm going to send for some coffee for you, and then I hope you'll answer a lot of other questions. It's too bad for you to be mixed up with all these troubles. How old are you?"

The coffee came and the "reptile" offered her a cigarette, and told her, very gently, how Robert Grenville had been knocked down in the city and lain out in the snow, and contracted pneumonia so that he could not answer questions for the time being.

Elizabeth goggled. "Not that beastly wharf place he promised not to go to?" she demanded.

A very short while put Macdonald in possession of all that she could tell about Debrette's letter, and her cry, "oh, that beastly man!" led him on to another question. She had seen Debrette? "I saw the man with the white streak in his beard," she replied. "Only once, but I'm never likely to forget him somehow. He was queer."

"I am very sorry to have to involve you in all this grim business, Miss Leigh," said Macdonald, "but now Grenville is knocked out—temporarily—the only people who seem able to identify the bearded man who approached Mr. Attleton are yourself and Mr. Rockingham. Debrette is dead. I am afraid I shall have to ask you to see his face and tell us if he is the man whom you saw in Park Village South. I know it will be pretty horrible for you, but it would help us a great deal. We have got to find out who killed Mr. Attleton."

Elizabeth looked at him with horror in her eyes.

"Must I? If I've got to, I will, but I shall hate it."

"I know you will. I wouldn't ask you if it weren't necessary. I dislike the necessity almost as much as you do. You're much too young to have such a request made to you—but it's very difficult. I want to know who knocked Mr. Grenville down, too."

"So do I!" said Elizabeth trenchantly. "He *was* a goop! Fancy going to the beastly place!"

"He certainly was a goop," agreed Macdonald, and then went on to ask her about the Attleton household and all that she knew of Sybilla and Mr. Burroughs and Mr. Rockingham, phrasing all his questions so neatly that Elizabeth talked on in her own idiom, quite unembarrassed, and with a sense of relief at unloading her mind to any one so sensible. Macdonald, listening to her spontaneous speech, liked her. She seemed a jolly, healthy-minded youngster, and the report he had received by telephone from the man on duty outside the Attletons' house had told him of the pluck and energy she had displayed over Weller's accident—which made him regret the fact that in this case he could not afford to look at anybody without suspicion. Every event could be interpreted in more ways than one. Weller might have fallen downstairs with a cut-glass jug in his hands, or he might have been the victim of some trick. As Macdonald knew from experience, a cord stretched ankle-high along a staircase can send a man flying headlong, to break his neck, perhaps, in the fall. Elizabeth Leigh had been in the house when the accident occurred, and might have brought it about as easily as any one else. On the other hand, she herself might have been the intended victim of a very dastardly scheme; a burning car and a door which would not open could easily have put an end to her admittedly charming self—and Weller *had* opened the bonnet of her car and looked inside the tonneau shortly after Elizabeth had entered the house.

Nevertheless, Macdonald felt something of an ogre when he took her to the mortuary, and led her into the grim, bare apartment where Debrette's body lay. Uncovering the face he stood beside her, and felt her small cold hand suddenly thrust into his own—the action of a frightened child. The dead face had the nobility of a sculptured mask, the lines smoothed out, the closed lids resting on sunken cheeks, a half smile, mysterious and peaceful, seeming to invest the worn features with an expression of content.

Looking down at the girl beside him, Macdonald saw her shake her head. "I can't tell," she whispered. "He didn't look like that—except for the beard. He was much darker. I mean his skin was dark. This poor thing looks so peaceful and happy, and the other was fierce, somehow. I don't know. It might be. He's like and yet he isn't."

With that Macdonald had to be content, and indeed he might have been more dissatisfied if Elizabeth Leigh had immediately identified that peaceful face. Death is a great alchemist, purging away the grossness which disfigures many a living face, sapping the colour, smoothing the contours. Was it likely that a young girl could look unmoved on that pale mask, and say, "This was he" of a man whom she had only glimpsed once?

After Elizabeth Leigh had left, Rockingham went in his turn to look at Debrette's inscrutable visage.

For a long time he studied the face, his own frowning and uncertain, but at last he turned to Macdonald and nodded.

"Yes, it's the same man I saw, undoubtedly. He's immensely changed. Now he looks more suitable for a stained glass window than for a hangman's rope, but I've seen enough of death to make allowances for a good deal of the change. I'm certain on this account. I noticed that one eyebrow was higher than another—in life it gave his face a grotesque look. It shows quite plainly still."

Macdonald nodded. "Yes. I noticed it. He's had a knock above the eye sometime and the scar still shows. You're satisfied—in spite of the fact that he looks ready for a halo—and a niche?"

Rockingham frowned and drew back.

"You have a nasty tongue. Niches—what a devil the man must have been! Well, that's my opinion. Let's get out of this."

Once outside, Rockingham asked:

"How's Grenville? Any real hope?"

"Plenty of it, thanks be!" replied Macdonald. "He's over the worst. A day or two will make it possible to interrogate him—and then we ought to be able to tidy up what I regard as a very unsatisfactory case, so far as my department is concerned, anyway. Grenville gave us the slip, you know, but that house he lives in has more doors than any house ought to have, and Furnival's Court is about as easy as a rabbit burrow to watch."

Rockingham looked at Macdonald with troubled eyes.

"To watch?" he queried. "Then you thought that Grenville *was* involved in all this?"

"He touched the case at every point," replied Macdonald. "You, who have followed it from the beginning, must have realised that. What induced you to come to us in the first case?"

"The fact that Grenville found Attleton's suitcase at the Belfry," rejoined Rockingham soberly, "but if there's any truth in what you suspect, wouldn't it be better if he didn't recover?"

"That's not a question I can ever ask myself," replied Macdonald, "but in this case it doesn't arise. He's going to get better, and then a few questions which I can't answer for myself are going to be answered. At present, our case is based on surmise—logical reconstruction if you prefer the term. Every one seems to be satisfied with the effort except myself, and I'm told that my natural name is Thomas. Before you go, there's one other question I wanted to ask you. I've been looking at Attleton's passport. I see it was issued last December. Can you tell me if he ever lost his passport, and applied for a new one?"

Rockingham pondered for some time.

"Not to my knowledge," he replied at length. "If he had done so—of recent years—he would probably have told me so. He went abroad fairly frequently. Could the passport office tell you?"

"I expect they could," replied Macdonald.

Rockingham seemed preoccupied with some other point and did not ask Macdonald for the reason of his odd question. He went on after a moment.

"You asked me—quite rightly—what time I left Grenville yesterday evening. I told you a few minutes after six. If you were having the place watched, you knew what time I left."

"Yes," agreed Macdonald. "Our man agreed with you. Six five he made it. After which you mounted a number thirteen bus in the Strand, which got held up when the Fascisti tried to demonstrate in Trafalgar Square at six thirty-five. You arrived home at seven three. The moral of which seems to be that it is quicker to walk than to go by bus in London during the rush hours."

The frown cleared from Rockingham's face.

"Then you *were* having me shadowed. I suspected it but was never certain. Well, I never expected to be trailed by Scotland Yard, still less to be grateful for the kind attention."

"Sorry to disappoint you," said Macdonald, "but you were not being trailed on our account."

"Then how the deuce can you be certain that I *did* get on a thirteen bus and stick in the Strand to let the Fascisti pass?"

"I can't," replied Macdonald cheerfully. "I merely note your own statement of your movements, and compare it with known facts."

"Bearing in mind the possibility that I might have knocked Grenville over the head, and thrown Debrette into the Thames, and still have got back to The Small House by seven o'clock?"

"Exactly," replied Macdonald. "There's a lot to bear in mind in this case."

Rockingham laughed aloud, and then sobered down again.

"Thank the Lord that Grenville's getting better," he replied. "It's one of the few good points in an otherwise ghastly mess-up. What about friend Thomas Burroughs?"

"An exceedingly dark horse, apparently of no traceable pedigree," replied Macdonald. "I can't make up my mind if his brain is a very subtle instrument, or a minus quantity."

"Judging by his bank balance, I should say the former," rejoined Rockingham.

XVI

ON THE EVENING AFTER ROCKINGHAM HAD GIVEN IT AS his opinion that the dead man in the mortuary was indeed the man whom he had seen speaking to Attleton, Macdonald got out all his notes on the case and went through them with all the concentration of which he was capable.

A good many points had been cleared up during the course of the day. Debrette's hiding-place had been traced down by means of information which had filtered in through various channels, and now it was clear that for the past fortnight he had been living in a room (described as "an American flatlet") in Camden Town. The owner of the house—an unpleasant-looking Jew who called himself James Stuart—could give no information about his tenant beyond the fact that he had paid a month's rent in advance when taking his room. This fact was, from Mr. Stuart's point of view, the best sort of reference obtainable. The room contained a bed, a hanging cupboard, a table and a chair; its amenities included a sink and a gas-stove, and it had a Yale lock on the door. The house in which it was a unit consisted of similar rooms similarly let, tenanted by strange shabby folk who were out all day, and who knew nothing of one another. Jenkins, who first investigated the house, said that he doubted if one of the tenants could look the law in the face, and none of them was willing to admit any knowledge of "Mr. Barbler," the name by which Streaky Beaver was known to his landlord.

The only things found in the room which were of any interest to the police were the script of a play which Bruce Attleton had written shortly before his death, and Bruce Attleton's watch, the latter identified by number by the makers. This last piece of evidence weighed down the scales of probability in the eyes of the "P.T.B.'s" that Debrette was guilty of the Belfry crime, and that he had also knocked Grenville over the head, and himself slipped into the river from the treacherous snowy surface of the wharf as he tried to dispose of Grenville's body in the Thames.

Macdonald, with all the evidence before him, was in a quandary. In one respect he needed time—and plenty of it. He might obtain an adjournment of the inquest once, but the process could not be repeated indefinitely without good reason. If all the evidence were to be produced now, a verdict against Debrette seemed inevitable—the reasoning (which Macdonald himself had pieced out), was complete.

Yet time was what he needed. To trace down, through the complex registrations of Somerset House, an individual named Thomas Burroughs who refused all account of himself was no simple matter, and Macdonald was far from satisfied over the excellent explanation given by that gentleman of his presence at the Belfry. In addition were the complications of Weller and his "accident," and the abortive fire in Elizabeth Leigh's car. Whether time were on the side of the law in the matter of Mr. Robert Grenville, Macdonald was less sure. Despite his firmly expressed optimism of the morning, he was beginning to doubt. The last bulletin had been far from reassuring, and if Grenville died before he was capable of being questioned, it looked as though the case would have to be decided by the balance of probabilities—a process which Macdonald distrusted, having met too many wild improbabilities in his dealings with criminals to be satisfied with anything but first-hand proof.

Sitting smoking his pipe, his papers arranged on the table in front of him, Macdonald looked the most imperturbable of beings, apparently settled down for a good evening's work. At the back of his mind he was waiting for something to happen—waiting for the word "go." The activities of the past few days, when event had crowded on event all too quickly, were the preamble to a climax which he hoped he had himself precipitated.

He thought over the position of his "contacts" as a chess player might ponder over his pieces. Grenville and Weller in hospital—both hors de combat (Knight and rook, two powerful pieces). Burroughs was at large, with Reeves watching him. Sybilla Attleton was at home (in her silver boudoir perhaps). Elizabeth Leigh was at her club, Neil Rockingham at The Small House, whence he had lately telephoned to Macdonald for news of Grenville, as had Elizabeth Leigh. In his little house in Chiswick the "Old Soldier" lay defying death, watched over by the faithful "young Alice," who had talked all too freely to her favourite Mr. Bruce.

The telephone rang at Macdonald's elbow and he caught it up and heard the urgent voice at the other end.

"Macdonald? Rockingham speaking. Can you send a man down? Something rather odd…" A report sounded over the wire which set the receiver vibrating, a veritable cannon shot it seemed, startling in its intensity.

Macdonald heard a clatter at the other end—the receiver falling apparently—and the line went dead. Plugging in to another line he called "Car ready—and follow instructions." Another second and he was calling "Exchange? Trace that call. Quickly."

It seemed ages before the reply came, but never had the telephone authorities worked more quickly to give Scotland Yard
the help it wanted.

No "spoof" calls to fool Macdonald—he had met that game
too often. Rockingham's voice, speaking from The Small House,
and a shot. Macdonald was downstairs and in a police car a few
seconds after Exchange had spoken, and the chauffeur, his foot
on the clutch and hand on the wheel, let the big car shoot forward while the traffic was held up for them. They shot round
Parliament Square and up Storey's Gate with a police gong clanging, past Wellington Barracks and the Palace and up Constitution
Hill at a pace which disturbed many a gaily-clad theatre goer.
They cut across Hyde Park Corner by the prohibited central
road and into the Park against the traffic lights—assisted in this
by the point-duty man who had heard the gong approaching.
One person at least was enjoying himself on that rush across
London, and that was the C.I.D. chauffeur, one of the finest
drivers Macdonald had ever seen. To cut straight across London
without a speed limit, to disregard all established canons of
the road, and to hurtle round Hyde Park in this style, was an
experience after the driver's own heart. At Stanhope Gate they
were again assisted by the point-duty men, and dashed into
Mayfair in a manner reminiscent of a smash and grab raid. As
they approached the mews where The Small House was situated
another note competed with the police gong—the deep-toned
bell of a fire engine—and by the time they drew up outside
Rockingham's house, the escape ladder was being set against
the red brick walls.

Police—sprung up from nowhere, it seemed—were keeping back the crowd which always materialises in London when

any unusual incident occurs, and as Macdonald jumped out of the big police car, the officer in charge of the fire engine said to him:

"We can't get any answer, sir, and there are steel shutters to those lower windows."

"I know," said Macdonald. "I'll go up through the bedroom window. No one seen entering or leaving the house, Fuller?" (This to the C.I.D. man who had been on duty in the mews.)

"No one, sir. Mr. Rockingham came home at four o'clock and he's not been out since."

Macdonald went up the escape ladder with the fireman close behind him, smashed the window and unlatched it, pushed up the sash and was through in a trice. There was a smell of burning in the air, and the two men dashed through the immaculate little bedroom and into the sitting-room across the landing. Here was a scene of chaos. Drawers had been pulled out and overturned, glass-fronted bookcases smashed and the contents scattered, chairs, tables and china flung here and there. An electric stove, still burning, was pushed up against the writing bureau, gradually setting fire to the hard rosewood. Macdonald, after one look round, made for the door.

"He's not here—leave that for your men to deal with. Come on."

Kicking the stove away from the bureau as he passed, he ran on, searching the little house. Bathroom and cupboards were inspected in a trice; downstairs they went and through the dining-room, lobby and offices, with the same result. No one, alive or dead, was there to account for that wrecked room upstairs.

"There was blood on the landing floor," said Barnes, the fireman, and Macdonald retorted impatiently:

"I know there was—on the stairs, too. There'll be a cellar somewhere—wine cellar or something. Over there, in that corner."

Macdonald knew what he had been doing when he had enlisted the assistance of the fire brigade in a venture for which he would have to stand responsible. Forcing doors was a business which came frequently into their activities. If a locked and bolted door stands in a fireman's way it is up to him to get it open, and the ancient door which guarded the wine cellar of The Small House gave way with a rending sound of torn woodwork to the fireman's hatchet.

Steps descended from the doorway to the cellar below where wine racks stood, a few holding bottles but mostly empty. A torchlight showed the small apartment to be empty, but Macdonald said:

"There's a way out somewhere. Must be. There's nowhere in the house where you could hide one man, let alone two. In the roof there, above the rack—give me that lever."

The trap-door yielded to a sound of tearing wood, and as it gave, Barnes heard another sound—that of a motor engine backfiring. Macdonald, his head and shoulders through the trap-door, shouted back, "Get your engine running and turn her round—it's in the mews parallel to the other. We may catch him at the corner. Meet me at the Mayfair Mews corner."

Barnes dashed back to the front door, having caught the idea in a trice. If the engine of the car which had just left the garage was running badly, it might be possible to head it off in the twisting Mayfair streets, and no driver, however desperate, would ram a fire engine. Also, if it came to a pursuit, the Brigade's bell would clear a path through the streets more efficiently than any police gong. Every driver in London would pull aside and make way for that warning note.

By the time Macdonald had run across the garage and gained the open doors, he saw the car which had just got out making speed up the empty mews. He ran after it to the corner and saw it turn off towards Grosvenor Street, but it was still backfiring, and the driver seemed unable to accelerate. Macdonald's whistle shrilled a warning in the hope that the car might run so badly that a constable might jump for the running-board, and then the fire engine came up, having backed up the mews and turned at the corner with a neatness incredible in such an apparently unwieldy vehicle. Jumping on to the running-board as it slowed beside him, Macdonald said, "He's turned east down Grosvenor Street. See what you can do."

With bell clanging, the magnificent engine accelerated and the vehicle leaped forward like a live thing. They saw their quarry, only a hundred yards ahead now, swing north into North Audley Street, but the driver now had his engine under control, and he accelerated in a manner which meant business.

"One way street ahead, sir, he daren't try that," said the man who was holding on beside Macdonald sounding the bell as they went. "That'll mean Oxford Street. He can't go far there. The traffic jams for the lights—don't we know it!"

Eastwards into Oxford Street they turned—a clear run to Selfridge's eastern corner, and then the dark car ahead found a way through the cross stream from Duke Street, and tore on.

"Force him into the pavement if you can draw level—here's a clear stretch. Lord, what's he doing now? He's going to turn down Marylebone Lane, and give us a run for our money. No, he isn't, he's pulling up. I know his game."

The game was evident. Realising that he was fighting a losing battle in competing with the engine behind him, which had everything in its favour while he had nothing, the driver had decided to "abandon ship" and take to his heels down a lane where neither fire engine nor police car could pursue him. Macdonald knew something of the network of little streets around old Marylebone Lane—the one his quarry had chosen was the little footway known as St. Christopher's Place, connecting Oxford Street and Wigmore Street by means of a narrow passage at the Oxford Street end. Whoever it was Macdonald was pursuing (and he realised with a flash of grim humour that even now he was not quite certain—there might be a body in that abandoned car), this man could run. He went down the little pavemented street at a pace which would have done credit to a freshman competing for a place in his college half mile, and was across Wigmore Street with Macdonald (once a trained runner, but now on the wrong side of forty) close behind him. At the junction of Marylebone Lane, on the north side of Wigmore Street, Macdonald had to swerve to avoid crashing with a portly pedestrian, and he lost a few yards. The flying figure in front swung round to the right and then turned sharply into an alleyway leading to a small yard. Instinctively Macdonald feinted, and crouched low as he overran to the far side of the opening instead of turning sharp into it, and a shot went over his head. Almost bent double, he jumped, leaping forward with outstretched arms and head low, and caught his antagonist round the knees as a second shot went wide. The two men came down together, and a third shot rang out as the hand which held the pistol struck the ground in falling, and a deep groan followed. A second later Macdonald was able to see the

face of the man he had pursued. With black wig awry, and run-
nels of sweat making light lines down the swarthy cheeks, Neil
Rockingham's ghastly face looked up at him. A phrase flashed
across Macdonald's mind as, panting, he bent instinctively to
the work of first aid to the wounded, "Logical reconstruction
number five."

*   *   *

When Macdonald got to bed that night, the rush of events had
put one question out of his head. What logical reconstruction
lay at the back of the events of the evening? Rockingham, before
he died, had confessed to the murders of Attleton and Debrette
and had asked for a priest—a fear in his glazing eyes which
Macdonald never forgot. Rockingham was a Roman Catholic,
it seemed, and feared to die unshriven. It was not until he sat
on his own bed, long after midnight, that Macdonald argued
out the final bid, not for victory, but for escape which had been
Rockingham's last move.

   With the trap-door in his own ancient wine cellar connecting with a stable building now turned garage, Rockingham had
an easy getaway. He knew that Macdonald would find it, and
had staged a scene to indicate a desperate fight—with himself
as victim, removed by the trap-door to the garage. He had put
through his telephone call to summon the police—and then
found that the engine of his car had let him down. With the
perversity that an engine will sometimes exhibit, it choked and
would not start up. Macdonald thought of the murderer working
at the maddening engine, knowing that by his own challenge,
pursuit would be upon him—a grim thought.

"He wanted to be too clever, and must have his 'curtain' at the end," thought Macdonald. "Losh, he nearly had the laugh of me, though, with his never-failing tricks. He admitted once he studied medicine. Dissecting, Drama and Devilment. Cold-blooded devil!"

XVII

To some extent Macdonald had forestalled the criticism he anticipated from Colonel Wragley and the inevitable question, "What tangible evidence have you against Rockingham?" by having written up a series of notes concerning his own observations and deductions, which, while mainly theoretical and tentative, had led him to his project of rattling up his private suspect in the hope of making him show his hand.

Macdonald admitted that he had formulated no fewer than five theories as to the possible originators of the Belfry crime, the last of which proved to have been the right one.

(1) The obvious reading of the evidence was that Debrette, having blackmailed Attleton, killed him at the Belfry. Theory disproved (to Macdonald's mind) by Debrette's inexplicable foolishness in showing his face with the identifying beard after the murder had taken place, when Debrette knew that he had been seen by three people who could both describe and identify him.

(2) That Grenville, some of whose evidence was uncorroborated, killed Attleton. Theory disproved by the fact that no weapon was found on him or near him at Dowgate Wharf by which the blow that laid him out could have been self-administered, assuming that he had first killed Debrette.

(3) That Burroughs, acting in conjunction with Sybilla, killed Attleton, disproved by the fact that Burroughs was under detention when Debrette and Grenville were found at Dowgate.

(4) That Burroughs and Weller acted in conjunction, and Sybilla manœuvred Weller's accident, Elizabeth Leigh being also involved.

(5) That Rockingham killed Attleton, and also found time to conceal his body in the Belfry while, according to his passport, he was in France and not in England.

Macdonald's theorising, in all cases based on the evidence he had culled, was equally elaborate for all five reconstructions, but in the case of Rockingham he hit the nail on the head with a very shrewd guess which turned out to be accurate.

Motive. Inheritance of the Marsham fortune, whose existence was learnt by Attleton from young Alice, the information being passed on by him to Rockingham. This involved the assumption that Rockingham was the grandson of Mary Anne Brossé (née Marsham). It also involved something else, to Macdonald's mind—the possibility that Debrette was also Madame Brossé's grandson and senior to Rockingham in succession. The Chief Inspector considered that the two crimes of Attleton's death and Debrette's were originally meant to have been more confused, as the identification of Attleton's body must have seemed very improbable to the murderer.

At this stage in Macdonald's elaboration of his own previously written up notes, Colonel Wragley took off his glasses and asked for further enlightenment as to the Chief Inspector's reasoning, and Macdonald replied:

"Rockingham argued thus, it seemed to me. The body was so well concealed that it was highly improbable that it would be discovered until his own time-bomb (to call it so) caused the fire. After the fire the identification of the body might have been impossible, and it thus left two possibilities—that Debrette killed

Attleton or vice versa, but neither could have been regarded as a claimant to the fortune since a murderer cannot profit by his crime. If things had gone according to plan, Debrette would doubtless have vanished and never have been seen again, leaving another unsolved mystery. When I suggested to Rockingham that Attleton's masseur could identify his body, Rockingham was horrified to the verge of fainting, perhaps by horror at the whole story—or perhaps by seeing his plans go awry."

"The whole thing is so demented that its ingenuity staggers me," groaned Colonel Wragley, and Macdonald went on:

"Rockingham was a dramatist, sir. Hence his ingenuity, but he was also a bit demented to think he could bring it off—but he very nearly did. It was Debrette's beard…"

"Yes, yes, yes. I'm sick of that beard!" snapped Wragley. "Having assumed a motive—and it appears you were right, according to Rockingham's confession, though you had no business to be, you might tell me, in short words of three letters, how he pulled it off."

Macdonald, disregarding the implied official criticism of his report, settled to work:

"Rockingham, more astute than most murderers, undertook an impersonation of a man who really existed, and who was to be involved in the crime. Owing to the nature of his household, living without a resident servant, he could absent himself from home without raising comment or having his absence observed. He took the lease of the Belfry, made up as Debrette, and it is obvious how a wig and beard, and dark make-up, added to the glasses, would alter that bald-headed fresh-faced appearance of his. During all this time he managed to keep in touch with his cousin Debrette, and supplied him with money to lie low, probably with the additional promise of a part in a future play. The identity thus established, and the scene set at the Belfry, having telephoned to Attleton on some blackmailing charge frequently enough to have become a known nuisance, Rockingham had finished his first act. Doubtless he bothered Attleton through some knowledge of the latter's indiscretions which he acquired in his Fidus Achates character. It was obvious that Rockingham, as Attleton's most intimate friend, would have had opportunities of knowing his life and habits…"

"Undoubtedly," said Wragley. "I pass Act One. It doubtless included the letter to Mrs. Attleton and the copy of the unfixed snapshot—a neat idea, that. Convincing but fugitive."

"Very neat," agreed Macdonald. "On the day fixed for the murder, Rockingham got Attleton to telephone to him from Victoria and induced him to go to Charing Cross, possibly with the bait of bowling out the blackmailing Debrette. They both went to the Belfry from Charing Cross (in a car procured by Rockingham) and Attleton was murdered there. Rockingham then locked the place securely, and went to Calais by the afternoon boat, using the passport I saw on his desk at The Small House."

"Have you proved this passport business yet?" asked Wragley.

"Yes, sir," replied Macdonald. "Sufficiently well to justify our assumption."

"Yours," corrected Wragley, and smiled at last.

"It is very difficult to tamper with the dates on a passport," went on Macdonald, "however neatly done it always shows on examination. Neither is it easy to obtain a second passport under a false name, despite popular belief in that strategy. Yet if Rockingham went to France and returned immediately, he must

have had a second passport under which to mask his activities.
He could have obtained one by stating to the passport office that
the one he held was lost or destroyed by accident. This is a not
infrequent occurrence, and the passport office issues a new one
to reputable persons in such circumstances. Quite simple, when
you think it out. Rockingham left England on Wednesday, March
18th, using one passport. He returned immediately, using the
second, went to the Belfry, completed his exceedingly nasty plans
for concealing the body—and showed himself in the character
of Debrette to Grenville. The next day he returned to France
using passport number two and stayed there until the following
Thursday, when he returned openly on official passport number
one, and roused the alarm through the medium of Grenville,
on the principle that the man who goes to the police is the last
to be expected of double dealing."

"His whole plan shows an effrontery which simply passes
belief," said Colonel Wragley, and Macdonald agreed, but qualified his agreement by adding:

"His plan, though complicated, was so thorough that he
very nearly succeeded. The evidence pointed most strongly to
Debrette, and once Debrette was silenced there *was* no direct
evidence against Rockingham. It was all presumptive, and if he
hadn't lost his nerve at the end, I doubt if he would ever have
been convicted. If you, sir, are hardly willing to believe it, now
that Rockingham has confessed to the two crimes on his death-
bed, I doubt if any jury would have believed the case against him
when it was riddled by a strong counsel. We could have proved
the possibility of his guilt, but it would have taken us a very long
time to get chapter and verse. The whole matter of his Brossé
descent is complicated. His mother, Marie Antoinette Brossé,

married a South African named de Haan—a British subject. This de Haan changed his name to Rockingham, quite legally, by deed poll, and our Neil Rockingham was born in England, the son of two respectable British subjects. It seems probable that all the time Rockingham knew Attleton, he never gave away his knowledge of their relationship. It was only of recent years that Rockingham could have ascertained the fortune which he believed would pass to the nearest heir, and he then took steps to eliminate those standing between him and that enviable position. Nothing more can be proved about the deaths of Attleton's brother and Anthony Fell. For all we shall ever know, Attleton himself may have been involved in them—in which case he had a very real fear of blackmail in the matter of the mysterious Debrette."

"Yet so far as I can see, Rockingham confused the issue so completely by his complications that I fail to see how he could eventually have profited," argued Wragley. "If his scheme had gone through there would have been no proof that Attleton was dead."

"I think that would have been substantiated later," replied Macdonald. "Some time or other Attleton's head will be discovered to put the seal on that problem—the dramatist's curtain—and eventually Neil Rockingham would have discovered, to his intense surprise, that his grandmother was Mary Anne Brossé, née Marsham. If Debrette had been convicted of Attleton's death, Rockingham would have felt quite secure."

Macdonald paused here, adding:

"It was, from my point of view, a very difficult case, because it was my own reasoning which led me to the conclusion that Debrette, on whose body the Brossé Missal was found, had been

responsible for Attleton's death in order to inherit the Marsham
fortune. If I had immediately concentrated on proving Debrette's
Brossé descent, I should only have strengthened the chain of
reasoning which I felt was too good to be true. The business
of the assault on Grenville could be explained in two ways,
of which the first was the simpler—that Debrette tried to kill
Grenville because the latter could identify him as the tenant of
the Belfry. On the other hand was the supposition that Grenville
was attacked and left for dead because he could state that the
real Debrette, examined at leisure and at close quarters, was not
the man he had seen at the Belfry.

"Rockingham aimed for a rapid double when he knocked
Grenville over the head, and threw the unfortunate Streaky Beaver
into the river with one of the famous Louis de Vallon de Brette
letters in his pocket. Yet I had no positive evidence on which to
arrest Rockingham—simply a balance of probabilities, and, on
the face of it, Debrette seemed a far likelier suspect. I wanted to
shake Rockingham up and get him to show his hand, so I tried
the effect of two stimulants. I asked him if Attleton had ever lost
his passport and obtained a new one on that account, thereby
showing him that my mind was running in the right direction so
far as his own activities were concerned, and I also assured him
that Grenville was recovering rapidly and might be questioned
quite shortly. I doubted if, assuming that he was guilty, he would
have the nerve to sit quiet and do nothing in face of those two
snags. Even though there is an obliging lady in Paris ready to
swear to Rockingham's residence with her for the period during
which he was busy with his criminal schemes, the sum total of
possessing a second passport, and of outfacing the man he left
for dead at Dowgate Wharf, were too much for his optimism."

"And Rockingham counted among his accomplishments the ability to write a continental hand, and to disguise his voice under a foreign accent?"

"Undoubtedly—but his mother was an Alsatian, and probably taught him his letters. That could be assumed from the original argument that he was of Brossé stock."

"It was a pity he didn't use his talents on the stage and leave real life melodrama alone," said Wragley dryly.

"He had a criminal mind and a dramatist's facility for plotting," replied Macdonald. "It was not over-acting, but overplanning, that gave him away. Many murderers have repeated their technique. Rockingham wanted room for his very subtle mind to have full play."

It was several weeks later that Macdonald was allowed his first long talk with Robert Grenville. The latter, regarded almost as a star turn exhibit by the hospital authorities for having recovered when death seemed inevitable, was still lean and wan of face, but surprisingly full of spirits when Macdonald went to see him. (The latter had seen Miss Elizabeth Leigh departing from Grenville's room before he entered it, and guessed that Grenville would be feeling cheerful.)

"Hullo, Long-in-the-Jaw," said Grenville blithely, "I want to get my bit said quickly so that I can shoot questions at you. You can guess most of it, and don't say 'Mugs will be mugs' because I know it. Old Neil R. rang me up five minutes after he'd left my digs that evening, saying, 'Can you come quickly? I'm at Cannon Street Station. I've been following Elizabeth. God knows what she's doing. Sybilla Attleton's just passed me, and I want to go and look at that damned wharf. I don't trust things. Straight down Dowgate Hill...' He rang off there. My God, I went! I jumped on a bus as it passed, and I hared down Dowgate Hill to the wharf at about fifty per. I passed old Neil R. just before I saw the Thames—and that's all I know about it. Well, I ask you, what would *you* have done?"

"Don't ask me. I'm no expert at these crises du cœur. I'll give Rockingham top marks for being a quick worker. After he'd settled you and Debrette, I suppose he rushed off in his car and parked it somewhere, and picked up a Number thirteen bus as per programme. Well, thanks for living through it, thick head. I should have been sadly cramped in style if you'd passed out before I picked you up."

"Hi, you blighter, don't you think you're going before you've told me all the jolly details," complained Grenville. "What about poor old fat-face—Thomas Burroughs. What was *his* to-do about?"

"Oh, just an invitation to hold the baby, by a dramatist who had a sense of detail. After all, Burroughs looked a likely runner-up at one time. Motive, and all that. Calculated to take our mind off other and more pressing details. There's a touch of pathos about the hole into which the unfortunate Mr. Burroughs found himself. I asked him for details of his parentage, lineage and so forth, and he declined to oblige with a noise and fury which seemed to indicate something. Our researches unearthed the appalling fact that he is a Jew. His father's name was originally Levi. Mrs. Attleton, it appears, loathes Jews, and Thomas knew it. He was willing to spend several more nights in his unpleasing cell rather than own up to his race."

"Well, I'm jiggered! To think of the dirt he ate while Sybilla reviled his forefathers and kinsmen to the third and fourth generation! I say, don't tell her. Let her marry him and then find out. I never could stick the woman."

"I never disliked any one more in my life," rejoined Macdonald, "but prejudices are no good in my job. I liked Rockingham to begin with. He seemed a pleasant, sound principled, rather nervous old stick-in-the-mud."

"My God, he was a cold-blooded horror! When he tied my head up that night in the Belfry he told me he had once studied medicine—"

"Yes. You told me so. That suggested he might have acquired some skill in dissection—and he needed it. Of course it was obvious from the first that he was a 'contact'—as you were. The two of you might have cooked the whole thing. If it hadn't been for the fact that Debrette had been seen at The Knight Templar I should have been disposed to believe that you and Rockingham had invented him."

"I know," replied Grenville soberly. "You never really believed I found that suitcase in situ, did you?"

"I doubted it," admitted Macdonald, "as I doubted the story of the poltergeist which hit you over the head in the Belfry when you and Rockingham were first together there. I suppose that he staged a Heath-Robinson booby-trap with bits of string—one round the meter for putting the lights out, and one to organise the fall of the easel across the door—into which you butted at full tilt, and knocked yourself silly so that you couldn't tell how-from-what. Your various vicissitudes all added to the complications. I've known too many guilty people who've got themselves attacked under suspicious circumstances to view such accidents in a really nice spirit."

"Thanks for loving sympathy," growled Grenville. "When did you leave off suspecting me and turn your attention to Rockingham?"

"Asked the journalist intelligently," said Macdonald. "My dear wooden-head, I suspected all of you, every one, from first to last. It seemed to me that you'd cooked up a beautiful lot of fool-proof evidence and handed it to me on a salver. That's what put me in a bad temper all through this case—I was simply busy picking up the bits you'd buried for me. I won't mention Debrette's beard again—it got my superior officer's goat—but I did refuse to believe that old balmy Barbler Debrette had had the brains and gumption to put the thing through. He'd been used by somebody—appearance and all. You, living off Fleet Street, might have known of him. Mrs. Attleton might have seen him tagging round stage-doors. Rockingham, as a dramatist, might have come across him, impersonated him, and paid him to lie low. I don't expect Rockingham ever thought Streaky Beaver would break his contract and show his beard at Charing Cross at a crucial moment—but Streaky Beaver was for it, anyhow, after he'd been used. Rockingham must have made an appointment with poor Streaky to meet him at Dowgate at the same time that you obliged and went running. What you call a quick right and left, and home again. Rockingham did you a good turn when he hung the cosh on poor Streaky's arm. Look here, it's time you went to sleep again. You're looking wuzzy."

"All right, nursie. Then Weller's accident was just a trip on the stairs and no more?"

"I take it so. He's resigned his job. Wise man."

"And what on earth was Rockingham's idea in putting that spoof call from Attleton over you?"

"Mainly mystification, but I think he hoped to confuse the issue as to who killed who, and tie us up in knots that way. I am certain that his original plan involved the deaths of Attleton and Debrette without either body being identifiable until he wished it."

"Clever devil!"

"Yes. Too clever. There's one other little point which may serve to point a moral in case you ever think of insinuating yourself into the position of sole heir to a fortune. The Old Soldier is still alive, and good for a few more years they think. When he was eighty he married young Alice—and made a will leaving his all to her. He's never acknowledged her as his wife before the world, but his wife she is. Rather a good ending to the story. She showed me her marriage lines with tears in her eyes. She really loves him!—and to think of the lovely story I concocted one night on the grounds that she was married to Weller, and that they were all in the game together. Which reminds me. Send me some wedding cake later—and good luck to you!"